Fat Witch Summer

LIZZY IVES

FAT WITCH SUMMER

LIZZY IVES

Cover Illustration by Amanda Julina Gonzalez

Map Illustration by Kalia Cheng

Author Photo by Zane Rubin

eISBN: 978-0-9962324-4-9

ISBN (Paperback): 978-0-9962324-5-6

ISBN (Hardcover): 978-0-9962324-6-3

Library of Congress Control Number: 2023900787

First Printed Edition 2023

If you were told not to try,
But you did it anyway,
This is for you

THE THIRTEEN STATES

Illustration by Kalia Cheng

NEW SALEM

WYCKTON

BROSIA

HASHILAND

NORTH HECATANEE

SOUTH HECATANEE

COTE D'AVEAU

SOLVILLE
(SUMMER CITY)

ELZBORAH

ELZBORAH CITY

MORGANSHYRE

IT'ISHLAND

MAHOLAND

REDROCK

BABAGONIA

CALYPSO

BELMAR

N
E
S
W

1

Thrash became a witch on the last day of school, in the library bathroom, because of course that's where it happened.

The Belmar branch of the Calypso Public Library was only two blocks from the high school, making it a convenient after-school pickup spot. Thrash avoided her reflection in the library's mirrored security doors, even though she didn't have any hidden enchantments for the mirrors to expose. She refused to apologize for her acne by hiding it with magic, or to glamour permanent eyeliner over her lids. Her one concession to vanity was her magenta hair, but she bleached and dyed it with real chemicals, not some magic ring.

Thrash had a love-hate relationship with a lot of things— with enchantments, with her "friends," with her name. Not Thrash, but the name her mother gave her. *Theodora Blumfeld-Wright.* It was grand and sophisticated, like her mom, who was the Protectrix of Belmar and never let anyone forget it.

When the mirrored doors finally slid open, Thrash came face-to-face with the portrait of her mother that watched over the lobby. She sped past the painting of steely-eyed Protectrix Osmarra Wright, who wore rows of glittering beaded necklaces in her portrait, the insignia of a decorated witch. Her hair was in its signature upswept bun, and she was wearing her favorite slimming purple suit. Thrash had a good one hundred pounds on her mom, not to mention the amateur dye-job. No one ever saw the resemblance.

At least the library was empty today, the only sound the quiet shuffle of enchanted book carts. Thrash allowed herself a brief, victorious smile at the thought that her classmates had been lured outside by the promise of summer, leaving her favorite table unoccupied. It was secluded (back corner), perfectly lit (garden window), with well-worn leather chairs that she could sit in for hours without getting uncomfortable. The perfect reading spot.

Thrash set her hat down on one of the chairs to claim the table and then wandered the stacks. She was on a mission to check out as many books as she could stuff into her hat, which was about two dozen. Now that school was out, her mom would be on her to go through Mum's boxes of things, and Thrash could no longer use homework as an excuse to put it off. It was time to build a long, fake summer reading list.

Conductive Metallmancy in Wandcraft sounded properly dry, as did *Allison Crowfeather's History of the Thirteen States*. Thrash picked out a few more academic-sounding titles and then snuck in a murder mystery for herself. Arms heavy with books, she returned to her table and froze.

Three girls were sitting there.

Three cool, beautiful girls.

Saki Anderson, tall and statuesque, was biting her nails while scrolling on her orb, glossy black curtains of hair falling around her face. Thrash heard Saki modeled on the side. She was only seventeen and her face had already graced magazine covers.

Emerald Atlandotir was the daughter of a mer-prince. According to the stories, her dad fell madly in love with a human and renounced his crown. Thrash wasn't sure if that made Emerald a princess or not, but she certainly had the proper posture of one. She held her chin high as she read, her pixie cut and wire-rimmed glasses just visible over the top of her book.

Then there was Cresca. Cresca King. Midnight skin, full lips, moonlight hair. Her arms and legs dangled over the sides of the chair like she was reclining on a chaise longue. While Cresca didn't have enigmatic beauty or royal blood, she had something far more coveted—effortless cool. As she twirled a strand of her long, silver-blond hair, Cresca's ring-clad fingers flashed in the summer sunlight.

The trio called themselves the Lunes. There was something that just screamed "coven" about them, even though none of them had gotten their knacks yet. Maybe it was the way their limbs were always intertwined, their fingers always in each other's hair. Some kids snickered at them, scrawled "the Loons" in yearbooks and on bathroom stalls, but the girls didn't care. Their magical, aloof air set them apart from the crowd—and near the top of the high school food chain.

"What about food?" Saki asked, looking up from her orb.

Thrash darted back behind the shelf, almost knocking a book cart off its course. The cart patiently rerouted around her, books floating off it to their proper places on the shelf. Thrash opened one of her own books and pretended to examine a family tree of flowering nightshades.

"Like, right now?" That sounded like Emerald. "I'm not really hungry."

"For the trip." Saki said that. "We can't just raid our kitchens."

"Blame it on your brothers," said Cresca. "Especially if you're planning to filch your dad's Scandi coffee. Which, for the record, I would not oppose."

"How would we make coffee?"

A pause.

"...Hotels have coffee makers," Emerald said. "I think."

"Can we pay for a hotel?" Saki asked.

"Such negative energy!" Cresca's voice was far too loud for a library. Thrash hadn't even meant to eavesdrop, but at this point, it was impossible not to. "We'll figure it out. We always do."

As the Lunes chatted about their summer plans, Thrash sank to the floor. She wished she had friends who planned road trips. Her friends were more like a study group who tolerated her at their lunch table. When Thrash moved to Belmar two years ago, she fell in with the academic kids, the ones who kept their heads down and worked hard, determined to do well even if they didn't develop a knack for magic.

Thrash peeked through the shelves. Her pointed black hat, complete with a half-dozen homemade buttons, rested on the chair, held hostage. Could she outlast the Lunes? The girls were still at the table—or at least, Saki and Emerald were. Where was Cresca?

"Hey, do you wanna sit at our table or something?"

Thrash scrambled to her feet. Cresca stood in the aisle, both hands on her hips in a way that reminded Thrash of one of her mom's "power poses." Not a silver hair was out of place, not a single pink nail chipped. Cresca wore fitted jeans and a white tank top that would have looked plain on Thrash but said "classic understated beauty" on Cresca.

Also, heels. Who wore heels to school?

"You don't have to sit on the floor," Cresca said. "You're free to join us."

Thrash hesitated. In the halls of Belmar High School, Cresca had a reputation for being friends with everyone and no one. She was queen of the disarming smile, the charming overture—until you got on her bad side. For the most part, Thrash kept to her nerds and Cresca huddled with her Lunes, doing whatever it is cool girls do all day (Compare outfits? Drink cappuccinos?). This was the most Cresca had ever spoken to her.

"Seriously, we have an extra chair," Cresca said. Her eyes were surprisingly warm. The color of butterscotch.

"Actually, I was just leaving." Thrash squeezed past Cresca before she could protest. "My mom's picking me up. Right now."

"Well, maybe next time!"

Thrash's cheeks burned. She wondered if Cresca's eyes were following her, but Thrash didn't dare glance back to check. Why did Cresca's kindness unnerve her? It would have been easier if she were mean.

Thrash took a hard right at the entrance, ducking into the library bathroom to hide out until her mom came, or at least until she figured out a Plan B. As she caught her breath at the bathroom sink, Thrash caught a glimpse of herself in the mirror.

Her favorite features were her cute nose, her heart-shaped face, and, usually, her cloud of magenta hair. Today, it resembled limp cotton candy. Thrash fluffed her hair with her fingers, trying to will more life into it. She didn't hate what she saw, but she didn't love it either. She lived with it. Just like Osmarra had to live with Thrash as her daughter.

The bathroom door slammed open. Thrash heard a loud crack followed by a rain of broken glass but couldn't reconcile it with seeing Cresca come in, clutching Thrash's hat. Had she snooped on her stuff or read her handmade buttons? Thrash thought of the bright blue one that read *I Love Big Books*. The "O"s looked like nipples and Thrash got in a fight with the school administration last year over whether the font was offensive. She could picture the Lunes snickering over it.

"Hey, I was trying to catch up to you because I think you forgot your hat..."

Cresca's words trailed away as her gaze swept to the bathroom mirror. It was completely shattered. A hundred Thrashes peered back at her from the jagged glass spiderweb. Had Cresca opened the door so forcefully it broke?

Neither girl moved or spoke for a long moment. Then Cresca stepped closer, examining the splintered mirror. She gave a long whistle.

"That," Cresca said, "is one hell of a knack. Congratulations."

"It's not a knack..." Thrash said, but uncertainty crept into her voice. Knacks were often a minor flash of magic, but this was never how Thrash had pictured her discovering that she had an aptitude for magic...

"It's definitely a knack," Cresca said. "You broke that mirror with magic. You're a witch!"

Thrash couldn't quite believe it at first. Did that mean she truly had magic in her veins? Being a witch meant Thrash would receive one of the three Gifts—Glamour, Growth, or Sight—to hone and strengthen the magic bursting inside her. If she was a witch, senior year would be filled with Magic Theory classes and applications to the Historically Magical Universities. If she got into New Salem University, her life would be, quite literally, magical.

Cresca was right, wasn't she? Thrash was a witch. A witch!

The thought was exhilarating, until Thrash remembered one hiccup.

Teenagers didn't get to choose their own Gifts. Mothers did.

"You look like you need a cigarette," Cresca declared, her hand fishing inside Thrash's hat. "You have any cigarettes in here?"

"What?" Thrash finally tore her eyes away from the broken mirror. "We can't smoke in the library."

"Relax, I always crack a window." Cresca stopped rummaging. "What are these?" She pulled out a worn deck of tarot cards and the color drained from Thrash's face.

"Please, don't, they're my mum's. My other mom. I—just please put them back."

Cresca tucked the cards back into the hat and handed it to Thrash brim-first. "Sorry, that was rude. I can be a little rude sometimes. I didn't mean to scare you. I just wanted to make sure you got your hat back."

"Thanks," Thrash said warily. Her heart was still racing from Cresca pawing Mum's cards. "I have to go. My mom is waiting."

"Sure, sure. See you around?"

Thrash just wanted to get out of there, but Cresca didn't move out of the way as she reached for the door. This girl was becoming a *literal* obstacle. Why couldn't she take a hint?

"Look, Cresca, you don't have to pretend to want to hang out with me. I don't need your approval or your pity or whatever. I'm good."

Cresca scoffed, but her eyes glittered knowingly as she stepped aside. "Whatever, girl. Tell your mom I say hi."

A gust of hot summer wind hit Thrash as she exited the library. She could already feel the sweat beading on her back—why was it always her back? Honestly, if she had a hate-hate relationship with anything, it was summer. While girls who looked like Cresca flaunted bare thighs and spaghetti straps, Thrash battled chub rub, sweat stains, and the glares of strangers. Summer was cruel to fat girls.

But the heat wasn't the only thing making Thrash drag her feet. She knew she should be celebrating her knack, but she would have to be strategic about breaking the news to her mom. Though magic wasn't tied to bloodlines, both of Thrash's moms were witches. Osmarra had the Gift of Glamour, and Duna had had the Gift of Sight. The tricky part would be convincing Osmarra to give her the Gift of Sight after what happened to Mum.

Swirling the misty surface of her orb until it was clear as glass, Thrash held the capture-ready crystal to her face and recorded a message for her mom, letting her know she was going to walk home and "enjoy the fresh air." Whatever that meant. It bought her an hour to come up with a plan, but as she walked, her mind wandered to the library bathroom, and she somehow spent the whole march home replaying her encounter with Cresca.

∾

Thrash took a bite of her steak and almost spit it out. It tasted bland and faintly spongy, less like a cut of meat and more like a slab of cauliflower—because that's what it was. She was eating *glamoured* cauliflower.

Thrash forced the bite down her throat, aware that her mom was watching her across the table. This was one of the hazards of having a mom with the Gift of Glamour. Appearances were deceiving, even at the dinner table.

"Isn't this a clever trick?" Osmarra asked. "I'm starting a new diet tomorrow. It's all based on eating with your eyes."

"Yeah, clever." Osmarra was always on a diet, even though Thrash was pretty sure the Gift of Glamour kept her hovering around a size 2. Compared to Growth or Sight, Thrash secretly thought Glamour was pretty flimsy. It lent itself to careers in politics or entertainment, two subjects Thrash had little interest in. She mainly saw her mom use her mighty powers of illusion to redecorate their home and keep her age somewhere in the inoffensive mid-30s. Sure, her mother's chestnut hair had a perfect wave, and her cheekbones could cut a diamond —but was that really the best use of magic?

At least the mashed potatoes were real. Tragically under-salted and butterless, but real.

"So, do we have any summer goals?" her mom asked. She took another bite of "steak" and chewed it with more relish than it deserved.

"Goals?" Thrash blinked innocently. "I thought it was called summer *break*."

"Very funny," her mom said, but she wasn't smiling. Osmarra sat up straighter and turned on her protectrix voice: "You don't realize how lucky you are to get three months off every year. That ends when you're a real adult, you know."

"I know."

"And while you have all this time on your hands, I'd like you to tackle the boxes in the stables." She said it casually, without even looking up, as if she were slipping Thrash a piece of paperwork that needed a sign-off.

"I have a lot of summer reading to do," Thrash lied, "but as soon as I finish, I'll start going through everything."

"If you leave it until the end of summer, you'll never get through it all."

Thrash shrugged and shrank back into her chair.

"Just start with one box a week," Osmarra suggested gently. "Do something easy, like books."

As if books weren't sentimental. Thrash thought of her dead mum's divination books, her star charts, her dream journals. How could she throw any of it away?

"What if I need the books some day?" Thrash tried to say it lightly, but Osmarra's arched eyebrows lifted. "Like, if I get my knack, and you give me the Gift of Sight—"

"You know how I feel about this," Osmarra said, her voice firm. "The Gift of Sight is a big responsibility."

Oh, Thrash knew. This was exactly why she dreaded telling her mom about her knack.

"I'm responsible," Thrash said. "I'm in every advanced class I can take. I keep my grades up and stay out of trouble. Shouldn't I get some credit for all the wild stuff I'm *not* doing?"

"You may *think* you want the Gift of Sight, but receiving any of the three Gifts would be a privilege. You should be grateful you were born in the Thirteen States."

Thrash had heard this spiel before—the Thirteen States was the most magical country in the world, drawing witches from every continent and society, a land where witches weren't persecuted, but *celebrated.*

The part no one wanted to talk about was how the witches who fled Europa arrived as refugees but died as colonizers. In 1791, the Founding Sisters pressured three Native nations into an uneasy alliance with their settlements that would come to be known as the Thirteen States. The magic of the next hundred years was wild, unregulated, and dangerous—until the Gifts were invented in the 1880s, ushering in the First Magical Revolution.

"I *am* grateful, but it's the twenty-first century—not the 1880s," Thrash snapped. The hypocrisy of it made her temperature rise.

Usually, her mother's eyes sparkled a brilliant blue, but

now they seemed dull, haunted. "You are too young to decide for yourself. This is why mothers choose the Gifts."

"Plenty of *parents* give their daughters the Gift of Sight," Thrash said. Though the Thirteen States was progressive in many ways, there was still matriarchal bullshit to deal with. "Some even let their children choose."

"This is not up for discussion right now."

"Just because Mum saw—"

"That's enough!"

In the space between heartbeats, fine lines flickered on her mother's face. Cauliflower replaced steak, potted plants disappeared, and the tablecloth dimmed from spun gold to drab cotton. By the time Thrash blinked, the illusions all settled back into place.

Osmarra adjusted and readjusted the napkin in her lap before finally speaking. "We'll have this discussion if you get your knack. Isn't the cutoff for next year's HMU prep track only a few weeks away?"

July 1st, to be precise, but Thrash didn't say that. If she *still* had to prove herself to her mom, so be it. She just had to endure one more year in this immaculate house, stripped of everything Mum, and then she was off to college. Only senior year stood between her and freedom.

Well, that and a Gift.

"Magic is a privilege," Osmarra continued, eyes on her plate. "And you would be lucky to receive any Gift."

Thrash bit her tongue and nodded. For the rest of dinner, she picked at her food, suffering in silence *like a real adult*.

∿

Thrash pulled a tarot card at random.

Six of Cats.

Well, that was meaningless. Cats were essentially the wild cards of the deck, a suit representing uncertainty and chaos. Thrash set the card on her bedside table and asked her question again.

"What Gift will my mom choose for me?" Thrash closed her eyes and squeezed her mum's deck extra hard. *Please no flowers or rings. Give me some eyes. Tell me it's the Gift of Sight!*

She flipped up the top card.

Knight of Cats.

More cats? Thrash groaned.

Thrash traded the deck for her orb. Still no messages from Loral or Zamber. She had always been a bit of a loner, but it still stung to think that her old friends had moved on already. It had only been two years since Thrash and her moms had moved to Belmar so Osmarra could run for being the city's Protectrix. She won the election and spent 90 percent of her time "protecting" Belmar from bad budgets and policies. What Osmarra really wanted was a position that she didn't have to campaign for, that she could hold for life. She wanted to be a Named Witch of the High Circle.

Thrash's hand wavered over the orb. She could send a capture to Loral, who loved cats, and show her all the cat cards she kept drawing from the deck. Or she could tell Zamber about her fake summer reading scheme. He loved drama. But she hesitated. When had she last reached out to them? The Winter Solstice?

Thrash tossed the orb aside. She would make new friends in college. For now, she had to focus on her future—on getting into New Salem. NSU was the best school for magic in the Thirteen States. It was also on the east coast, and she would be lying to herself if part of the appeal wasn't putting an entire country between her and Osmarra. Thirteen states, in fact— three ruled by their own indigenous laws, but all ultimately answering to a High Circle and a Low Circle modeled after the Europan Fae Courts.

It also wouldn't hurt to travel outside of Osmarra's beloved Calypso for once. Thrash's longest trip had been the eight-hour car ride when they moved, and that was only from the northern half of the state to the southern. While Osmarra rode ahead on Tempest, Thrash and Duna drove the car down. The scenery was flat, beige, and forgettable.

What Thrash really remembered about that trip was the warm wind when her mum rolled down the windows, how it tousled the curly brown hair they shared. She could smell the baking sand, hear the faint chime of Duna's silver constellation earrings dancing on the breeze, feel the fizz of a super-sized lavender soda on her tongue.

Thrash grabbed the deck of cards again. She would try a different question, one that was more open-ended—and less tied to her mom.

"What does my future hold?" Thrash asked.

She flipped up the top card. It was a woman draped in blue robes, a sword in one hand and set of balanced scales in the other.

The Justice.

Relieved, Thrash sank back into her pillows. *The Justice* wasn't just a tarot card; she was one of the most famous Named Witches, a powerful seer whose predictions saved the nation from natural and political disasters. Thrash had three biographies on The Justice on her shelf and had read them all. Not only was The Justice the pinnacle of what a witch could achieve with the Gift of Sight, she had also honed her skills and earned her name by hunting down murderers. How badass was that?

There was a gentle knock at the door. Thrash shuffled *The*

Justice back into her deck, stuffing Duna's tarot cards under her pillow. Osmarra disapproved of her using them.

"Hey, Theo—"

"It's *Thrash,* Mom."

A long pause, and then, through the door: "I have something for you."

"I'm in the middle of something."

"Thrash, please." It was a small victory, one almost immediately undone by her mother's low, dangerous voice. "Unlock this door."

Thrash groaned but rolled off her bed. She had only just gotten her mom to agree to the locks a few months ago; having them revoked was not an option.

Osmarra stood in the doorway, hair down and sans necklaces. Her blue eyes flitted to Thrash's sweatpants. A wrinkle of displeasure planted itself in a familiar spot on her mom's forehead. Black sweatpants were perfectly acceptable for sleeping —so why didn't they feel good enough when her mom opened the door?

"What is it?" Thrash asked.

"I'm sorry dinner got a little tense. I meant to give you this at dinner. It's something I think will help you out over the summer."

Thrash hadn't even noticed her mom's hand tucked behind her back until suddenly a velvet jewelry box sucked up all the space between them like a black hole. Osmarra liked "gifting" Thrash things that she not-so-secretly wished Thrash would use. What would it be this time?

Osmarra gestured for Thrash to sit at her vanity, an ancient thing made of ravenswood and glass. Osmarra tried to throw the mirror away once, but Thrash saved it from the curb and lugged it back upstairs by herself. Thrash liked objects that had personality. Her room was filled with thrifted gems that

Osmarra considered eyesores, including a collection of metal goblets (decorative until Thrash got them tested for lead) and an iron cauldron she used as a sock drawer.

Thrash sat on the stool and met her own gaze in the speckled mirror. Her mother knelt beside her and placed the box in Thrash's hands. The dark velvet was surprisingly stiff.

"Now I know you don't like wearing rings..." her mom said as Thrash lifted the lid. Inside was a simple necklace. A silver letter *T* on a silver chain, presumably in case Thrash ever forgot the first initial of her name.

"Complexion smoothing, bag reduction, contouring, *and sunscreen*." Her mother's tone was almost comically reverential. "All in the same necklace."

"Wow. That's... a lot."

"Now, I know the glamours won't show up in the mirror, but we have to try it on."

Osmarra draped the pendant and then closed the chain around Thrash's throat. As Osmarra leaned back to admire the necklace, Thrash's eyes weren't on the silver *T*; they were on her mom.

In the mirror, Osmarra looked older, but no less beautiful. Stripped of her glamours, her bright eyes still projected confidence, happiness, and love—a love that wrinkles couldn't dim. As far as Thrash was concerned, this was her *true* mom.

But then Osmarra saw herself in the mirror. She touched her face self-consciously.

Then her eyes landed on Thrash.

"How long are we going to keep our hair like this?" Osmarra asked, fussing with her daughter's magenta frizz as if willing it to turn into long, tumbling locks.

"I don't know." Thrash suddenly wished she hadn't unlocked her bedroom door. She liked her hair like this. There was a reason she had been dying it since she was fourteen.

Osmarra pulled Thrash's hair back, twisting it into a bun that made her wince. "It would look so pretty if you just put it up every once in a while."

"Please, Mom. Do we have to talk about this right now?"

Osmarra let go of the bun, but her fingers still tugged Thrash's hair. Thrash swallowed, her throat catching on a lump.

"All I'm saying is that a new hairstyle could go a long way." Osmarra's fingers might as well have been around her neck. "It just requires some trial and error. But don't worry. We'll find something that frames your face better."

"Please, Mom, just *STOP*."

Osmarra gasped and released her, stepping back from the vanity. It took Thrash a moment to realize her mom hadn't backed off because of what she said, but because of what she saw in the mirror.

"My baby is a witch," Osmarra whispered.

A crack like a lightning bolt split the glass.

Osmarra wrapped her arms around Thrash in joyous disbelief. When Thrash met her mom's eyes in the mirror, tears of happiness glittered in them. She felt a pang of guilt for being so hard on her mom. Osmarra only wanted what was best for her; she just needed time to see that the Gift of Glamour wasn't it.

Right?

As Osmarra turned away to glamour her tears off her cheeks, Thrash looked into the mirror. Ripped in half by a large, ugly crack, two Thrashes stared back at her, eyes sinking like stones.

2

June 20th, the eve of the Summer Solstice.

Thrash dragged herself out of bed. Every night this week, the Gift of Glamour had infected her dreams with masks she couldn't pry off her face and dresses made of bright, glittering chains. Thrash looked at her reflection in the cracked vanity and touched her face, relieved it was her own.

That relief was short-lived when she remembered she would receive a Gift tomorrow. She only got her knack a week ago and she was already staring down the date of her Kindling Day party. Osmarra had gone into full hostess mode, orchestrating things so that Thrash could receive her Gift just in time for the solstice. Two parties in one—Osmarra's dream and Thrash's nightmare.

Osmarra also didn't shy away from pulling the strings to make the dates coincide. As the daughter of Belmar's Protectrix, Thrash apparently got to skip the knack verification process, which typically required an adjudicatrix from New Salem University. According to her mom, a Gift was on its way from NSU's library and would arrive today.

Thrash found her mom on the cream-colored carpet of their pristine living room, pedaling an invisible bike. It wasn't magic; it was high intensity interval training. The program was called "The Amazonian Method," tailor-made for warrior moms who didn't have enough hours in the day.

In center of the living room, the family orb glowed with pink light and said in a soothing male voice, "And rest for ten... nine...eight..."

Osmarra rolled back onto her hands and knees and managed to wipe the sweat from her brow in one graceful motion. She spotted Thrash and smiled.

"Good morning! You're up bright and early."

"I was just going through a few of Mum's boxes," Thrash lied. Even though she had been on her best behavior the past week—making dinner twice, keeping her room spotless—she still couldn't bring herself to sort through Duna's things.

"Is that what you're wearing tonight?"

Thrash blanched, looking down at her jumpsuit. She loved this piece of clothing: as comfortable as pajamas, but the black color made it pass as formal wear. Her mother would never appreciate this, but it was just short of miraculous to thrift a jumpsuit that fit in all the right places—especially when you were plus-size.

"...and one," the orb intoned. "You are fierce! You are a goddess! Stand tall and prepare for one minute of spring squats, starting...now."

Osmarra dropped into a squat for a few seconds and then hopped into the air. As she jumped, she said, "What about...the lace dress?"

Thrash frowned.

"The flattering one...from the ribbon cutting..."

"Thank you for your feedback." Thrash felt cute in her outfit, and she wasn't going to change it.

Her mother either didn't notice her attitude or was sweating too hard to care. Thrash knew it was a long shot, but she hoped her Kindling party wouldn't be a battlefield where she and her mother waged this pointless war. She had a more important fight to save her ammunition for: the Gifting.

Osmarra landed in a deep squat, exhaling with a sound like someone stepped on a half-inflated sunball.

"I just want...what's best for you."

"Are we still talking about my outfit?"

Thrash had been trying to get Osmarra to talk to her about her Gift all week. Every time she tried to make her case for Sight magic, Osmarra either diplomatically side-stepped or worse, reassured Thrash she knew what was best for her.

The orb flashed pink. "You are *glowing!* Rest for ten...nine..."

"Pause Amazonian Method," Osmarra said. The glowing orb relaxed into a swirl of pale mist. Osmarra stood and plucked a small white towel off the glass coffee table. As she dabbed her forehead, she turned to Thrash.

"I know you're worried about your Gift but have a little faith in me. It wouldn't be a proper Kindling if I spoiled the surprise."

Osmarra took a step back, looking long and hard at her daughter. Thrash shifted uncomfortably, but then her mom said, "Actually, I was being too harsh. I like this outfit. It's very 'you.' I was too quick to judge it."

"Thanks." Thrash's heart lifted just the slightest. Maybe she wasn't giving her mother enough credit.

Someone knocked at the front door.

"Oooh! I think I know who this is!"

Osmarra hurried to the front door and dispelled the house wards with the wand she kept in a decorative bowl on the credenza. Thrash peeked around her mom as a woman in a chipper blue uniform wished her a good morning. She held a scroll in one hand and a brown paper parcel under her arm. This was no ordinary courier; her neck bore beaded necklaces. Thrash didn't know how to read their code, but the number of chokers and the material of the beads heralded a witch's education, rank, and even specific accomplishments. This woman was an oathtrix, tasked with executing magical contracts and pacts.

Osmarra solemnly swore to take full responsibility of the Gift, to cast the spell tomorrow morning and then return it swiftly. She swapped the wand for a silver pocketknife and pricked her finger. The oathtrix unfurled the scroll, and Osmarra squeezed her pinky, letting a drop of blood fall on the dotted line.

As soon as the door closed, Osmarra rushed into the living room with the wrapped package.

"No peeking," Osmarra said with a sly wink. She positioned it in a place of prominence on the mantel above the dormant fireplace. Belmar was a mid-sized coastal city; no one ever used their fireplaces. "Now, I'm going to go take a shower. There's oatmeal on the stove and fruit in the fridge. I have to start getting ready before the staff arrive."

"The *what?*"

Osmarra squeezed her daughter's shoulder and leveled Thrash with her most reassuring smile, the one that made Thrash feel anything but reassured. "Stop worrying. You only become a witch once. Enjoy it."

"Wait—how many people are coming? I thought it was just Gram, Aunt Masha, and the twins?"

"I invited a few protectrix from nearby cities. And most of my team. And a few other people I need to impress—but I also invited some of your classmates! Won't that be fun?"

"Oh my Goddess, Mom, why would you do that?"

Osmarra jogged upstairs without a backward glance. "It's
so easy to make friends at your age! Enjoy it while you can!"

Thrash collapsed on the sculpted white couch. She yelled,
"I won't!" right as the bathroom door slammed shut.

Thrash's backyard was pristine but utilitarian, a rectangle of
grass lined with inoffensive flowers. Her mom's latest home
renovation project was the brand-new porch; Osmarra had
been really into "projects" since Duna died. The wood was so
fresh it was still bleeding sap. Thrash could smell it from her
bedroom if she left the window open.

Guests started trickling into the backyard as the sun
dipped toward the horizon, its red-gold light the color of faded
hair dye and fire. Thrash's heart beat faster at the thought of
the impending bonfire. That was the "kindling" part of the
Kindling Day, and it officially started at sunset. The Gifting
would follow at sunrise.

"Come greet your guests!" Osmarra chimed, steering
Thrash toward the gate. She looked the part of a queen with her
dark hair braided into a crown, her slim purple dress embell-
ished with intricate gold threadwork. It already felt like the
longest day of the year—and not because it was the solstice.

Thrash only dimly recognized her mother's guests, but she
shook hands, recounted the résumé version of her life, and
received presents that would aid her when she went off to an
HMU. Thrash accepted candles, herbs, and notebooks,
graciously placing the craft in the bottomless trunk. Made of
solid leviathan bone and decorated with silver constellations,
her mom had used it to move all their furniture from their old
house. The trunk was the most expensive thing they owned—

which was probably why Osmarra wanted it on display. Because really, a table would have been fine.

Eventually, Thrash snuck away to the refreshment table. Her mom had gone all out, renting a hundred jeweled cups and saucers painted with purple rings, green flowers, and blue eyes —the symbols of Glamour, Growth, and Sight. A dozen floating teapots danced around guests, their spouts nudging at empty cups like nosy cats.

Thrash picked up a cup just so she had something to occupy her hands. A floating teapot tipped hot cinnamon tea, a Kindling classic, into her cup. Thrash wondered if levitation was within the powers of a Glamour witch, or if a hidden wand channeled power to the self-pouring pot from beneath the table.

Tea in hand, Thrash scanned the sea of unfamiliar adults. A few kids ran past, wearing golden ribbons in their hair and waving sticks like wands. They'd get to play until the sun went down, a Summer Solstice tradition. The holiday was supposed to be about soaking up abundance and releasing burdens. How did that annoying ditty go? *Dance! Sing! Take a big swing! Cast off your sorrows and cast off your rings!*

Thrash moseyed over to the edge of the party and joined Tempest, her mother's familiar. It was easy to find him; he was the huge black stallion surveying the crowd with mild disgust.

"How are the apples?" Thrash asked, gesturing toward a tower of blood red apples on a silver platter.

"Go talk to your peers," the horse replied.

"I literally don't know anyone here." Thrash blew on her tea and took a sip. It was fiery, but not because it was too hot to drink. "Wow. I think my mom spiked the tea. I'm not sure if I'm impressed or horrified."

"It's a special occasion. What do you humans say? Shears?"

"...Cheers?"

"That's the one." Tempest snorted, but then he looked at Thrash with dark, heavy eyes. "This is a big day, little witch."

"I know."

Tempest's ominous stare made Thrash wonder if she was missing something. Or maybe he was just being cryptic. You never knew with familiars. The spirits offered pacts of great power to witches, but no one knew what they wanted in return. Osmarra could see through Tempest's eyes and use his magic to adjust her illusions, even on herself. Their relationship was symbiotic, and a little creepy.

"Oh Goddess, what is *Blossom* doing here?" Tempest cried suddenly. "With a mane that shabby, they really should have left her in the stables. I suppose I must offer her an apple. Excuse me."

Tempest trotted away, and with him, Thrash's excuse to not talk to anyone else. She searched the crowd for someone, anyone, from her lunch table study crew, but none of them had shown. Thrash tried to swallow her disappointment with a swig of tea. Her hand wobbled as she sipped it.

Then she felt a friendly tap on her shoulder. She caught a whiff of sugary perfume as she turned around—right into Cresca's arms.

"I told you I know a knack when I see one!" Cresca embraced Thrash in a half-hug, her silver locks grazing Thrash's cheek. They felt just as soft as they looked. "You're a witch, bitch! Congratulations!"

"Thanks?" As Thrash pulled away, she self-consciously adjusted the seat of her jumpsuit. "Did, uh, my mom invite you?"

"I hate to be the one to tell you this, but your mom invited our entire high school class."

Thrash almost spit out her tea. She wasn't sure what was worse—that her mom invited everyone, or that almost no one came. Then again, the summer before senior year always tore a rift between magical and non-magical friends.

"It's a shame you don't smoke," Cresca said. "You look like you need a cigarette."

"I'm good. Where are your, uh, friends? Are they here too?"

"Yeah, I hitched a ride with Saki's parents. Her cousin Dai came along, FYI. He's a sophomore at NSU and they will not shut up about it. They're over by the dessert."

Thrash spotted Saki sulking by her family. A young man, presumably Saki's cousin, was in the middle of some captivating anecdote. The circle that had formed around him leaned in. Dai looked like he was dressed for a job interview. Saki, on the other hand, was wearing short-shorts and an oversized NSU hoodie. She looked like she wanted to disappear into it.

Cresca scanned the backyard, then nodded toward the gated entrance. "Looks like Em just got here."

Thrash couldn't help it; she craned her head to get a look at royalty. Everyone at school called Em's dad a DILF, but the only thing remarkable about the mer-prince's appearance was a faint golden shimmer to his olive skin. Beside him, Em's mom smiled politely at the onlookers. She was a famous Named Witch they called The Gardener, but her gleaming gold chokers were the only hint that she was a renowned fabricatrix. For their astonishing pedigree, Em's parents looked like any ordinary couple, complete with their daughter trailing behind, trying to distance herself from them.

Osmarra circled the famous couple, waiting for her moment to pounce on The Gardener. Thrash knew, because her mom had talked about it for three nights straight, that Osmarra wanted to rope Em's mom into the Gifting. The spell required a blind coven—three witches of any type of magic— to cast. Osmarra knew it was a longshot to get The Gardener but having a prominent witch as one of the casters was a bragging right worth chasing.

Em split off from her parents. She started toward Cresca, but when she noticed Thrash, she pivoted and headed over to Saki instead. Thrash was disappointed but unsurprised. Call it a coven or call it a clique, the Lunes' mystique came from exclusion.

Cresca frowned. "They'll come say hi eventually. Actually, speaking of that, I have a present for you."

"You didn't have to get me anything. I didn't even expect you to come."

"And I didn't expect you to have your Kindling in under a week." Cresca's eyes twinkled. "In the library, you didn't seem super thrilled to get your knack, or to tell people about it..."

Thrash sipped her tea, avoiding Cresca's implied question. She had her own questions, like why was Cresca so damn interested in her after two years of swimming in totally different ponds?

"Look, I think we're both no-bullshit people," Cresca said, her voice suddenly low and urgent. "I'm just gonna say it. We all have our knacks. Me, Em, and Saki. But we haven't told anyone."

"Wait, really?" When did the Lunes get their knacks? Why were they keeping them a secret? And why should she care?

"It's complicated," Cresca said with a shrug, but even as she said it, she studied Thrash's face.

"And your present to me...is telling me this?"

"Not exactly. Look. What would you say if I told you that you could choose your own Gift?"

"I'd say that's impossible."

"It only seems impossible because all of this"—Cresca waved at the surrounding party—"is designed to convince us this is the only way. Why should parents choose our Gifts for us? Just because some old crones decided it should work that way a hundred years ago?"

Thrash swallowed. "I don't love it either, but that's just the way it is."

"It doesn't have to be." Cresca lowered her voice and whispered, "Drive with us to NSU. We're going to break into the library, steal our own Gifts, and cast them on ourselves."

Thrash's head spun. Had she heard that right? She wasn't sure she was understanding, and the spiked tea wasn't helping.

"I know it sounds wild but listen. We have Em's car and an NSU student ID, courtesy of Saki's cousin. All we've gotta do is get ourselves Gifts before July first, and we're golden for senior year."

"...Is this a prank or something?" Thrash asked. She glanced around, half-expecting to see Cresca's bored besties capturing this on their orbs.

Cresca frowned. "No. Why would you think that?"

"Because this is so random. I barely know you."

"We'll get to know each other along the way."

Did Thrash *want* to get to know the Lunes? Something about this plan didn't sit right with her—beyond the obvious logistical concerns of hitching a ride with three girls she barely knew and stealing from the top university in the Thirteen States.

"Oh, wait, I see," Thrash said. "You only have two people for the spell, but you need three. Your plan won't work without a fourth person."

Cresca chewed her lip. That was all Thrash needed to know.

"Not interested." She tried to walk away, but Cresca skipped a few steps ahead, throwing herself into Thrash's path.

"Wait! Wait. I get it. You're probably like, 'Why should I help these girls?' And that's fair. But we have more in common than you think." Cresca took a deep breath. "I was simplifying earlier when I said we were all hiding our knacks. I actually *did* tell my dad, but he won't send for an adjudicatrix."

"What? That's awful. Can someone even do that? Legally?"

"Do you think I'm the first witch to fall through the cracks?" Cresca's gaze fell. "If I don't steal a Gift, I won't get one."

Neither one of them said anything for a long moment.

"So, now that you've heard my tragic backstory..." Cresca held her chin a little higher, a hint of smile on her lips. "Will you run away with us? And choose your own destiny?"

Thrash had to admit, she was tempted. As she considered everything Cresca had said, she caught a glimpse of the crowd parting to let an enchanted fire pit float to the center of the lawn. Osmarra guided it with a silver wand in her hand and a genuine smile on her face.

"I can't," Thrash finally said. If nothing else, it would break her mom's heart.

"Even if your mom gives you the Gift of Glamour?"

Cresca's words hit Thrash like a gut punch. How did she guess? Or was Osmarra's vanity so notorious, and her disregard for Thrash so obvious, that everyone except Thrash already knew tonight's inevitable outcome?

Thrash stared into her teacup. If she looked into Cresca's eyes, she might cry, and she refused to cry on her Kindling Day.

"I'll live with it," Thrash said. "Thank you for your offer, but I don't want to go with you."

"Whatever you say." Cresca shrugged, but the spark had gone out of her eyes. She seemed defeated. "Just remember that we need at least five days to get there, and that doesn't factor in driving back. We should leave soon. If you change your mind."

With that, Cresca backed away, her rings dull in the twilight.

When had the sun disappeared?

One by one, guests placed branches in the fire pit. Thrash wasn't sure she tracked the metaphor. Did the sticks represent the community that supported her? Or the new life that awaited her after the Gifting? Whatever it represented, she found it strange that the culmination of her Kindling Day involved her burning everything to ash.

As Thrash's palms began to sweat, Osmarra glided between guests. Thrash hadn't seen her mother look so carefree since...well, since before Mum died.

"What if she gives you the Gift of Glamour?"

Thrash wiped her hands on her pants. Goddess, her fingers itched to pull a tarot card. As the Lunes approached one by one and added their sticks to the kindling, she couldn't help but notice how the pile of branches began to resemble one of the most ominous cards: *The Tower*. A warning of upheaval—and destruction.

"Don't be strangers!" Osmarra called, gesturing for everyone to come closer to the pit. The circle of guests tightened like a noose. With a flick of her mother's wrist, the lanterns around the backyard dimmed. The murmur of conversation faded with the light, replaced by silent anticipation.

"Thank you all for joining us for this sacred sunset." Osmarra took a deep breath and unleashed a dazzling smile that dispelled some of the seriousness in the air. "It's all gone by so fast, hasn't it? As a parent, you dream your daughter will get her knack, and then one day you wake up and your caterpillar has become a butterfly. It's hard for us parents to accept, but like the sun and the seasons, all things must change. It has been a privilege, my beloved Theodora, to watch you become the young woman you are today."

If the applause was any indication, Osmarra's oratory skills hit the mark. Thrash plastered on a smile, trying to look like she deserved the praise—though she could've done without the caterpillar comparison. Beneath the commotion, Osmarra turned to Thrash, speaking so only she could hear:

"I am so proud of you."

That got Thrash. Her love for her mother rose and caught in her throat. But before any tears could come, Osmarra pressed two pieces of flint into Thrash's hands.

Reverting to her protectrix voice, Osmarra turned to the crowd and announced, "With this fire, you take the first step toward becoming a woman. And a witch!"

Thrash swallowed. Her heart thundered in her ears, drowning out the applause. Like her mom said, it was all moving too fast. In the twilight, the sea of onlookers swayed, their faces as indistinguishable as charcoal smudges. It was only when she latched onto Cresca and her kind brown eyes that Thrash stepped back onto stable land.

Thrash raised the cold, flat stones. She felt like she was watching someone else's hands as she struck the flint. The fire pit, enchanted to catch fire with the smallest spark, erupted into a dazzling blaze. The heat lapped at Thrash's dazed face, intoxicating and sickening.

"And now the reveal!" Osmarra reached her arms into the fire. Guests gasped, the sounds of horror turning into awe and delight as Osmarra pulled a pristine white cake from the flames. Thrash's mom winked at her. More applause.

Far back from the fire, Tempest's big black outline nudged

someone forward. The crowd parted and spat out a waiter, who took the two-tiered cake out of Osmarra's hands. The man disappeared and reappeared a second later with the round white cake on a silver platter, a platter Thrash had shined for her mom earlier that week.

Thrash held her breath as Osmarra picked up the cake cutter.

Osmarra beamed at her daughter, because of course she knew the outcome. When Thrash saw the clean knife emerge with a purple smudge, her heart withered.

Glamour, the only Gift Osmarra could envision for her fat daughter. Osmarra pushed the plate of purple cake into Thrash's hands and her stomach turned. Her mom's wide smile was suddenly grotesque, like the warped masks in her dreams.

Thrash wanted to scream, she wanted to run—but all she did was stand there, surrounded yet entirely alone.

In the crowd, only three faces weren't smiling. Cresca, Saki, and Emerald didn't clap or cheer. Arms linked as if holding each other, the Lunes were stone-faced, their jeweled eyes heavy. Cresca gave Thrash a sad, knowing smile. A smile that said, "It's not too late to accept my invitation."

In that moment, Thrash was desperate enough to take it.

Em's dad squeezed her shoulder, a flash of scales just visible beneath his flannel sleeve. "Time to go, kiddo."

"The cake *just* got cut," Em whined. "Can't Saki's parents drive me home?"

"We have to get your dad home." Em's mom pulled her away from the girls and steered her toward the gate.

Were people already leaving? Was the party already over? Thrash suddenly noticed all the impatient guests checking their watches and beginning their goodbyes. In the background, caterers surreptitiously broke down tables. The evening was slipping away.

Whatever Thrash was going to do, she had only hours to decide.

Thrash sat cross-legged on her starry bedspread, nervously shuffling Duna's tarot deck. It was just past midnight; she couldn't sleep, but she also couldn't bear to deal herself a card.

Besides, she already knew what her future held. Four years of studying Glamour at an HMU and then some unbearable career in a field of magic she had zero interest in. Thrash didn't want to be a politrix like Osmarra or a trend-chasing designtrix. She couldn't see herself in entertainment as an actrix or a directrix either. Maybe she could stomach a job in security or even espionage, but she didn't want to spend her life hiding.

Osmarra thought she knew what was best for Thrash, but apparently she didn't really *know* her at all. Her mom had condemned her to a lifetime of superficial magic, of using Glamour to conform, manipulate, and hide. The only magic she would ever use, the magic of lies.

Thrash's anger crept up like a fever. She leapt off the bed, shuffling as she paced, but the longer she paced around her room, the angrier she got. How long until she broke another mirror?

Actually, breaking things sounded great.

Thrash set Duna's deck down on the vanity and eased open her bedroom door. She listened for a long beat. When she convinced herself Osmarra was sleeping, Thrash crept down the carpeted stairs and into the kitchen.

Osmarra always lectured her about midnight snacks, so Thrash decided now was the perfect time to indulge in one.

Leftover hors d'oeuvres piled in glass containers crowded the refrigerator so that Thrash couldn't even see the suspended metal wand at the back of the fridge, which channeled magic to keep it all cool. Her stomach grumbled, and she realized she had been so nervous at the party that she hadn't eaten a single bite.

One particular food caught her eye, though.

Thrash pulled the top tier of the cake out of the fridge and cut herself *the largest* slice. Like, a-quarter-of-the-cake large. She smiled, maybe for the first time that day, as she stabbed her fork into the slice and took her plate to the living room. She sat on one of the rigid, colorless couches, breaking Osmarra's rule that food wasn't allowed near them.

As Thrash hate-ate the purple sponge, her gaze wandered over the untouchable furniture in the sitting room where they never sat. The room looked far more ominous at night, from the dull glow of the curtains to the strange shadows cast by the central orb. Watching over it all was a book wrapped tight in smooth parcel paper. The Gift.

Thrash set her plate on the couch. It accidentally tipped, and her silver fork scraped so loudly that her head whipped to the stairs.

All quiet.

Thrash picked up the Gift. It was lighter than she expected for a spell book, but if it only contained a single spell, maybe it was a short book. Every crinkle of the wrapping paper made Thrash's heart leap into her throat. Before she could talk herself out of it, she tore the rest of the paper off like Mum had taught her to rip off old bandages.

Beneath the packaging paper was a simple tome bound with pitted leather, *The Gift of Glamour* embossed in silver script across its cover. Thrash turned it over. It was just a collection of words, and yet so much more than that. Could a book change the course of her entire life?

Thrash had to look inside.

She held her breath as she opened the book, but there was no paper, no pages.

It took Thrash a moment to realize what she had in her hands was a false book, hollowed out and filled with craft.

Thrash counted five black candles and three pouches made of fine purple velvet nestled between the candles. Did she dare open them?

How could she not?

The first pouch held three golden amulets shaped like abstract suns. They didn't look like any craft Thrash had ever seen, but books about witchcraft were heavily regulated and typically owned and leased out by schools. She gleaned what she could from her moms over the years, but it would be up to her prep classes next year to start filling in the gaps.

In the second pouch, Thrash found a delicate box with a dozen pins mounted inside. Each pin was two, maybe three inches long, with small gemstones at the heads that reminded her of the beaded chokers witches wore.

From there, it only got weirder. She opened the third pouch and found a glass vial filled with pearly beads. Thrash squinted at them in the dim light.

Teeth. Not beads, but teeth. It was a vial of *baby* teeth.

Were they...*her baby teeth*?

Thrash almost slammed the book shut, but her curiosity was a hunger she couldn't ignore. Thrash set aside the baby teeth and removed a false tray.

Behind it was a clay doll shaped, undeniably, like Thrash.

Feeling dizzy, she crammed the items back into the hollowed-out book. This couldn't be the Gift of Glamour. Pins and baby teeth? A simulacrum of some sort? There was nothing about Glamour in there. It made no sense.

Thrash had so very few answers, but at least there was one thing she did know.

She could not let her mom cast the Gift of Glamour on her.

Ever.

3

Cresca laid awake in bed. It was her knack acting up again. Her bones thrummed, vibrating until she couldn't stay still for another second.

She hopped out of bed, slipped on her rings, and grabbed a half-empty pack of cigarettes. The only thing that made the bone-rattling feeling go away was releasing that energy with a toss.

"Where do you need me to go at this hour?" she whispered, slipping a single cigarette out of the box. Normally, she would toss a branch, but her dad gave her weird looks when she started bringing nature inside. It was a waste of money to throw a cigarette, but it had to be something with a little "outside" in it. Tobacco was once a plant, after all.

Cresca allowed herself a moment to smell the cigarette, and then, with a sigh, she flipped it into the air. It landed, predictably, facing the door.

Cresca picked up the cigarette, cracked her bedroom door, and slipped out into the hallway. She crept past Nana's bedroom, her fingers shaking. Her grandma said throwing things and trusting how they landed was a superstition, not magic, but Nana hated magic and blamed all their problems on it. Cresca needed to believe her knack was real. A Gift couldn't enhance magic if it wasn't there.

Cresca focused on what she did know, which was that her bones wouldn't quiet until she got where she needed to go. At the end of the hall, she tossed the cigarette again. It pointed to the front door.

Cresca looked through the peephole and saw a short, fat, white girl trying to peer through the blinds of her living room window.

Thrash?! Cresca picked up the front door wand with shaky hands, then undid the house wards. When Cresca opened the door, Thrash almost jumped out of her skin.

"Goddess, Thrash, are you robbing us?" Cresca whispered.

Thrash was dressed in black from head to toe. She pulled off her black beanie, releasing a cloud of magenta hair.

"I was trying to blend in."

She said it so seriously that Cresca almost laughed. Damn if she didn't admire Thrash's...pluck? That word was too squishy to describe her. Maybe grit, or nerve. It was what old crones called gumption, back in the day.

Thrash's eyes flitted to Cresca's legs, and she realized she had automatically slipped on her rings but completely forgotten pants. Eh. Her bottoms were cute. Could be a bathing suit.

"Sorry, I should've sent a capture or something," Thrash mumbled, cheeks turning red. "I should've warned you I was showing up."

"I *did* notice your bottomless trunk on our sidewalk." A few feet behind Thrash, an expensive ivory chest glittered in the moonlight. It made Cresca feel a little self-conscious about her modest house with its cracked security mirror on the front door. She really hoped her knack was real, because witches landed the best jobs, no matter what her grandma said.

"Does that mean what I think it means?"

"I'm going with you," Thrash blurted. "To the library at New Salem University."

"And you want to leave...tonight?"

"My Gifting is at sunrise."

"But what about your mom?"

"I left her a capture," Thrash said. "I tried to make it sound like I got cold feet and I would be back for the Gifting later. I told her not to follow us, but I made it sound like a spontaneous thing..."

Cresca bit her lip. This fantasy had lived so long in her brain—now that it was actually happening, could she go through with it? Cresca's dad always claimed her problem was "follow-through." He was a history teacher and coached the high school's sunball team. All his life lessons rang like locker room pep talks. Their latest argument, about her knack, ended with the conclusion that Cresca was "lazy, frivolous, and mouthy."

Meanwhile, Thrash waited on her porch for an answer, her eyes wide and hopeful.

"Let's get that chest in here before someone robs *you*," Cresca said. Her body buzzed, and it wasn't from her maybe-a-knack. They were leaving. They were truly, finally, leaving.

And Cresca was a little bit terrified.

Thrash tapped her foot nervously as she lingered in Cresca's kitchen, admiring the wood cabinets and the very orange, very floral 70s wallpaper. Cresca was making tea because she claimed it would take Em and Saki at least half an hour to

sneak out, get the car, and haul themselves to her house. As
Cresca pointed out, it was "only" 2:00 a.m.

"Sunrise is 5:40 a.m.," Thrash pointed out. That gave them
three hours before Osmarra woke up—and that wasn't
factoring in her mom's tendency to be early for everything. It
was honestly a miracle that Thrash had been able to creep past
the stables and Tempest, who was passed out after a night of
apples and indulgence.

"We have time. Just relax." Cresca struck a match and bent
over the stove to light the burner.

"How can I relax when we're supposed to leave and you're
not even wearing pants yet?"

Cresca laughed. The flame caught and flared on the stove.

"Why don't you light it with a wand?" Thrash asked.

"Wands are expensive."

Thrash paled. Was that an insensitive question? This was
why she didn't trust herself around other human beings.
Cresca's enchanted rings cost a fair amount, and wands
weren't *that* expensive, especially disposable ones...but what
did Thrash really know about money?

Cresca left the pot to boil and started rooting around in the
cupboards. Thrash's gaze roved the kitchen shelves, which
held a mixture of cookbooks and knickknacks. Osmarra
would've called it cluttered, but Thrash found Cresca's house
cozy and packed with memories. Her eyes settled on a homemade calendar. Bathing suit-clad and smiling, the Kings posed
for a photo by the ocean. Thrash didn't see any beaded collars;
she wondered if anyone in Cresca's family had magic.

Thrash leaned in. Mr. and Mrs. King smiled, their arms
wrapped around an eight or nine-year-old Cresca. Absent were
her signature platinum locks; instead, two yellow bows
corralled Cresca's frizzy black hair into pig tails. By her side
stood a skinny teenager in a crocheted bikini and matching

white hat. She smiled coyly at the camera. Did Cresca have an older sister?

Then Thrash noticed that the calendar wasn't turned to June, but to August—and was almost ten years out of date.

"Black or green?" Cresca asked, tossing two tea boxes to the table. The sound made Thrash wince; the last thing they needed was a waking parent. "I know it's not fancy, but—"

"Black. I think I'm gonna need the caffeine."

Cresca continued buzzing around the kitchen, collecting mugs and spoons and napkins and cookies. It was maddening. Thrash could feel every wasted second dripping down the drain. And Cresca *still* hadn't packed her hat.

Then Cresca froze. For a brief second Thrash wondered if maybe Cresca's knack had to do with reading thoughts, but then she heard a distant click. Like the sound of a door closing.

"Bathroom door," Cresca mouthed.

The hairs on Thrash's arms and neck rose. Wordlessly, she went to the stove and turned off the gas. Cresca nodded. So much for teatime.

They crept out into the living room. Still empty. Cresca pointed at the bottomless trunk and in her lowest whisper asked, "Can I throw my stuff in there?"

Thrash hesitated. She had grabbed the chest because she figured the Kindling Day presents might be useful, but she had also thrown in the Gift of Glamour. Thrash had spent the whole walk here justifying her impulse decision to take the Gift. First and foremost, Thrash had no idea if Osmarra could cast the ritual on her from a distance, and she didn't want to find out. Taking it was also a huge middle finger to Osmarra. Plus, that Thrash-doll was *creepy*.

She didn't regret her decision to get the Gift of Glamour away from Osmarra, but she also didn't want Cresca finding the Gift. It wasn't exactly the stealthy choice; Thrash didn't want Cresca thinking she had already ruined the plan. For now, it was easier not to tell the Lunes and complicate things.

Thrash was still working out how to politely decline when Cresca rolled her eyes.

"Whatever. Sorry I asked." Cresca grabbed a knit blanket off the back of a couch and threw it over Thrash's trunk. "The hallway's old and creaky, so watch where I step."

Thrash followed Cresca down the dark hallway, past a parade of framed team photos of a smiling Mr. King surrounded by beaming athletes. She had never had Mr. King as a teacher, but he had a reputation for being tough but fair, with a zero tolerance policy for goofing off in class.

Light peeked out from under a closed door. Thrash held her breath. It felt like she was stepping through the beam of a searchlight as she stepped past the bathroom door. But the door didn't swing open.

At the end of the hallway, they slipped into Cresca's room. Inside, it was like a mall had exploded. Clothes spilled everywhere. Thrash counted three "closets"—a wardrobe bursting at the seams, a small mountain that was probably once a chair, and the floor. Cresca's desk and bedside table were coated in beauty products, many of which Thrash could not identify (and looked like they doubled as instruments of torture). One wall was devoted entirely to a giant collage.

"I know, it's a mess," Cresca whispered. She grabbed a white pointed hat off a hook on the wall. A familiar crochet pattern decorated the brim—Thrash had seen it in that family photo, on Cresca's older sister's head. White in its prime, the hat was aging into a cream color. She watched Cresca stuff skimpy tank tops, shorts, and sandals into it.

"Three bathing suits?" Thrash asked.

"I like to be prepared."

"For what? A monsoon?"

Cresca only smiled.

Thrash eyed the dreamy collage. Among the swirling images, she recognized famous Glamour witches, among them beautiful actrix and trendtrix. Scattered with cutouts from fashion magazines were photos of classic witch symbols—crescent moons, beaded chokers, broomsticks, and of course, the pointed hats that had once been outlawed in Europa. Rings, the symbol of Glamour, appeared in bursts like fireworks.

"Hey, catch!"

Thrash turned just in time to catch Cresca's orb, which pulsed twice with white light. A message.

"Can you check if that's Em and Saki?" Cresca asked as she wrestled some underwear out of a drawer and added it to the hat. As Cresca reached under her bed and dug out a pair of jeans, Thrash cupped the orb with one hand and swirled her fingers over it. The cloudy interior dissipated and revealed Em's face. She looked like she was in a car.

"Get in, witch!" Em yelled. "Let's hit the road and get this adventure start—"

Thrash dismissed the recording, but the damage had already been done. Em's exuberant face faded away and the crystal turned opaque once more.

"Well..." Cresca said as she tugged on her pants. "They're here."

"Do you think that was loud enough to wake up your dad?"

When Cresca looked up, her smile was gone. She magically fastened her hat to her head with both hands.

"Only one way to find out."

～

Thrash wasn't sure if it was a good omen or a bad one, but the bathroom light was off when they stepped back out into the hallway.

"Toothbrush?" Thrash whispered.

"I'll buy one or borrow one if I have to."

Borrow a toothbrush? Thrash made a mental note to never leave her toothbrush unattended in any future bathrooms they might share.

Cresca's orb, clutched in her fist, glowed with a new message. Thrash shook her head. *Don't answer it.* Cresca nodded and peered through the living room blinds instead. She gave Thrash a thumbs-up. As Thrash picked up the bottomless trunk, she marveled that they had gotten away so easily.

"Where do you think you're going?"

Thrash almost dropped the trunk. In the dimly lit living room, Cresca's dad stood up from the couch. He loomed over Thrash and Cresca at six-foot something. Clothed in shadows and a pair of athletic shorts, he crossed his beefy arms, awaiting an explanation.

"Hey, Dad. This is my friend, Thrash," Cresca said. For once, Thrash wished she had been introduced as Theodora. After all, Thrash wasn't the name of someone you wanted your daughter running off with in the dead of night. "Thrash, this is my dad."

"Um, hi, Mr. King. Nice to meet you."

Cresca's dad didn't even look at Thrash. Staring daggers at his daughter, he said, "Cresca, you can't do this to your grandmother."

"Do what?"

Mr. King's eyes flitted to Thrash, but only for a second. "You know what."

"Relax, Dad. Thrash is a new friend. We're just going on a road trip."

"In the middle of the persecuting night?"

Cresca stood her ground. "We're leaving early to beat the traffic."

Mr. King laughed, sudden and sharp as a bark. Thrash glanced at the hallway and wondered how long it would be before someone else emerged. They had to get out of here.

"Cresca, I'm at the end of my rope with this behavior."

"What behavior?" Cresca batted her eyes innocently, but Thrash detected a vicious undercurrent. If Cresca pushed her dad's buttons, would their road trip end before they even made it out the front door? "Oh, do you mean how you called me lazy, frivolous, and what was it? Oh, yeah, 'mouthy.'"

Mr. King's face fell, the fight leeching out of him. "I can't keep doing this."

"Doing what?"

"I don't want to fight you. Please, just tell me where you're going."

"For your information, this is an educational trip. We're going to New Salem University."

Thrash closed her eyes. How long before Osmarra pried their destination out of Cresca's dad? This was the beginning of the end.

Mr. King shook his head. "You expect me to believe that?"

"Fine..." Cresca's eyes flickered for a moment. "We're going to Slumber City."

Mr. King sighed and rubbed his hands back and forth over his shaved head, probably picturing all the underage drinking associated with the ironically named party capital of the Thirteen States.

"Why on earth do you want to drive to that cesspool?" Mr. King asked, but he sounded sort of relieved.

"Literally, to party," Cresca said, tossing her hair. "I'm seventeen and it's summer! I just want to go on a road trip with my friends—who, by the way, will totally watch my back and make sure no one slips me any drugs."

"Drugs?!"

"I love you, Dad," Cresca said. "Tell Nana it's not personal. I'll check in every day and see you in two weeks."

Then they walked right out the front door. Thrash couldn't believe it. She looked back over her shoulder, but Mr. King didn't move or yell after them. He seemed disappointed in Cresca, but not determined to control her. What must that be like?

As Thrash carried the trunk, Cresca slipped her hand beside Thrash's, attempting to take the handle from her.

"Thanks, but I got it," Thrash said.

"Em's car is around the corner. We have a spot." Cresca's hand pressed against hers in a stubborn battle of wills. Thrash sighed and released the handle, allowing Cresca to help carry the load.

Before they reached the end of the street, a car hovered up beside them. Thrash's vision filled with five feet of chrome and magnificent, tropical blue. The roof of the boxy convertible peeled back with appropriate suspense and revealed two pointed hats, Em's a woven straw number and Saki's an indigo velvet. While Em craned to wave at Cresca, studiously avoiding meeting Thrash's eyes, Saki stared at Thrash so hard it felt like she was willing her to turn around.

"Hey, can you land?" Cresca asked. "Thrash brought a bunch of goodies for the road, but we need to get this chest into the trunk."

Behind the wheel, Em picked up a metal wand. "You got it."

Em traced a pattern Thrash recognized from driver's ed, and the classic convertible dropped unceremoniously to the ground, hitting the asphalt with a crunch. Wheels would've cushioned the fall, but the last time this car had wheels was 1976. This was part of why Osmarra, and the NatPo, preferred familiars—they were more reliable than revitalizing old vehicles with magic.

After Cresca and Thrash lifted the bottomless trunk into the boot of the car, Thrash hopped over the door and landed in the back seat. Saki immediately whirled around.

"That's Cresca's seat."

"Oh. Sorry." Her cheeks heated up. Is this what the entire road trip would be like? Was it too late to turn back?

Thrash scooted over to the seat behind Em. Unsure where to look or what to say, she studied the interior of the convertible. The backseat was spotless, and the pearlescent fabric upholstery felt stiff and cold to the touch. Thrash ran her hand along the raised ridges of the shimmering leather, noticing a pattern of repeating diamonds—almost like scales.

"Is this dragon hide?" she gasped before she could stop herself. Osmarra was well-off as a protectrix, but she should've known Em's parents were real rich—like, dragon-leather-in-your-restored-car rich.

"Relax, it's faux hide. Everybody buckled in?" Em didn't pause long enough to give anyone a chance to reply. "Saki, hit it!"

Saki hesitated. With her long ballerina legs, she looked cramped in the passenger seat.

"Um, which playlist do I hit?"

"*Fuck the Parents,*" Em said.

The car speakers blasted electro-string in a language Thrash didn't recognize. Between the loud music and the lukewarm Lunes, Thrash had enough second thoughts to fill the bottomless trunk.

Em grasped the wand and the car jolted back into the air.

Thrash eyed the horizon line. Was the inky sky already brightening, or was that just her imagination?

Em flicked the wand and the music blasted louder. With another spell, the car took off. Thrash might have been comforted to know it was only 2:47 a.m., and that Em's playlist had not, in fact, woken up half the neighborhood. She was thankful for one thing at least: they were finally on the road.

4

Thrash's stomach started grumbling for real food around 7:00 a.m. While Cresca had drifted into peaceful slumber in the backseat, Thrash hadn't slept a wink. Her eyes scanned the rearview mirrors as the landscape outside her window transformed from shrubby coastal hills into cracked salt plains. *Thank You For Visiting Calypso!* read a sun-bleached sign with a witch in a bikini tipping her hat at drivers.

"I guess we're in Redrock now," Thrash commented. They were making good time.

"If you're looking for the official welcome sign, it's likely on the main highway, Leyline 791," Em said. "This is the old route. In the fifties, it was a thing to drive this road from Calypso to Wyckton. Coast to coast."

Thrash knew that already, but she nodded along. Last year, she had Modern Magic History with Em, which covered the period from the Founding Sisters landing in Salem to the Second Magical Revolution in the 1970s. Em had been an insufferable know-it-all, the kind who pushed everyone out on a group project and then acted like a martyr when she did all the work herself. Thrash reminded herself that she only had to survive a week and a half of this. It took about five days to drive to New Salem, Wyckton—but with only ten days until July 1st, they would be cutting it close.

Thrash slipped her orb out of her hat. When she touched it, the crystal ball pulsed six times in her hand. Thrash didn't need to play the messages to guess who hand sent them. Osmarra was going to murder her.

Em gasped, pulling Thrash's attention away from the orb.

"I haven't eaten at a Sunny Bucket in, like, forever!" Em cried as they drove past a billboard with a smiling egg rising out of a bright red bucket. "How many miles away? Did it say? Did anyone catch it?"

"Not sure..." Saki said, her hand draped out the window, surfing the breeze. "But I could eat."

Thrash opened her mouth to object and a handful of her magenta hair landed in her mouth. Maybe that was a sign that she should keep her mouth shut. Thrash was trying her hardest not to be prickly on day one, even with her hair flying in her face.

Another billboard for the Sunny Bucket sailed by. Saki read aloud: "In five miles, take the Lost Paradise exit."

"Maybe we should keep going," Thrash blurted. She shifted in the backseat, pinned by her seatbelt. "We're making great time. I'm fine eating snacks."

Saki and Em shared an unreadable glance but didn't say anything. Thrash's gut twisted. She wished Cresca, who she had at least gotten to know a little bit, wasn't sound asleep by her side.

"Actually, real breakfast sounds great," Thrash murmured.

"There are so many options," Em continued, as if Thrash

hadn't spoken. "Though, I'm probably just gonna get a sunny bucket. And maybe extra hash browns..."

As Em and Saki chattered about the menu, Thrash stared into the glowing orb. Thrash hated that she had folded so easily, but she told herself she was upholding an unspoken peace treaty. Peace with the Lunes would keep the drive bearable, or at least that's what Thrash told herself as another billboard flew past, another egg and another red bucket. Thrash returned the orb to her hat, her mom's captures unplayed and unanswered.

Em guided the car off the leyline. Clustered around the offramp, the town of Lost Paradise seemed anything but lost: it *screamed* for attention. There was a bar (*Two-For-One Tuesdays!*), a dusky purple motel (*Orbs in Every Room! Mermaid-Safe Pool!*), a craft station (*Affordable Wands! Sage Water!*), and, of course, the heavily advertised Sunny Bucket. A reflective blue sign boasted that Lost Paradise had a population of only 250.

The car hovered over to the gravel parking lot alongside the Sunny Bucket. With a flick of her metal wand, Em severed the connection between the car and the magic it was channeling. The car wavered in the air, and then dropped into the gravel with a crunch that made Thrash's teeth clack together. Cresca yawned and stretched like a cat.

"Oooh, yum, a Sunny Bucket!" Cresca hopped over the door. That was the other flaw of these old cars: once they were grounded, the doors couldn't open without scraping against the pavement. That was why it was mostly old, revitalized convertibles flying around. Thrash noticed Em struggling to get out of the driver's seat. Long-limbed Saki leaned over and helped her out.

As Thrash held open the restaurant door for the girls, she wondered if she had ever felt as cheerful as the relentless smiling eggs painted on every glass window. Inside the diner, she found the clock, also shaped like an egg. It read 7:16 a.m. Hopefully they could be out by eight.

After they scooted into a red vinyl booth, an acne-faced waiter dropped off their menus without a word. He had red hair the color of watery ketchup.

Thrash flipped through the spiral-bound menu. She had read novels shorter than this.

Cresca yawned and waved over their teenage waiter. "Four coffees, please."

"We should definitely order at least one bucket," Em declared, her nose deep in the menu. "It's four eggs and a pound of hash browns. They shape the hash browns into a bucket. Ergo, the sunny bucket."

"It's not a real bucket?" Thrash joked. No one laughed.

"How are you ladies doing?" the waiter asked. Thrash did a double take. Their waiter had the same ketchupy hair but gone was the acne. He had sprouted a jawline and an extra six inches of height.

"Two egg whites, scrambled, and two sides of bacon." Cresca leaned over to Thrash and whispered, "Be warned: Saki grazes on our meals. Get used to it, and maybe order an extra side."

An extra side of what? Thrash hadn't even made it past page four. When the boy's eyes landed on her, Thrash said the only thing she could: "I'll do the bucket, I guess."

"Me too," Em chimed.

"How do you want your eggs?"

"Sunny side up!" Em replied. "You gotta get 'em sunny side up, it's the best. Trust me."

The waiter looked to Thrash.

"I'll do that too. Thanks."

The waiter turned to Saki, who was staring off into space and hadn't even cracked her giant menu. Em nudged her.

"Oh..." Saki said. She blinked a few times, as if waking from a dream. "Sorry. I'll just have the coffee. Thank you."

The waiter jotted it down. As soon as he disappeared behind the counter, Cresca leaned in conspiratorially: "Did our waiter grow up?"

"Right?" Em said. "That's what I was wondering too!"

"If enchanted rings can do *that*," Cresca said, leaning back to glance at the waiter's hands, "we're screwed. Older, hotter boys that are secretly eleven? I'm done."

Thrash watched their waiter as he fetched a coffee pot. There were some things magic couldn't replace, like a smiling human face, or the feeling of being cared for by human hands, even if those human hands were just pouring coffee. All the cost-cutting, time-saving magic would be happening in the kitchen, where non-magical cooks used wands far from the eyes of customers.

The kitchen door swung open, and their original waiter emerged balancing three plates. The girls glanced back and forth between the boy with the coffee and the boy with the plates.

"Older brother!" Cresca cried. "Of course!"

Em nodded. "Occam's razor. The simplest, least magical explanation is probably correct."

The Lunes laughed over the mix-up as Waiter Sr. poured fresh coffee and Waiter Jr. set down the ceramic plate piled with hash browns and eggs. The sunny bucket was like a messy, edible science fair volcano. It was one of the most beautiful human creations Thrash had ever seen.

As they all dug into the food, Em stuffing hash browns into her smiling face and Saki stealing small, thoughtful bites of everyone else's food, Thrash almost forgot that she was an outsider, almost forgot the ticking clock.

Almost.

The coffee and the hearty food gave Thrash a second wind. She felt not only livelier, but friendlier.

When Waiter Jr. passed to refill mugs with steaming coffee, Cresca put her hand over her mug. Cresca's rings flashed, but this time Thrash noticed a small, black crescent moon tattoo just above her knuckles. On her middle finger. Where had she seen that before?

Thrash glanced across the table as Saki lifted her mug and Em swirled her fingers over her orb. They all shared the same simple black crescent tattoo on their left hands. As she watched Cresca's fingers fidgeting on the linoleum tabletop, Thrash felt an irrational pang of sorrow at the thought that she wasn't one of the Lunes—even though she had never wanted to be one.

Cresca suddenly shot up from the table, her fingers tapping her hips. How much caffeine had she had?

"I need a smoke," Cresca announced. "Be right back."

"I'll go pay." As Em scooted out of the booth, she spun a plain metal band around her finger. Must be her credit ring. Thrash had one for emergencies, but she had accidentally left it at home.

With Cresca outside and Em up at the register, suddenly it was just Thrash and Saki at the table.

Saki sipped her black coffee, squinting at Thrash over the top of her orb with precisely zero subtly.

"I've heard you model on the side..." Thrash ventured.

"That's just a rumor."

"Oh." Beneath the table, Thrash drummed her fingers on her jeans. "Um, so what are you into, then? Do you have any hobbies or anything?"

Apparently that was a sore spot, because Saki's eyes narrowed and she burst out, "How do you know Cresca? I have been Em's best friend since first grade, and I've known Cresca since third grade when she moved two blocks down the street."

"Um, I honestly don't really know her?" Caught off guard by Saki's directness, Thrash felt like she was stumbling in the dark. "Cresca just kinda happened to be there when I got my knack. And I guess she needed a fourth person for the Gift ritual."

"Yeah..." Saki didn't look smug or angry. If anything, she looked a little panicky, darting glances around the diner. Looking for the other Lunes to come to her rescue?

Thrash knew that feeling.

"So, you like your coffee black, huh?"

"I have perfect taste," Saki said by way of explanation. "It's like musicians who have perfect pitch."

"Is that your knack?" Thrash asked.

"I think so..."

"Is that great or terrible?"

Saki stopped looking for the Lunes. She leaned in, her voice an excited whisper. "If food is perfectly cooked and perfectly seasoned, it's *amazing*. But when I taste everything that's wrong all at once, it can be so...not harsh, exactly...um..."

"Overwhelming?" Thrash asked. Saki nodded. "At least you don't psychically break mirrors with your mind when you get upset."

"Cresca mentioned that..." Saki paused thoughtfully. "Pretty badass."

"Thanks," was all Thrash could manage. She, Thrash, was

badass? She hated to think that popularity had any power over her, but the thought of Saki Anderson, the school's ethereal beauty, finding Thrash cool went to her head like a sip of champagne.

She was still giddy and a bit disoriented when Cresca bounded up to the table, smelling faintly of soap and cigarettes.

"Pick up your hats and finish your coffee," Cresca declared. "There's a unicorn farm near the southern border of Redrock and Ji'ishland, and I *need* to take a few captures or I'm gonna explode."

"I'm just saying that I don't think a unicorn farm is what you think it is," Thrash told Cresca.

According to the egg clock, it was only 7:55 a.m., but a detour was the last thing they needed. Cresca just shrugged and waved goodbye to the waiter-brothers as they left the Sunny Bucket. The cook even stuck her head out of the kitchen window to bid them farewell. Her hair was red, streaked with gray.

"Wow, it's really a family affair," Cresca commented.

"Don't change the subject." As soon as they stepped outside, Thrash gripped the brim of her hat, fastening it to her head. Without magic binding their wide-brimmed hats to their heads, the wind would've stolen them long ago. "Unicorn farms aren't exactly ethical."

"It's not like they're making unicorn hamburgers." Cresca cringed. "That would be gross. I'm practically vegan."

"Except for eggs," Thrash deadpanned.

"And bacon!" Cresca flashed a wicked smile.

"All those farms care about is selling unicorn horns and

unicorn hair. Do you really think hornless, bald unicorns are a good photo op?"

Before Cresca could reply, Saki yelped behind them.

Em was in a heap on the ground. Thrash's brain flashed with an image of her mum Duna collapsing at the bottom of the stairs. Her heart spiked. She rushed to Em's side.

"Oh Goddess, are you okay?" Thrash asked.

"Ah, it's nothing," Em said through gritted teeth.

"Do we need to go to a hospital?" Thrash looked back and forth between Cresca, whose mouth was still frozen in a shocked O, and Saki, who was elbow-deep in her hat, rummaging around for something.

"No, no. You sound as bad as my parents." Em waved Thrash away. "I just didn't know we were leaving last night so I didn't take a soak, and now my stupid half-mermaid legs are throwing a fit."

Thrash felt a pang of sympathy, and guilt. She had never seen Em's legs. They were always tucked away under hefty peasant skirts.

Thrash tried to offer Em a hand up (she kept turning it down) when Saki let out an "Ah ha!" and pulled out a collapsible metal cane. Saki snapped the pieces into place like she had done it a hundred times and the cane floated off the ground, hovering in the air like a magic broom of old.

"Absolutely not," Em said.

"Are you able to drive?" Thrash asked. Her black hat was beginning to bake in the sun. She could literally feel the minutes ticking away as the sun inched upward.

"No," Saki answered firmly, right as Em finally stood back up to full height.

"Can anyone else drive?" Thrash asked.

Cresca scoffed. "Do you have your license?"

"No, but I thought you did?"

"Nope. Em's the only one who can drive."

"The motel has a pool that is mermaid-safe," Saki said. "And it's only a few blocks away. We'll soak your legs and then you can drive *safely*."

Thrash watched helplessly as Saki packed up the cane and Em stubbornly inched forward. What had Thrash gotten herself into? Part of her wanted to protest, but what was she gonna do, argue it was safe to drive right after Em took a fall?

Cresca fell back beside Thrash. "Girl, it's fine. This is just a slight detour. We're still going to make it to NSU. I've got the whole thing planned out."

"I'm not worried about the plan," Thrash said, though she was secretly a little concerned on that front too. "I'm worried my mom will catch up to us."

"You need to seriously stop thinking about her." Cresca grabbed Thrash's hand and tugged her toward the faded purple motel.

But Cresca didn't know about the stolen Gift of Glamour hidden in the bottomless chest in the boot of Em's car. She didn't know Thrash had stolen two priceless objects from her mom, which, in retrospect, maybe wasn't the smartest idea.

"Thrash," Cresca urged. "This is silly. Your mom isn't chasing us like some Ji'ishland bounty hunter."

If only she could believe that was true.

INTERLUDE

Tempest hated mornings only slightly more than he hated human children. He was bloated; he was parched. That was the cost of a mortal body, he supposed.

As Tempest shook out his marvelous coat on the way to the water trough, he wished he hadn't eaten quite so many apples at the party last night. It was a crime that the Gifting was at dawn. He could do without all the fanfare and secrecy of the Gifts, but he had to acknowledge that the Gifts were practically all that separated a witch from a typical today.

Thrash told Tempest it was rude to say "typicals" presently, but how else was he supposed to distinguish between those with magic and without? "Non-magical persons" had a terrible ring to it. It made Tempest feel every one of his two hundred and forty-seven years in this physical body. Tempest longed for the early days of the Thirteen States, when a witch could channel magic and a typical could not. He would never understand why witches invented wands, rings, and other

enchanted accoutrements that gave their magic away.
Everything had gone downhill since the Second Magical
Revolution.

As the red glow of dawn soaked the stable, Tempest tried
to picture pesky little Thrash, who had just learned to walk
yesterday, receiving her Gift this morning. Osmarra was likely
trying to pry Thrash out of bed this very instant. Everything
was a fight between those two. There had been no peace since
Duna's death.

The stable door banged open. A disheveled Osmarra
rushed inside, last night's updo coming undone around her
wild eyes as she clutched her orb.

"Theodora is gone," Osmarra said, thrusting her orb in
Tempest's face. "Watch."

The swirling mists dissipated, and Thrash's face filled the
glass. The child's voice was a whisper.

"Hey, Mom. Don't panic, but some friends invited me on a
trip and—and I'm going. I'll be gone for a week or two, but I
promise we'll be safe, and we'll be back before the deadline. I
just need some time to think. I hope you understand. Anyway,
love you. See you soon."

Tempest snorted. "While I do admit the party could have
had a better turn out, I didn't think it was *that* bad."

"There's more," Osmarra said, rubbing her temples. "The
Gift of Glamour is gone."

Tempest straightened. "Now *that* is an intriguing wrench."

"Is she doing this to punish me?" Osmarra cried. "She has
no idea what could happen to me if the High Circle gets wind
of this. At a minimum, we'll both face Realignment."

Ah, Realignment, what humans considered a humane,
therapy-driven alternative to their barbaric prisons of
centuries past. Tempest rather thought humans had gone soft

over the years. He saw evidence of this in how Osmarra sheltered Thrash, bending over backward to smooth the road ahead for her.

"We cannot allow her to open it," Osmarra continued. "This could end my career and destroy her future—"

"We won't let it get that far."

Osmarra nodded, but as she sat down on a hay bale, her confidence wilted. Despair stained her face like runny mascara.

"I thought I raised her better than this. What does it say about me that I can't even control a stubborn teenager? How will I earn my Name if I can't even handle my own daughter?"

Osmarra glanced up at the ceiling, blinking back tears. Tempest nuzzled her arm. Humans needed that sort of thing from time to time, even though it made Tempest feel like a glorified nanny. Osmarra often came down to the stables after a few glasses of wine and told Tempest her fears that Thrash was too quiet, too friendless, and too immature for her age.

What no one seemed to understand was that to Tempest, humans were *all* children.

"Start with what we can control," Tempest suggested. "Avoid notifying the High Circle that Thrash missed the Gifting. If we never report that the Gift is missing, no one need ever know she took it."

Osmarra was nodding now. Tempest tugged on strings of magic, opening the curtain that separated them and allowed Osmarra to see through his eyes. She wiped away her tears and began fixing her face, erasing the bags under her eyes with a minor work of Glamour.

"What will they call us?" Tempest intoned, leveling Osmarra with his dark eyes.

Osmarra sat up a little straighter. "The Triumph."

"Let's earn our Name." Tempest's nuzzle became a nudge

toward the door. Though she would never realize it, a shakeup might be good for Osmarra. "Fix your hair, eat some breakfast, and think like a protectrix. Who does she know who owns an automobile?"

5

"Girl, you can just borrow one of my swimsuits."

"No, thank you," Thrash insisted. If Cresca suggested she change into one of her skimpy bikinis one more time, Thrash was going to throw her book at Cresca's flawless forehead. And this thriller was from the library, so it was hard and pointy.

"Aren't you roasting in the sun?"

Thrash *was* roasting. She was wearing black jeans and a black shirt, because a) most of her clothes were black, and b) she had dressed for stealth last night. More than ten hours and no sleep later, Thrash admitted the outfit didn't seem like the best choice, but she wasn't going to let Cresca know that.

"I'm fine. We're leaving soon anyway, right?"

Cresca just shrugged and leaned her lounge chair back. Her silver bikini, which matched her enchanted hair, glinted in the harsh sun. Thrash unfastened her hat and used its brim as a fan while she watched Em paddle around the saltwater swimming pool, still wearing her long skirt even though it must have weighed her down.

Another reason Thrash didn't like summer: water and water activities. She would rather stay inside and curl up with a book than wade into a lukewarm or freezing pool (they only came in two temperatures, in her experience), especially a pool whose black tiles conveniently hid grime and who knows what else. One night at the High Moon Motel cost about as much as breakfast—which, honestly, told Thrash all she needed to know about this place.

As Em swam, Thrash struggled to focus on her thriller, *Song of the Silent Daughter*. The threat of a fictional murder just couldn't compete with the reality that Osmarra could be closing in on them this very moment. Plus, she was distracted by the Gift of Glamour lurking in the trunk of Em's convertible. Thrash wondered if she should show the girls the hollow book and the peculiar craft inside it, but how secure were they really at this semi-public pool? The only thing separating them from passing eyes was an iron fence that had been painted white, then teal, then white again to battle rust. And the rust was still winning.

Em splashed Saki, who was dangling her legs over the edge of the pool. Saki sighed, stood up, and stowed her orb back in her indigo hat. Thrash thought Saki would join them on the chairs, but instead she turned sharply and cannonballed right on top of Em. They both came up for air a few seconds later, gasping and giggling.

"I can't believe I once thought you were all so glamorous," Thrash joked. Cresca snorted.

"You of all people should know 'glamour' is a lie." Cresca lowered her sunglasses and met Thrash's eyes. "We all have our issues."

"Are there any other 'issues' I should know about?" Thrash asked.

"Like with Em, you mean?"

Thrash stammered, "I didn't mean to call it an 'issue—'"

"I know what you mean. The half-merperson thing can be inconvenient, sure, but Em is a smart cookie. And stubborn. She's just dealing with two very overprotective parents."

"I can't relate," Thrash said. A second later, Cresca laughed.

"But, like, *really* overprotective." Cresca leaned in and whispered, "When Em told them she got her knack, they decided to pull her out of school. They want to homeschool her so they can hold her back. She won't get a Gift until next year."

"Woah."

"Yeah. They treat her like she's super fragile, which is ridiculous. And then Saki has the opposite problem." Cresca absentmindedly braided her long silver hair. "Saki's parents actually told her she can choose her Gift. People trusting their daughters, weird, right? But the problem is, Saki can't decide. I don't know if you noticed, but she has really bad anxiety."

"Oh." That explained a lot. This was the sort of thing she wanted to know about the Lunes. It was one of the reasons Thrash preferred book characters to real people: you just knew all this stuff, the *real* stuff that made people human, without the years of effort befriending them.

"Don't worry. As Saki gets to know you, she'll warm up. And Em will chill out. We all need to work together if we're going to pull this off."

"Speaking of pulling off the plan..." Thrash hated the idea of being the pushy one, but she wanted more concrete answers. "What *is* the plan?"

"Well, when we get to NSU, I'm not too worried about getting inside. We've got Dai's NSU ID card. That can get one of us on campus and into the library, but the bigger problem is getting the Gifts out. Dai told Saki there's some powerful Sight magic protecting that building."

"...So do we have a plan for that?"

"One word." Cresca tilted down her sunglasses and smiled. "Or should I say, one *herb*. Warproot."

"Isn't that *illegal?*"

Thrash's eyes darted around the pool area, which was still mercifully empty. In the same way the mirrors stripped away Glamour magic and salt damaged Growth magic, warproot was a plant that, when burned, interfered with Sight magic. Though Cresca was only planning to use it to scramble Sight wards, there was a clear reason it was illegal—warproot was dangerous because it interfered with the Thirteen States' complex network of econotrix, healrix, and protectrix that all relied on Sight magic to keep the country running smoothly.

"Relax, it'll be fine," Cresca said, sliding the sunglasses back up her nose and hopping off the chair. "We're just gonna stop by my sister's place. She has a warproot connection. Want a soda or anything from the vending machine?"

"Uh, no, I'm good."

As Cresca strolled toward the motel lobby, Thrash felt nauseous. She lowered the brim of her hat and closed her eyes, but she wasn't able to banish the image of the dimly lit Realignment Center in the basement of her high school. For burning an illegal substance like warproot, they would all be facing a long stint and heavy fines. Thrash also didn't love the idea of a detour to Cresca's sister's house, wherever that was. If Thrash had learned anything from reading thrillers, the more people involved in a crime, the more likely it was to fail.

The sound of splashing water intensified. Thrash opened her eyes, expecting to see Em and Saki horsing around, but they were both clutching the edge of the pool.

"I'm not doing anything to the water," Em said to Saki. "Are you?"

Saki shook her head. "Could it be an earthquake?"

That's when Thrash noticed the choppy pool water.

Though Em and Saki both held totally still at the side of the pool, waves clamored around them. Thrash thought of seasickness and then had to wonder...if water was a reflective surface, would her knack break it like a mirror? Could her mood be affecting it?

As Em and Saki inched cautiously toward the pool steps, Thrash closed her eyes. If her knack was tied to stress, she had to calm herself down. *Don't worry about Cresca,* she thought as she took a deep breath and closed her eyes. *Don't worry about Saki and Em, or NSU, or warproot, or Mom.* Thrash exhaled, releasing the tension inside of her, a mix of sleep deprivation, insecurity, and minor annoyances.

When Thrash opened her eyes, Saki and Em were out of the pool, and the water no longer had a mind of its own. Em wrung out her skirt and a whole bucket of water drenched the pavement. Thrash caught just a glimmer of scaly skin beneath the fabric. The two girls plopped down on lounge chairs beside her, oblivious that Thrash's knack had affected the pool.

"It must have been a small quake," Em explained. Saki nodded. "A state with 'rock' in its name probably has some geological activity."

"Speaking of Redrock, are we ready to hit the road?" Thrash tried to keep it light, but even she could hear the strain in her voice.

"We have to dry off first," Em declared, rolling her towel into a neck pillow. "Just give us fifteen minutes. It's summer. We should enjoy the sunshine."

"Summer" and "sun" were words Thrash mainly associated with "sweat" and "burn," but she laid back on her lounger and let her eyes drift close. What was another fifteen minutes? She could be cool. She could relax. Going with the flow might even do Thrash, and her knack, some good.

A few minutes drying off in the sun became a few hours napping, and then a whole night staying at the High Moon Motel because "we already paid for the motel" and "we'll need to sleep anyway." At least Thrash convinced the lobby boy to give them a room facing away from Leyline 791. Em begrudgingly moved the car around the back, where the walls had faded to the color of used chewing gum. Thrash didn't know when the motel was built, but it must have been pre-1970s. Architectrix created most modern buildings out a mixture of Growth magic and natural materials, usually woven glass, uppercrust stone, and pinefiber.

The girls ate snacks for lunch and dinner. They wasted more time at the pool. When it was time for bed, Thrash was assigned to share a bed with Saki because, "she's a kicker." It was no surprise that Thrash fell asleep angry, all fantasies of wanting to get to know the Lunes replaced by wanting to murder them. She dreamed of fingers tattooed with matching black moons tearing into the Gift of Glamour, ripping off the leather cover and flinging pages everywhere.

The next morning, Thrash opened her eyes and saw Cresca sitting at the foot of her bed, looking into her orb.

"I was starting to think someone put you under a sleeping spell," Cresca teased.

"What time is it?"

Cresca shrugged. Saki was already out of bed, sitting at a desk and writing something next to a glass jar that read *The Good Shit Jar*. Thrash groped for the starched sheets. The fabric's texture was more chalk than fabric, the sheets bleached so many times they made Thrash feel dirty.

"Breakfast at the Sunny Bucket?" Cresca asked Thrash.

"Can we get the food to go?" She didn't need to know what time it was to know they should already be on the road.

"I'll go scope it out." Cresca leaped off the bed with a spring in her step, confirming what Thrash suspected —*morning person*. Meanwhile, Thrash was still rubbing the sleep from her eyes as she grabbed her hat and headed for the bathroom.

She closed the bathroom door and pulled out her toiletries, balancing them on the precariously narrow edge of the sink.

"Hey!" Em yelped. Thrash blinked a few times before spotting Em submerged in the bathtub. She was wearing a bra and boxer shorts but nothing else. Thrash caught a flicker of iridescence as Em scrambled to sit up and tuck her legs under her as fast as possible.

"Have you ever heard of knocking?" Em snapped.

"I'm sorry!" Thrash blurted, already packing up her toothbrush. "I was just gonna brush my teeth!"

"No, it's—just give me a sec and I'll get out. I've been in here for like an hour." Em looked away and pushed her wire glasses up her nose. "Can you turn around while I get out, though?"

"Of course, totally." She felt her cheeks burn as she pivoted on the spot. Thrash heard Em pull a towel off the rack. "But just so you know...I really don't care. About your legs."

Other than the soft shuffle of terrycloth on skin, Em, for once, was silent.

"But I get if you care," Thrash hurriedly added. "Like, people always tell me I should wear whatever I want, but if I wear shorts, people stare at me like they've never seen cellulite before. Some days I just don't want to deal with that."

Em didn't reply for a long moment. Thrash heard the soft swish of her adjusting her towel.

"It's all yours," Em said. She darted out the door before Thrash could reply.

Thrash sighed, unzipped her toiletry bag, and turned on the shower. She just couldn't get it right with the Lunes.

With the sound of running water as a cover, Thrash plucked her orb out of her hat. She conjured the first of the many captures from yesterday. Within seconds, Osmarra's image emerged through the swirling mists.

"Theo, it's your mother. I got your message, but this behavior is so unlike you. I'm worried about you." To Osmarra's credit, she did look genuinely worried. Thrash had glimpsed her fake-worried face many times before on public captures. "Running off with a group of strangers? Not telling me or Tempest where you're going? I know you said you need some time to think, but you can think at home."

Thrash scoffed at that.

In the capture, Osmarra tucked a stray hair over her ear, her hand shaking slightly. "I don't understand why you took the Gift, but please promise me you won't open it. Please be safe, or even better, come home. I love you."

The rest of Osmarra's messages were all variations of the same plea. Sometimes, her mom varied her tactics, but they all contained the same underlying warning: stay away from the Gift of Glamour.

Bang bang bang!

"Are you taking a shower?" Cresca called through the door. "Can I come in? I need to pee!"

"One second!" Thrash didn't even have time to question if this was a normal thing friends did—she dropped her orb and scrambled to yank off her clothes. She had never hustled so fast in her life as she leaped into that shower and shut the curtain.

"Okay, you're good!"

Thrash let the lukewarm water hit her. *Act normal.* Of course, this was anything but normal for her. Realizing her orb was just sitting there on the floor, she held her breath and listened for almost a full minute until she heard the toilet flush. Cresca washed her hands, humming to herself. No sound of her playing messages from the orb.

It was only when Thrash heard the blessed sound of the door closing shut that she finally allowed herself to melt into the hot water, which she now realized had gone from tepid to scalding. At least she had kept her cool. Mostly.

When Thrash emerged post-shower, she expected to walk into the same lazy-morning vacation scene she had left. Instead, she found Saki curled in a chair, biting her nails, while Em paced back and forth. Cresca immediately pounced on Thrash, waving her orb in her face.

"Your mom is here!" Cresca said. "It's over."

The words drove a spike of panic through Thrash's chest. *It can't be over.* Over meant the Gift of Glamour for Thrash, and she would not—could not—let that be her future.

Instead of letting her fear drag her under, Thrash swatted Cresca's orb away and asked, "Where is she? What exactly did you see?"

"She's at the Sunny Bucket, interrogating the waiters," Cresca said. "Your mom either didn't see me or didn't recognize me, I don't know. The staff was distracted dealing with her, so I just turned around and ran back here."

Suddenly, it clicked. "Em, how did you pay for breakfast?"

"I don't see how that's relevant..."

"Protectrix have access to the magic that tracks purchases made with credit rings. That must be how she found us. We should've used cash."

As Em sputtered to come up with a reply, Cresca tossed clothes into her hat.

"Well, this was a nice mini-vacation, girls," Cresca said. "See you all in Realignment in the fall."

"No way. We can't give up this easily." Thrash tried to catch Cresca's gaze, but she wouldn't take her eyes off her hat. When Thrash looked to Em and Saki for support, both girls had their eyes on the spongy brown carpet. "We have a plan, remember?"

"I didn't plan for *this*," Cresca said.

"So we change the plan. We adapt. We don't just give up the second it gets tough." Thrash looked around desperately for something to work with, but all she had was cheap motel furniture and the Lunes themselves. She thought back to what Cresca had told her by the pool, how in some ways this road trip was about more than just the Gifts—it was about Em proving her independence to her parents, and Saki trying to figure out what she wanted for herself.

"Saki, what Gift do you want?" Thrash asked, knowing full well Saki couldn't decide.

Curled up in the motel's desk chair, Saki peered up at Thrash and tucked a ribbon of black hair behind her ear. She murmured, "I don't know."

"Then what are you going to do if we turn around and go home today?"

Saki gripped her knees tighter.

"I don't..." Saki started nodding. "I need more time. To figure it out..."

"Em, what Gift do you want?"

Em took the bait. "I guess I never let myself get that far, but I think I'd want Growth, actually. There's so much you can do with it."

Thrash turned to Cresca, who looked like a deer in head-lights. "Well, Cresca? You roped me into all of this. When we get to NSU, what Gift do you want?"

Cresca picked up her hat, but she didn't put it on to leave. Instead, she pulled out a pack of cigarettes. Cresca took out a cigarette and fiddled with it. Thrash noticed all the girls' eyes were locked on Cresca's hands.

Thrash held her breath—if she could convince Cresca, the other girls would surely follow.

"Glamour," Cresca finally answered. She tucked the cigarette back into the box and put it away. "Okay, we've outsmarted parents before. Let's think through this..."

"Well, my mom probably talked to your dad," Thrash said. "That would mean she thinks we're going to Slumber City. That route veers south. If we go north, we might be able to avoid her—but we have to sneak out of here first."

"What if we all hide in the bottomless chest?" Cresca suggested.

Em leaped in, "Nope. No way. Magic that collapses space like that basically flattens you like a piece of paper and folds you a bunch of times. You can't close it on a living creature. Just ask my hamster."

Saki knit her brow. "You don't have a hamster."

Em spread her palms, resting her case.

Cresca tapped her chin, lost in thought until she turned suddenly to Em.

"Before we settle up in the lobby and drive out of here, you could disguise yourself with your knack!" Cresca said.

"I would rather not." Em glanced at Thrash and then back to Cresca. "It's *embarrassing*."

Cresca twisted a bright gold ring, the one around her index finger. "I mean, if you can't pull off a disguise, I guess I could do it."

"No, no, it's fine," Em said, waving Cresca away. With one last wary glance at Thrash, Em closed her eyes tight and concentrated.

Em's hair disappeared.

Thrash gasped; she couldn't help herself. But Em's dark hair wasn't really gone. An outline of it was just visible, a few swirling wisps of color, almost like the soap bubble. With a *pop!* Em's hair reappeared, now teal green.

"Tah dah," Em said with zero enthusiasm. "My knack."

"...Does it always make that sound?" Thrash asked.

"Unfortunately, yes." Em resumed her pacing, cracking her knuckles one by one. "I know what you're thinking, Cresca, but I don't know if I can change the color of something as large as a car."

Cresca grinned, bright as the rising sun. Thrash didn't know Cresca well, but she already recognized that look.

It was the "I have a plan" look.

6

Thrash peered past the curtain, careful to keep her face obscured by the fabric. From the window of their second-story motel room, she could just see the bright blue convertible, one of three cars resting in a patch of dirt that could charitably be called a parking lot. Behind her, Cresca studied a map while Saki fiddled with the motel wand for boiling water in a glass pitcher.

Outside, Em shot out of the stairwell. Her disguise wasn't much—no glasses, a bright green pixie cut instead of a brown one—but from a distance, she worked it. Em glanced up and down the line of motel room doors and then turned her attention to her car.

Em's hands formed into fists at her sides.

A minute passed.

The color of the car didn't change.

"What's going on out there?" Cresca called.

"Nothing," Thrash replied. "That's the problem."

Cresca couldn't help herself; she crept over to the window and pulled back the curtain. In the parking lot, Em took a few steps toward the car and opened her mouth. Thrash couldn't read lips, but she recognized a few curse words.

"Maybe the car is too big?" Cresca fiddled with a strand of her hair. "I should've known this wouldn't work—"

But as Em pounded the hood of the car with an angry fist, the blue convertible disappeared. Well, most of it. Thrash could just make out a faint bubble-like sheen where the car should have been. In a heartbeat, it appeared again. Black as a familiar.

Cresca clapped her hands. Em leaned down, tried to hug the hood (but settled for kissing it), and then dashed back toward the stairs. Instead of going up, she rounded the corner of the building and disappeared.

Em should be on her way to the lobby, which was on the other side of the motel, the side facing the leyline. She would return the aluminum wand that unlocked their room and pay the bill. Her instructions were to pay in cash.

Thrash noticed she was gripping the curtain. She released the scratchy fabric. Maybe they would actually avoid Osmarra and escape without any trouble.

Thrash stepped aside so Saki could peer out the window and admire the car's new paint job.

"Wow..." Saki said. "She did it."

She did, didn't she? Em's knack was useful, and it made Thrash wonder if hers could be too.

Cresca rolled her shoulders and shook out her arms. "You witches ready to run for it when we see Em?"

"I hate running," Thrash said. "But yes."

Cresca smirked as Saki kept staring out the window. Being lost in thought seemed to be business as usual for Saki—until she stepped back sharply from the glass and gasped.

Thrash raced forward. Outside, Tempest trotted slowly past the motel, his dark eyes combing over the doors and windows. Osmarra surveyed the property from his back. She was wearing her double-breasted black uniform, the one she wore for special state ceremonies, with the purple sash across the chest. A black-clad witch atop a black familiar—everything about her appearance reminding others to obey.

"What are you doing? Get down!" Cresca grabbed Thrash's hand and tugged her to the floor. The spongy carpet wheezed when Thrash landed on her knees, crouching beside Cresca under the windowsill.

"Should we warn Em?" Thrash whispered. Why was she whispering? "Wait, no, her orb is in her hat. And a capture's a stupid idea."

"Maybe your mom will just look past the car and move on?" Cresca sounded hopeful.

Saki peeked over the windowsill. Thrash and Cresca both held their breath. Seconds felt like hours as Saki wordlessly watched whatever was unfolding outside.

Saki sank back down to the carpet. "I think...she's heading around the building."

"Is that it?" Thrash asked.

"She...stared at the car for a while."

That was the last thing Thrash wanted to hear, but she tried to stay calm and think it through. What would she do if she saw a convertible that almost matched the description of the one she was looking for? She wouldn't knock on every door of the motel.

She would go to the lobby.

Thrash hoped Em's disguise was good enough. Because that's all there was left to do, really. All they could do.

Hope.

～

Thrash picked at a loose thread on the gross carpet while
Cresca served as lookout. Thrash hated waiting, and this
waiting was the worst kind. She was intimately familiar with
the grim sort of wait, which she associated with stiff bedside
chairs and bleak hospital waiting rooms.

Or maybe it was the smell of cheap, terrible coffee that
reminded Thrash of Duna's hospital stays. Osmarra often sent
her down to the cafeteria to fix Duna a cup of coffee—no milk,
double sugar—when she wanted alone time with Mum.

Thrash noticed Saki hovering in her peripheral vision, a
single-use paper coffee cup in each hand.

"Coffee?" Saki asked.

Thrash accepted the cup. "Thanks, Saki."

"I'm worried about Em," Saki blurted. The coffee in her
hand almost sloshed over the edge.

"If anyone can take on my mom alone, it's her." Thrash
took a sip of her drink and added, "Wow, this is perfect, Saki."

"It's not perfect," Saki said. Then she softened and added,
"But you're welcome."

At the window, Cresca gave a sharp inhale. "She's here!
It's Em!"

Everyone scrambled to their feet. Thrash fastened her hat,
Saki trashed her coffee, and Cresca threw open the door, her
whole body behind the motion.

"No actual running," Cresca hissed. "Not unless you see
Thrash's mom. Remember, look casual. Move quick."

Thrash followed Cresca as they flew down the concrete
steps and hustled to the convertible, Saki almost tripping over
her long legs. Teal-haired Em arrived at the car at the same
time, her face drained of all color.

"I don't think she recognized me, but we gotta go," Em
whispered. "Get in and stay down."

Thrash didn't waste a second. She leaped into the backseat

and tried her best to duck down and wedge her body in the space behind the driver's seat. A moment later, Em mercifully scooted up her chair, and within seconds the convertible lifted off the ground.

"Cresca, get lower," Em hissed. "What did we decide about the leyline? Do I take it? Or go through the wildlands?"

"It's up to you," Cresca bit back. "How do you feel about off-roading with your parents' car?"

Thrash toppled to the side as the car burst forward. The last thing she heard Em say was, "Whatever puts as much distance between me and that freaky horse, let's do it."

Fifteen minutes later, Thrash peeled herself off the floor of the car.

They appeared to have made it out of Lost Paradise without drawing Osmarra's attention. There was no sign of Tempest in the rearview mirror and no reason for her mom to assume they had gone north. According to Em, they were making good time and already in Ji'ishland, one of the three Native states that retained its own code of law. Ji'ishland was infamous for disbanding its wandslingers—the non-magical police every state armed with stun wands—and replacing them with special laws that allowed citizens to police themselves.

As Thrash clicked her seatbelt back into place, Cresca pulled a map out of her hat and scanned it.

"We should just be entering the wildlands," Cresca said. "The Tsin Protected Wildlands."

Oh great, now they were illegally driving over protected lands. Add that to their list of crimes, committed and yet-to-be-committed.

"The *T* in Tsin is silent," Em piped in. "Which is ironic, because people sometimes call the mountain range that runs through the park the Devil's Tits. Not sure if that's because of the heat, or the rumors that the wildlands are a den of criminal activity."

"One murderer hid out there twenty years ago," Thrash said. "Not quite a den."

"One murderer *that we know of.*" Cresca winked.

As the convertible climbed, the sand turned from red to purple. Rugged hills grew into modest mountains, though Thrash didn't think they resembled tits. The nickname seemed a little desperate. However, she could see how the endless caves and crevices might attract outlaws on the run. After all, here they were, practically outlaws-in-the-making.

"Doesn't your sister live right outside Queen City?" Em asked Cresca. "That's near the northern edge of the wildlands, right?"

"Yep," Cresca said, her eyes on the pale cacti people called bone succulents. They looked like long, knobby femurs planted in the sand. "Speaking of relatives, that was a close call with Thrash's mom. We should all probably check in with our parents."

Thrash opened her mouth to defend herself, but Em cut her off. "Already did this morning. They think that I'm staying at Saki's house for a week. I told them that if they wouldn't let me go to sleepaway camp, the least they could do was let me and Saki camp in her backyard."

"My parents know I'm here." Saki gathered up her knees and hugged them to her chest. "They say a trip is exactly what I need to figure out what I want…"

"Your parents are adorable," Cresca quipped. "But we need to make sure they don't talk to Em's family. Oh, and Thrash, maybe you can send your mom a capture that throws her off

the scent? We need to get to NSU without any more inter-
ruptions."

Thrash liked the sound of that. Maybe Osmarra showing
up was a blessing in disguise if it got the girls to wake up and
realize this wasn't a vacation.

Saki twisted around in her seat. Her eyes settled, unnerv-
ingly, on Thrash.

"How did you realize that the Gift of Glamour wasn't right
for you?" Saki asked, as if Thrash must already have a breezy
answer to such a stomachache of a question.

"I don't know. Glamour just...isn't me." Thrash was highly
aware of Cresca—who wanted the Gift of Glamour—sitting
beside her.

Saki's eyes narrowed. "But how do you know what's *you?*"

What was Thrash supposed to do, share her deepest
thoughts and desires on the spot? She almost wanted to laugh
at the irony that Saki Anderson, whose vacant eyes convinced
people she was mysterious and deep, might actually be lost
inside.

But as Saki waited patiently for her answer, eyes crowded
with genuine doubt, Thrash realized maybe it wasn't easy
being Cresca and Em's third wheel. Maybe there wasn't much
room to breathe in this dynamic, to speak up and take up
space.

"I try to listen to myself," Thrash finally answered. "Instead
of listening to what other people think of me."

As Saki contemplated that, Cresca chimed in, "What we
should be listening to is *music.*"

"Amen," Em added. The word sounded like an eyeroll. "I'm
feeling either *Banshee Bangers* or *Torture Chamber Muzak.*"

"*Bangers,*" Cresca answered, cutting off Thrash before she
had a chance to speak. Whatever. The electric violins and
screeching vocals didn't allow for much conversation anyway.

As the convertible climbed a steep slope, Thrash stared out the window at the passing rock formations, thinking to herself that "the Devil's Tits" would be an excellent name for a playlist, or a band, or an expletive. Ah well. Four more days. And then she would be free.

By sunset, Em's black convertible approached the northern edge of the wildlands, which had grown flatter and more desert-like. They had driven all day without seeing any signs of civilization. No craft stations, no campgrounds; nothing but skeletal cacti, vivid against the purple-brown dust flats and the red rays of the setting sun.

The mood in the car reflected the mellow landscape. Em mercifully switched from banshee ballads to softer, more nostalgic tunes a few hours ago. The Lunes had mostly fallen into a comfortable silence. Beside Thrash, Cresca slouched against the doorframe, reading on her orb. Thrash wished she could read without getting carsick. Instead, she settled for watching Em's wand hand as she drove.

"Hey, Em?" Cresca shifted upright in her seat. "You wanna pull over for a sec?"

"Do you really want me to stop here, among the creepy succulents and murderers?"

"Trust me."

Em gave an annoyed little growl as she slowed the car to a halt. Thrash felt on edge the moment the car stopped. Without the sound of wind through her hair, she could hear all the faint chirps and skittering sounds of the desert coming alive at dusk. It wasn't just criminals hiding out in all those caves; Em had educated them on all the creatures that called the wildlands home, from corpse mice whose bite could take down a buffalo-wolf to nasty pygmy dragons covered in venomous spikes.

Em twisted in the driver's seat to look back at Cresca. "Well?"

"Girl, your parents don't think you're at Saki's. They put out a bounty. They're offering money for tips about your location." Cresca kept reading. "And there's a hefty reward for 'the safe return of our *special* daughter,' whose '*fragile* condition necessitates a swift journey home.'"

Em groaned and pressed the palms of her hands to her eyes. "*Oh My Goddess,* they made it sound like I've been kidnapped!"

"I'd turn you in for this kind of money," Cresca said with a whistle. "It's, like, literally a mer-king's ransom."

"Speaking of, without credit rings, how much cash do we actually have?" Thrash asked.

Everyone pulled out their wallets. Together, they had $140. Actually, $160 when Saki remembered she had an "emergency twenty" in her bra. That might cover lodging, but not lodging *and* food. And now that there was a bounty on Em's head, motels didn't seem like a safe option. When Thrash suggested sleeping in the car, Cresca cracked, "Maybe if we fold Saki in half."

"At least we can sleep at your sister's place tonight," Em said.

Cresca gnawed her lower lip.

"Cresca?"

"I don't think Coco and I are on *that* good of terms," Cresca admitted.

"We've been driving all day, I've got a bounty on my head, and we're out of money." Em picked up the wand and traced the ignition pattern. The car charged ahead—without Cresca's input. "I get that it's awkward between you two, but this is our only option."

"Fine." Cresca sank in her seat. But something else was bothering Thrash. She squinted at Cresca in the dying light.

"So, you don't think your sister will let us stay the night..." Thrash said. "But you think she'll just hand us the warproot?"

"I never said she was just gonna *give* it to us," Cresca murmured.

"Then what was the plan?" Thrash said. "*Rob your sister?*"

"Look, I said it's fine—we can try to crash with her. And you two," she pointed at Em and Thrash, "can send captures to your parents and get them off our backs. All good?"

Thrash felt dizzy. Did Coco even have the warproot? How could Cresca be sure? She was too scared to ask. This was *not* the plan she thought she was signing up for, but she was in too deep. At this point, she just wanted to keep moving and stay ahead of her mom.

And get out of the wildlands before they found out what creatures came out at night.

Thrash spotted the ranch right as the sun dipped behind the mountains, draping the valley in shadow. The old house had a wide, welcoming front porch and a quaint tapered roof. As the car crept closer, Thrash saw that the generous porch was actually missing a fair number of floorboards and the roof was shedding shingles. The adjoining horse paddock, seemingly horse-free, had been transformed into a junkyard craft studio. Wind chimes made of glass and metal scraps decorated the gate, along with *2 for $20* potted succulents that stuck out of clay pots the color of Ji'ishland's purple dirt, like little bones poking out of portable graves.

Em pulled up in front of the house and parked alongside an old truck resting on wooden blocks. The truck had seen better days, but someone had revitalized it with several cans of matte purple spray-paint. Black detailing along the side reminded Thrash of tribal tattoos. As Thrash hopped out of the back of Em's convertible, she squeezed between the two vehicles and past a name stenciled along the side of the truck. *Madame Wiki.*

Oh, and the front of Madame Wiki? Covered in spikes.

"Your sister seems...colorful," Thrash commented. Cresca snorted, unfastened her crochet hat, and tossed it into the backseat.

"That's not her truck."

Cresca breezed past Thrash and led the pack of girls up the creaking porch steps. There was a mirror built into the front door like in most homes, but Cresca deftly sidestepped to avoid its enchantment-stripping gaze. She knocked so hard on the door that flecks of chipping white paint came away on her knuckles.

The front door opened a crack.

Coco King peered at them, a slimmer, harder version of her younger sister. Wearing a floral robe draped over daisy dukes and a crop top, Coco's bohemian outfit clashed with her rough surroundings and the severity of her shaved head. Thrash knew, logically, she must be around twenty-five—but Coco's clothing seemed so young, and her eyes seemed so old.

Coco searched Cresca's face for a moment too long. Then her eyes finally widened with recognition.

"Cresca?" Coco breathed. "I didn't recognize you with *that hair.*"

"Good to see you too," Cresca quipped. "It's only been, what, three years?"

"Why are you here?" Coco asked, taking in the rest of the girls. "Who are they?"

"We're on a road trip and we wanted to crash at Grandma and Grandpa's place." Cresca examined her nails like this was no big deal. "We've gotta save our money for Slumber City."

"This doesn't seem like a Dad-approved trip."

"You would know a lot about those, wouldn't you?"

Coco weighed her sister carefully.

"I think you should turn around and go home," Coco said. "This isn't a motel."

"Wow, you sound like Dad," Cresca laughed. The glee in that laugh sounded downright deadly. "I guess when I get home, I'll have to tell Dad about how you're running this place into the ground, and how he should really kick you out, like he's been threatening to do for years..."

Coco's eyes narrowed. Her mouth remained a thin, mirthless line, but Coco unlocked the latch and stepped aside to let them in.

The inside of the house smelled like dust and old perfume, but some aggressive incense was working overtime to cover it. The mismatched furniture looked like it had been hauled right out of the junkyard. Coco waved them over to two lived-in couches, which was when Thrash saw two flags pinned across the wall. Thrash recognized the dark purple flag with two white candles as the banner of the Magic Liberation Movement. The orange flag under it, emblazoned with an image of a broom broken in half, was the symbol of the radical, backward wing of the MLM. Thrash wondered if it was too late to run back out the front door, because a broom breaker flag could mean only one thing:

Coco King hated magic.

7

Coco didn't offer them a seat or a glass of water. Everyone stood awkwardly in the living room, clustered around a rusty metal coffee table that might have once been the hood of a car, unsure how to proceed.

Right as Thrash was about to back out the front door, Cresca spun and plopped onto one of the couches. No one else moved.

"How's the revolution going?" Cresca asked, nodding to the orange flag.

"Great," Coco said. No elaboration.

As Cresca and Coco continued their stare-off, Thrash eyed the broom breaker flag. They were the extremists of the Magical Liberation Movement. Thrash had watched news captures of the broom breakers erecting pyres and stakes outside the Circle chambers in Elzborah City, their flame-orange flag evoking the Europan witch burnings of the late 1600s. Though the Magical Liberation Movement was originally founded to push for equal treatment of people with and without magic, the broom breakers made it hard for everyone to get behind them.

However deep Coco's anti-magic beliefs ran, Cresca's assumptions began to make more sense in light of them. It all fell into place: Cresca's hesitation to stay here, her hunch that Coco might have warproot, and her suspicion that Coco might not just hand it over to her sister and her wannabe coven.

"You know, we've had a really long day on the road," Em said. "Would it be okay to use your bathroom?"

Coco eyed them all warily. Clearly, she still wasn't entirely committed to letting them stay the night. "Down the hall. Last door on the left."

Em hopped up off the couch and scurried down the hall, presumably off to soak and maybe even search for the warproot.

"Nice hunting staff," Cresca said, gesturing to a tall staff leaning by front door. It was almost five feet of tarnished silver capped with orange ribbon. Staffs channeled more magic and packed more of a punch than wands, but they were also more expensive and cumbersome. Big game hunters used them— but why did Coco have one?

Cresca twirled a strand of her silver hair around her finger. "I thought that *typicals* in the MLM didn't use magic?"

Thrash cringed. Non-magical person was more polite than typical, though NMP had morphed into nimp somewhere along the line. Thrash didn't need a degree in linguistics to know there were several offensive slang words for non-witches, who made up roughly 80 percent of the population, and that this said a lot about what modern society valued.

"Believing in freedom from magical oppression doesn't mean we live entirely without magic," Coco replied.

"We?" Cresca asked.

"The staff belongs to my *wife*." The corner of Coco's red lips quirked. "Her name is Rongo."

Thrash's eyes flicked to Cresca's face for a sign of recognition, but her face was carefully blank. "Congratulations."

"Thanks."

"Were you ever going to tell Dad? Or Nana?" Cresca tried to sound nonchalant, but Thrash could see her nails digging into her thighs. Thrash wanted to shake her out of it and say, *Stop antagonizing our host.*

Coco squinted at her sister. "Dad knows."

"Cool. So, you just didn't bother to send *me* a capture?" Cresca didn't even try to hide the bitterness in her voice anymore. "You know, you can fight for the revolution or whatever *and* call your family occasionally."

"Oh, because you tried so hard to reach out to me."

"I was eight when you left!" Cresca snapped.

Coco said nothing, but her eyes simmered like two dark embers. Thrash was convinced Coco was about to throw them out the front door when a voice from another room boomed, "Coco?"

"I'm fine," Coco called back. "Just some unexpected visitors."

Thrash tensed as loud, creaking footsteps ambled down the hallway. A tall woman ducked through the doorway, two long black braids swinging as she wiped her hands on a camo-print apron. Thrash saw flashes of tattoos on her brown skin. And she was big. Thrash knew the world saw her body as taking up too much space, but this woman was a size you couldn't sneer into nonexistence. She commanded the room just by being in it.

"Who are our guests?" Rongo asked, leaning down to kiss Coco's frigid cheek.

"This is my little sister, Cresca, and...her friends."

Rongo studied them for a long moment, but then her face broke into a toothy smile.

"You must stay for dinner!" Rongo's voice rumbled, warm as a summer thunderstorm. "I insist. Take off your hats. Get comfortable. No one leaves Rongo's house hungry."

Thrash caught the first whiff of something savory wafting from the kitchen. A decent meal and a little hospitality were exactly what she needed. Maybe this pitstop wouldn't be awful —maybe it would even be awesome.

That's what she told herself, at least, as Cresca and Coco glared at each other, their arms crossed like shields.

While Rongo toiled in the kitchen, Coco directed Cresca and Saki to fetch two more chairs for the dining room. She tasked Thrash with clearing the table. The far end of it was littered with old mugs and crafting supplies.

As Thrash moved the clutter from the table to the sideboard, the heaviest item by far was a device made of two wooden blocks and a metal lever. Thrash picked up a stack of flyers and realized it was a crude printing press, used for cranking out pages that read, in bold black text:

Free the Witch, Ditch the Gifts!

Thrash read the words again. Free witches from Gifts? Beneath the blazing words, an illustration of a book on fire almost made Thrash crumple up the pamphlet. The real freedom witches needed was the freedom to choose.

"I'll take those, thanks," Coco said, plucking the stack of flyers from Thrash's arms and ferrying them to another room.

The flyers wouldn't let Thrash rest. The words needled her as she worked. It wasn't until Em returned—just in time to call dibs on the rocking chair—that Thrash remembered the warproot. She wanted to ask Em if she found it, but with Coco now setting the table, she bit her tongue. Best to act like normal, friendly guests until they found what they needed.

"So, where did you girls say you were heading, again?" Coco asked as she set a chipped plate down in front of Cresca.

Cresca didn't bat an eye. "In Slumber City, you mean? We're staying at a hostel in the Banque des Voleurs."

"Huh. You know, I lived in the Cote d'Aveau for a few years, actually. Slumber City isn't for the faint of heart."

Coco dropped Saki's plate to the table with a loud smack. Saki flinched in her chair. Coco just smiled, her teeth tinged yellow. Thrash wondered if Coco's vice was coffee or cigarettes.

"No offense, Cresca, but your friends don't exactly look like Slumber City girls."

Em, who had been openly glaring at Coco since she startled Saki, snatched the last plate out of Coco's hand before she could set it down.

"That's very presumptuous," Em said. Coco raised a single eyebrow at Cresca, as if to say Em just proved her point.

"Coco?" Rongo called through the kitchen doorway. Thrash didn't know a lot about cooking, but she did recognize the smell of it burning. "Can I get a hand?"

"On my way." Coco pinned them into their chairs with her eyes before disappearing into the kitchen.

Before anyone could relax, fire detection wards started screeching. Red glyphs appeared on the ceiling, casting pulsing red light over the table. Between the alarm sounding and the banging cabinet doors in the kitchen, Thrash figured this was the best chance she would get.

"Em," Thrash whispered. "Did you find anything?"

"I saw a garden through the bathroom window," Em said. "Looks like there might be a door to it from the kitchen."

Saki leaned in and spoke for the first time since they had arrived. "Does anyone taste something weird? In the air?"

The girls exchanged glances. Thrash didn't taste anything. Saki frowned and closed her eyes, concentrating as she inhaled.

"Could you be smelling the smoke?" Em asked. Saki shook her head.

"It's sour and a little sweet. It tastes...like something isn't right."

Saki still looked lost in her own head when the wards quieted and Rongo emerged carrying three plates along one arm. Thrash spied purple mashed potatoes, fried cactus, and a tureen of date gravy. Coco trailed behind, clutching a rectangle of blackened meat between two oven mitts.

"I hope you like your jackaloaf extra crispy!" Rongo laughed, a booming but good-natured sound. "When the oven's acting up, I like to say the char adds flavor!"

"A new oven would also add flavor," Coco cracked. Rongo chortled and swung back around the table to peck her on the cheek. Thrash thought of Osmarra and Duna cooking together, and her heart sputtered.

As Rongo pulled up the chair between Thrash and Em, she cried, "I see we have another guest!"

"Sorry, I was using the bathroom earlier." Em fiddled with the edge of her lacy napkin. "I'm Cresca's friend, Em."

"Welcome, Cresca's-friend-Em." Rongo's dark eyes glittered as she offered an open palm to Em and then to Thrash. As everyone linked palms, it struck Thrash that she wasn't even sure she remembered the last time she sat around a dinner table with more than two people at it.

"Goddess, thank you for our plenty," Rongo said. "Thank you for the jackalopes that plague Coco's garden and the taro that Mama Rongo won't stop sending from the islands. Thank you for reuniting Coco and Cresca, and guiding her and her friends to us. Three Blessings!"

"Three Blessings," Thrash murmured.

Rongo began passing platters, and Thrash's mouth started watering. Warproot could wait until after dinner. As Coco carved Thrash a large slice of jackaloaf, the real reason they were here grew muddy as the gravy—which, by the way, was a perfect complement to the slightly sweet taro mash. Even Saki ate almost every bite off her plate.

"So, Cresca..." Coco said, picking the fried batter off a piece of cactus. "What's with the hair?"

"Enchanted ring," Cresca said.

"Sounds expensive."

Cresca gave her sister a smile thin as a knife's edge. "I saved my birthday money."

"We just bought our first orb, matter of fact, but Coco won't touch the thing."

"The government uses them to spy on us," Coco said with utmost seriousness. When she read the skeptical expressions across the dining table she added, "It's true. Think about it. They only let normal folks access magic through orbs they control. The Gifts are the same damn thing."

"What's wrong with the Gifts?" Thrash asked. The flyers were still bothering her—not to mention all the creepy craft inside the Gift of Glamour.

"Well, for a start, they're a tool for assimilation and oppression. Have you ever wondered why there are only three types of magic?"

"I thought it was because those are the strongest types?" Thrash replied. "Isn't that why people come from all over the world for Gifts? Isn't it why our standard of living is so high in the Thirteen States?"

"But what did we lose to achieve it all?" Coco countered.

"What about the witches who didn't conform? What about the Native magic we lost?"

Thrash wanted to reply, but the truth was she didn't know about those things. All she felt was an aching sense of frustration. If Coco was right and the Gifts were flawed, where did that leave her? It's not like she had another option.

Rongo beamed at her wife. "When Coco's not working on her art, she's trying to organize non-magical folks like us to rise up."

"But you see, that's the thing," Coco said with a pointed look around the table. "*Witches* should rise up too."

Saki shot out of her chair.

Rongo chuckled. "Not literally, child."

"I have to use your bathroom," said Saki. Rongo nodded toward the hall and Saki rushed away from the table. As Rongo exchanged a puzzled look with her wife, Thrash reached for the jackaloaf pan. She would miss this once they hit the road again. Saki's snacks did not a real meal make.

People didn't usually "get" Saki, so she wasn't surprised that the girls didn't understand her knack.

They didn't get that she knew, *knew*, that the sour-sweet taste in the air meant danger. If they tasted a carton of spoiled milk, they would know it was bad. It was the same thing. Saki just knew that the taste in the air was *wrong*.

The sour-sweet taste got stronger toward the end of the hall. The bathroom was the last door to the left, but there was another door on the right side of the hallway. Saki sniffed the mystery door and almost gagged on the sour taste.

Saki hesitated. What would Cresca do? Probably charge through that door without second-guessing it. Em would tell her to think it through. And Thrash? Saki was bad at befriending new people, but Thrash seemed sensible. Maybe Thrash would tell Saki to trust her instincts. Trust her knack.

I'm more than the snack girl, Saki told herself. Her mom swore by saying positive self-affirmations. *I have value. I contribute. Find the warproot for the girls and prove it.*

Saki held her breath, turned the doorknob, and plunged inside before she could turn back.

The room could be called a bedroom. It was a room, with a bed. But the bed was covered in hunting wands, foothold traps, snares, and small cages. A mid-sized orb, plus the box it came in, sat in the center of the mattress. On the walls, old film photos, certificates, and animal hides competed for space with a giant annotated map of the Tsin Protected Wildlands.

Saki examined the animal pelts. She grew up in the coastal suburbs; she didn't know much about animals. In the photos, a slightly younger, slightly thinner Rongo smiled at the camera with her fellow hunters. In one, she proudly hoisted a dead animal over her shoulder; in another, she beamed as she shook hands with a many-necklaced witch in indigenous regalia.

Rongo looked so happy, like hunting had given her real purpose. Nothing had ever made Saki feel that way. She could barely choose what to eat for lunch without feeling paralyzed by the decision, and now her mom and dad wanted her to choose a Gift for herself?

Saki sighed and read one of Rongo's framed certificates.

The Coven of Wildlands Protection hereby recognizes RONGOMAIWHENUA TUPU for Excellence in Fugitive Justice.

Fugitives? As in the *murderers* her friends kept joking about in the wildlands? Saki looked closer at the photos on the wall. Rongo wasn't posing with fellow game hunters; she was posing with Ji'ishland *bounty* hunters. That dark shape over Rongo's shoulder could have been an animal, but the longer she looked at it, the more the shape looked like a person.

Below the photo of Rongo shaking hands with the Native woman was an accompanying black and gold plaque:

Ji'ishland's Bounty Hunter of the Year

Saki felt sick to her stomach, and it wasn't because of the sour scent clinging to the air. Her best friend had a bounty on her head, after all. A mer-king's ransom, as Cresca had said.

Em.

"So, I sidled up to him, and I said, 'Sir, the Circles High and Low destroyed every last gun before I was born. I can't help you.' But then I flashed him this baby." Rongo rolled her denim sleeve up past her bicep, revealing a tattoo of a roaring camp-fire. "And then I said, 'Unless you want to check out this *fire arm.*'"

Rongo howled with laughter at her own joke and Coco playfully rolled her eyes. Coco had been about as inhospitable as the Tsin Wildlands at first, but together they were *funny*. Rongo was loud, unapologetic, and unafraid to take up space. Thrash couldn't help but like her.

The laughter was just starting to settle when Saki appeared with her indigo hat fastened to her head. Eyes wide and wary, she looked more like she was going to bolt out the front door than return to dinner.

"So then—"

"What kind of animals do you hunt out here?" Saki cut in abruptly. She still hadn't taken her seat. Their hosts eyed her warily.

Rongo cleared her throat. "Been snooping in my trophy room, have you? Well, if you're talking about the larger critters, we've got a few untamed American unicorn left, along with the majestic fanged tortoise, the fearsome buffalo-wolf—"

"I didn't see any in the wildlands when we drove through." Saki held Rongo's gaze for a second and then dropped it like a hot pan.

"Aren't fanged tortoises extinct?" Em added. "And buffalo-wolves are a protected species. I'm pretty sure you can't hunt them."

Rongo smiled and steepled her hands on the table, hands that looked like they could crush any one of those small critters with ease.

"You seem like smart girls," Rongo said, nodding at Saki, who sank into her chair. "And I'm not a liar, so here's the Goddess-blessed truth: I make a little money on the side hunting down people who escape the law. You may have heard some rumors about how that works in this fine state. With the Devil's Tits practically in our backyard, I occasionally haul out bad people who hole up in there."

"You're a bounty hunter?" Thrash asked, trying to keep her jaw off the floor. "Like The Justice?"

"The Justice was impressive, before she sold out to the NatPo." When Rongo grinned, Thrash caught a flash of silver. How could Thrash grow up to be Rongo? Where did she sign up? But then she remembered how pale Saki's face was in the candlelight. She looked like a gazelle that wanted to bolt.

"Bounty hunting paid better back then too. Before wand-slingers. These days, the High Circle is so keen to keep us under their thumb that they'll hand a stun wand to anybody. Not a ton of money in dragging folks out of the wildlands."

"Where *is* the money?" Thrash asked, a pit forming in her stomach.

"Personal bounties, mostly." Rongo shrugged. *Personal bounties like the one Em's parents had put out on her.*

"Coco, this meal was *so* good," Em said, pushing her empty plate away. "I feel really energized, really good to drive, actually. I think we'll just hit the road tonight and save you both the breakfast and the trouble."

Coco's eyes lit up. In a rush, she said, "Such a shame to see you go, but you know what's best for you."

"But surely you girls must stay for dessert!" Rongo crossed her arms and leaned back in her chair, which creaked ominously.

Coco shot a glance at her wife. "What dessert?"

"I'm sure we have something," Rongo replied through her smile. Coco didn't look amused. "In the ice chest?"

"We don't want to impose any more than we have already," Thrash said. When she stood up from the table, the Lunes took a stand with her. "We should get going. Thank you so much for dinner."

Thrash hustled into the living room. She grabbed her hat off the couch and fastened it without looking back, but she could hear Rongo behind her.

"Girls, what's the rush?" Rongo called after them. Her jovial tone made Thrash shiver. When she glanced back, Rongo leaned lazily against the doorframe to the dining room, like she had all the time in the world. "If you stay for a while, I can tell you my best stories! Did you know it was Rongo who caught the Grim Peeper?"

Thrash was only half listening. She tripped over a footstool on her way to the front door but caught herself just in time.

Thrash grabbed the doorknob. It didn't turn. She tried to jostle the knob and then the door but neither one would budge. Cresca nudged Thrash aside and rushed in to try it herself. When the front door still wouldn't open, Cresca spun around and spat, "You can't keep us here!"

Rongo's predatory smile grew wider as she stepped into

the living room. Thrash caught a glimpse of Coco lurking in the hallway, pulling her floral robe tighter around herself as her eyes darted between her wife and her sister.

"Well, that's the funny thing about being a bounty hunter," Rongo said. "I actually can."

"Wait, what bounty?" Coco called after Rongo as she stalked forward. Thrash stepped back until she felt the curtains of the front window brushing her back.

"I'm sorry your road trip has to come to an end. We're gonna take a little drive to the local NatPo station and get you back to your parents."

"Rongo," Coco said, her voice ice.

"My love, I know it's not ideal, but we have bills to pay."

"You want to turn my little sister over to the gnats?" Coco screeched. Rongo winced.

"Coco—"

As Rongo turned to placate her wife, Thrash saw her opportunity. She swept the window curtains aside and placed her palms on the cold glass.

The window shattered. Thrash recoiled from the crashing sound, expecting glass to fly in her face, but the window broke perfectly into a million little pieces like it was safety glass— even though she knew it wasn't.

As shards dropped from the frame like snowflakes, Thrash watched in what felt like slow-motion as first Saki and then Em hopped over the ledge. Cresca was yelling something at Thrash, then she was grabbing Thrash's hand and pulling her forward.

Thrash stumbled down the steps of the porch and plunged into the backseat of Em's convertible seconds before it lifted up off the ground. Thrash didn't have time to look back, but she heard Rongo's booming voice cursing and Coco shouting after her to stop.

As they flew away, Thrash heard the faint sound of a car door slamming. The truck on the wood blocks. Thrash twisted around in her seat. Darkness smothered the valley, rendering the ridges of the wildlands invisible. All Thrash could see was the light pouring out of Coco and Rongo's broken front window, and a second later, the flash of headlights. *Madame Wiki*. Not Coco's truck, but Rongo's.

"Go faster!" Thrash urged. Though the magic-channeling cars were silent, a few seconds after the car door slammed, Thrash heard head-bashing music blaring from Madame Wiki.

"She's going to catch us," Em replied, one hand gripping the steering wheel while the other grasped the wand. "We can't outrun anything powered by a staff."

If they couldn't outrun Rongo, they'd have to outsmart her. Thrash twisted back to face the front of the car and searched the darkness ahead. The headlights of Em's car illuminated a few outcroppings. In the distance, twinkling lights shot like comets across the flatlands. It wasn't just a road; it was a major leyline.

"We could hide," Saki offered. Thrash nodded, an idea dawning on her.

"Let's head for the leyline," Thrash said. "But when we get there, we pull over by some big rocks, shut off the car, and let Rongo pass us by. All she can follow are our headlights anyway. She'll assume we took the main road."

Cresca sat up a little straighter in her seat. "Em, if you can ditch Rongo and my sister, I will make you a hundred playlists."

"I will buy you coffee," Saki added.

"I will buy you a persecuting sunny bucket," Thrash said. "Just get us to the leyline."

"Done and done." Em swerved to avoid a sudden slab of jutting rock. Thrash watched the road ahead as if she could will them to teleport instantly across the desert. At least five miles stood between them and that leyline. Behind them, Rongo's beating drums and screeching lyrics encroached decibel by decibel.

The streaking headlights grew larger and more distinct. With maybe a mile to go, Thrash could make out the outline of the cars hovering through the valley.

Boom!

A patch of earth exploded. Cresca and Saki screamed as Em swerved away from the blast, throwing Thrash against Cresca.

Boom! Another bolt of bright white magic hit the ground, this time closer to the car. Dust and dirt pelted them from above. Saki ducked down, cradling her head between her knees.

Thrash pulled herself up by the seatbelt. She swore she could hear Rongo laughing, or maybe it was just her demonic music. When Thrash glanced back over her shoulder, all she could see were Madame Wiki's headlights, the orbs burning twin suns into Thrash's night vision.

Thrash leaned forward and hissed, "She's right on our heels!"

"I'm almost there," Em shot back.

"Almost where?!" Cresca cried. "She's going to kill us!"

Em ignored Cresca's panic and flicked the wand, shutting off their only light source. Without headlights to light the path, Thrash could barely see Em or anything else in the darkness ahead.

Em veered suddenly to the left, toward where the first explosion landed. The opposite of what panicking prey would do. The force of the turn threw Thrash's stomach up into her heart and made Cresca clutch her door. The turn was long, maybe a full 180 or 360 degrees, impossible to tell as darkness spun around them.

Then Em gunned it.

There was another *boom!* but this one landed far from its mark. Under the cover of the sound, Em snapped, "Don't make a sound," and then rounded a boulder and slammed on the brakes, bringing the car to a silent, sudden stop. Thrash lurched forward, and the seatbelt cut into her gut.

They hovered in place, the road only a few hundred feet away. Cresca whimpered quietly beside her.

Madame Wiki crept past the rock and their car, her bright headlights piercing the black haze. The girls held as still as possible. Thrash didn't move, didn't breath. She tried to will her body into nonexistence. When she looked down at her hands and she didn't see them, she was only dimly shocked to see it had worked.

Thrash, the girls, the car—all of them had turned translucent.

Madame Wiki slowed to a stop. Thrash had forgotten about the spikes, which looked like hungry fangs in silhouette. She couldn't make out Rongo in the darkness, but she could feel the weight of her gaze.

If Rongo had been looking for them in broad daylight, she might have noticed a strange shimmer in the air, almost like the oily multicolored sheen of four girl-bubbles and one car-bubble ready to burst. But Rongo didn't have the benefit of sunlight, and she was looking for four teenage witches in conspicuous pointed hats and a shiny black-and-chrome convertible.

After what felt like a century, Madame Wiki roared away and onto the leyline.

Em dropped everything—her arms, the wand, the car, and the cloaking spell—with the sound of a *pop!* Then Em threw back her head and let out a, "Wooooo!"

"That was amazing, Em," Thrash said, breathless. Thanks

to their knacks—their supposedly worthless knacks!—they were still free!

Only Cresca wasn't smiling.

"Shit. The warproot." Cresca rubbed her eyes. "What are we gonna do now? We can't go back there!"

"Um...actually..." Saki sat up, reached into her hat, and pulled out a glass mason jar. It was packed with dried herbs— well, one herb specifically. "I found this in Rongo's trophy room."

Cresca leaned forward and threw her arms around Saki, hugging her through the chair. "Holy shit, Saki! You did it!"

"I did it." Saki's hesitant smile widened into a giddy grin. "I did it...I got the warproot."

INTERLUDE

I t was another early morning for Tempest. Around 6:00 a.m., the sun made its entrance, assaulting Tempest's eyes with sharp golden rays. In a few hours, the valley would feel like an oven and his hair would frizz—though that was the least of the stallion's problems.

Last night, Osmarra received a tip from the Atlandotirs that their daughter was holed up on some desolate ranch outside the Tsin Protected Wildlands. Tempest and Osmarra immediately rerouted from Redrock, but the girls had somehow slipped right through the fingers of the bounty hunter who had claimed she had the situation under control.

No matter. Osmarra didn't want some freelancer getting tangled up in what was already becoming a messy pursuit. Osmarra was currently inside, negotiating with the big woman. Outside the ranch house, a dozen reporters perched like vultures, eager for an update on runaway royalty.

Tempest was mid-yawn when the bounty hunter's wife, a waifish thing in snakeskin boots and a sliver of a shirt, appeared lugging a large aluminum trough through the junk-yard gate.

"Now I just gotta get the hose," the woman muttered, dusting off her hands and rolling her wrists.

Feeling benevolent, Tempest plucked a few of the universe's strings and fresh water filled the trough. He had once been a storm spirit, after all. The bounty hunter's wife watched wide-eyed as the water rose. Ah, to never have seen real magic without frivolous wands and other nonsense.

Tempest said, "Thank you, my dear," and the poor thing yelped.

"Goddess above—you can talk?!" she said, backing away.

Tempest snorted. What, did the girl think Tempest was a normal horse? How insulting. Sure, most familiars didn't deign to talk to typicals, but in Tempest's experience most humans benefited from what he had to say.

The bounty hunter's wife muttered something about getting back to work and fled into the junkyard. Tempest sighed. Why did he ever expect humans to be anything but disappointing?

When Osmarra emerged from the house, she hurried down the porch steps. The reporters flocked to her, their capture crews not far behind with orbs encased in mirrored boxes.

"Protectrix Osmarra!" a reporter yelled, "Is your investigation related to the disappearance of Emerald Atlandotir?"

"I cannot comment on specific persons involved in the incident."

"Protectrix, now that this kidnapping—"

"Incident."

"Now that this *incident* has crossed state lines, would you say it's a matter of national, rather than state, security?"

Osmarra paused to consider it, even though Tempest knew she had already planned out a careful response hours ago. If

Osmarra made answering the questions look too easy, the reporters would think they could ask even more. Truth be told, they were worse than vultures. At least vultures contributed to the desert food chain.

"As the incident is related to a citizen of Calypso, the State of Calypso is fully capable of handling the incident without the aid of the National Protectrix," Osmarra answered.

"Protectrix Osmarra, is it true that one of the runaways is your own daughter?"

Osmarra didn't miss a beat. She threw back her head, earrings tinkling musically, and laughed.

"Now I've heard everything," Osmarra said, whisking away a tear, likely glamoured. A few of the reporters chuckled with her. "That's all the time I have for questions, if you'll excuse me."

Osmarra waved Tempest after her as she ducked into the junkyard, putting a wall of rusty pre-magic appliances and car parts between them and the reporters.

"What did the bounty hunter say?" Tempest asked.

"Nothing much. The girls are still claiming Slumber City is their destination, but why head north? The route doesn't make sense."

"A decoy destination," Tempest whinnied with delight. "We've underestimated little Thrash."

"That's not all. Did you see that shattered window? The bounty hunter says she broke it with magic."

"Impressive."

"Yes, yes, she'll be a powerful witch someday—but only if we can talk some sense into her." Osmarra's frown deepened. "You know, legally, I have to report that her knack broke the window. This is becoming a real mess."

"Nothing we can't clean up..." But as Tempest said it, Osmarra rolled up her sleeve, revealing a burn mark in the shape of a glyph. The Fae word for *violation*. The blood contract to return the Gift of Glamour was up.

"The High Circle is going to put the pieces together," Osmarra said. "Between the blood contract, the reporters, and the knack report. We have a day—maybe—before the High Circle realizes she stole the Gift of Glamour."

Osmarra rolled her sleeve back down. She drummed her fingers against her chin.

"This is so unlike Theo. Or at least, I thought it was. Maybe you're right. Maybe I've underestimated her."

"I'm always right."

Osmarra didn't acknowledge his remark.

"She disdains my magic for whatever reason," Osmarra said. She started pacing, her boots kicking up fine purple dust. "But this means she has a blindspot—*she* underestimates *Glamour*. We can use this against her."

White light glowed from Osmarra's coat pocket. She pulled out her orb and sighed. "Yet another capture from the Atlandotirs. I should send them an update. Then I'll put in the request for wandslingers for the Atlandotir case."

Tempest was happy to leave that to Osmarra. With a bow of his head, he trotted back toward the house. Maybe he could harass the reporters a bit. Throw them off the trail.

As Tempest retreated, a pair of watchful eyes reflected from behind a mountain of trash. Tempest realized it was the bounty hunter's wife. The hollow-cheeked woman had been listening.

How much had she overheard?

8

Em insisted on driving through the night while the rest of the girls tried to sleep in the car. Thrash draped a spare jacket over her arms like a blanket to protect against the wind in the back of the convertible. She could've used more space, but it was hard to complain when Saki sat bent like a folding chair in the front seat, her arms and legs tucked into her oversized NSU sweatshirt like a turtle.

After twenty minutes curled up in the back with her eyes closed, Thrash gave up on sleep. She opened her eyes, leaned back, and watched the sea of stars drifting above them.

What even *was* magic, precisely? Some believed it was a gift from the Goddess, who blessed witches, her chosen children. In school, teachers described it as energy surrounding everything, like the dark matter between stars or the tissue holding the human body together. The government talked about witches like they were tools for harnessing magic, and Thrash supposed it had been like that up until the Second Magical Revolution. The invention of wands and rings allowed everyone to harness magic to some extent.

What Thrash wanted to know was how her knack fit into this picture. Knacks were supposed to be minor, inconsequential glimpses of magic, useful for spotting a witch but worthless after receiving a Gift. But what was magic if not the ability to move and manipulate surfaces? Breaking that window certainly felt like magic—purposeful, direct, refined.

What it *didn't* feel like was the Gift of Glamour, Growth, or even Sight.

Cresca stirred against her doorframe, groaned, and sat up in her seat, stretching her neck from side to side. Cresca caught Thrash's eye and nodded to her. All this thinking about knacks and Thrash realized she still didn't know Cresca's.

"Hey," Thrash said.

Cresca caught Thrash's eye and whispered, "Hey. You look wide awake. Something eating at you?"

Thrash hesitated. "Knacks, actually."

"That window back there did not see you coming," Cresca said with a hint of awe. "We basically have your knack and Em's to thank for getting away from Coco and Rongo. And maybe Saki's knack, too, if her theory's right about having 'danger taste.'"

In the passenger seat, Saki shifted and mumbled, "I'm not asleep yet. And I *did* taste danger."

"Well, there you go." Cresca lowered her voice. "All of your knacks are pretty incredible."

If Thrash thought about it, she wouldn't say it. So she said it.

"What about your knack?" Thrash asked.

"Oh, completely un-incredible." Cresca examined her nails, which were suddenly examination-worthy. "Don't even worry about it."

But Thrash was a bit worried about it. Cresca's "plans" all sounded great until it became apparent that she was withholding key details. If Thrash and the Lunes were going to steal their Gifts, they all had to be on the same page. They all had to trust each other.

Cresca set down her hand and scooted closer to Thrash.

"What would you say if I told you that you have a very comfortable-looking shoulder?"

"I'd say you're blatantly trying to change the subject."

"Is that a 'yes, you can use me as a human pillow' or a 'no, my heart and shoulder are both made of cold, unfeeling rock?'"

"Sure." Thrash was too tired to argue about it.

Cresca unclasped her seatbelt and scooted toward Thrash across that thin patch of middle-seat that barely passed for a seat at all. Thrash wasn't big on personal contact, but the weight of Cresca's head on her shoulder felt cozy. She was relieved to have buoyant, non-angsty Cresca back after Coco's, even as Cresca skirted her questions. There was some weird comfort in learning that Cresca wasn't all unicorn farm selfies and perfect eyeliner.

"Hey, Cresca..." Thrash took a fortifying breath. "I didn't have a choice about whether or not I told you about my knack, but I'd like to think that by now, after all we've been through...I would have told you. Even if it was un-incredible."

Thrash wasn't sure if Cresca tensed beside her, or if it was just the natural turbulence of the flying car. What she really wanted to say was, *You can trust me.*

"I guess it's kind of like dousing," Cresca finally whispered. Thrash strained to hear her over the wind. "I toss something natural, like a piece of wood, and it leads me where I need to go."

"A navigation knack sounds really useful," Thrash said, thinking of Em and Saki stumbling through Coco's house searching for warproot. Why didn't Cresca use her knack to find it?

"It doesn't really work like that." Cresca sighed. "*It* tells *me* when it wants me to find something. I don't know. It's this feeling I have, and I can't really control when I have it."

Thrash thought of her own knack, which she wouldn't quite call "under control" either. Excitement and shame flooded her every time she unintentionally broke a mirror or caused a disruption, like at the motel pool. But at Coco and Rongo's, all the doubts fell away and Thrash harnessed her knack with purpose. It felt like magic—not like baby teeth to be discarded to make room for "real" magic.

Neither one of them said anything for a few minutes, until Thrash finally broke the silence and said, "Thank you for telling me."

"Mmmm," Cresca murmured, sinking deeper into Thrash's side.

Thrash wasn't sure if Cresca was asleep or in that fragile half-waking place, but for once Thrash had the opportunity to *not* break something. Holding very still, Thrash kept the questions to herself and let Cresca sleep, slowly turning them over in her head until she finally dozed off herself.

A few hours later, Thrash woke up to a face full of early morning sun. She squinted into the light and scrambled to sit up. Her mouth tasted like a muffin had died in it. She needed a toothbrush. Or a coffee.

The Lunes were all awake, absent their usual chatter and too-loud music. Thrash felt oddly touched when she realized that that was for her benefit, but the quiet didn't last long once Cresca announced, "Look who's finally awake."

"Welcome to Morganshyre!" Em cried from the driver's

seat. "The Cornucopia, the Horn of Plenty, the Overflowing Bread Basket of the Thirteen States!"

Saki twisted around and informed her, "It is a lot of grain, in a lot of colors."

When Thrash finally got her wits about her enough to take in the scenery, it almost stole her breath. Overnight, multicolored fields in shades of bright gold, soft pink, and verdant green had replaced the desert plains. The wind carried a scent like a freshly mowed lawn and...pastries?

Saki offered Thrash a battered pink box. She opened the lid and revealed a dozen croissants.

"I spent the night skirting the northern edge of Ji'ishland, avoiding all major cities," Em explained as Thrash bit into her pastry. Flakes flew everywhere, courtesy of Em's broken convertible top. "I wish we had time to veer south and go through the Cote d'Aveau. I've heard the Gulf of Meczica has water so clear it's like walking through an aquarium. And that green sand? I need it!"

"We just passed the welcome sign for Morganshyre," Saki added. "You were asleep...we didn't want to wake you up..."

"No worries." Thrash was overjoyed, in fact. Morganshyre was practically the East Coast! At least to a West Coaster like her. It was halfway across the country. Halfway to Wyckton. Halfway to New Salem University.

Cresca leaned forward to address Em. "Girl, do you need to stop for, like, a bathroom? Or a nap?"

"I could always stop for *brunch*," Em said. "The upcoming exit said it has food and craft. As I recall, I am owed a breakfast, a sunny bucket, and a thousand playlists."

"Witch, you know it was one hundred," Cresca replied. "Next you're gonna be saying Thrash owes you an actual Sunny Bucket restaurant."

"Does she not?"

Everyone laughed as Em steered them toward the next exit, but their laughter died as soon as they drifted to a halt at the first stop sign.

There wasn't much of a town near the off-ramp, just a few brick buildings clustered on a concrete square in a sea of wild grass. The paved roads had seen better days; the aggressive grass clawed up through the asphalt like it had been buried alive.

But what stole the girls' laughter was a poster taped beneath the red stop sign. An illustration of Em stared back at them along with huge black text that proclaimed *TROUBLE*. The flyer listed Em's name, height, weight, eye color—and, of course, the reward.

"That's four years of tuition." Cresca whistled.

Em gunned it. A single road cut through the tiny town and led back to the leyline. As they sped past the brick businesses, Thrash saw trouble posters for the rest of the girls too. A hundred paper eyes, including Thrash's own, stared at them from lampposts and storefronts and benches.

"What do we do now?" Saki asked as they flew back onto the leyline. Even with their printed faces firmly in the rearview mirror, Thrash didn't feel entirely at ease.

"I think we just keep following the leyline," Em said. "Off-roading's not exactly an option here. Someone will notice if I drive over their crops."

Beside Thrash, Cresca shivered. She was practically trembling in her seat.

"The map. Where's the map?" Cresca rooted through the seatback pocket in front of her and grasped under her chair, her hands shaking.

"I think it's in your hat," Thrash said.

Cresca cursed and unfastened the hat, yanking out the map

and her cigarettes. She spread the map out over her thighs and ripped open the cigarette box with her teeth.

"You wanted to see my knack in action?" Cresca said. "Here you go."

Cresca pulled out a cigarette and tried to block the wind with her free hand. Thrash still half expected her to light it, but instead she tossed it a few inches in the air and let it fall on the map. Cresca paused, chewed her lip, and tossed the cigarette again.

Cresca looked up from the map, her brown eyes heavy. "It says to turn around."

"What?!" Em cried from the driver's seat. "Seriously? Why?"

"You know I don't know!"

As the girls debated their next course of action, Thrash peeked over at the map. There was really only one main artery cutting through Morganshyre, Leyline 115, and they were on it. Cresca's cigarette landed perfectly on the leyline, the end of it pointing west. They had driven all night to get ahead of Osmarra and Rongo, and now it was telling them to go *back*?

"No, yup, I taste it," Saki said suddenly. "That's the taste of danger."

"Are you kidding me?" Em shrieked.

"Turn around!" Cresca shouted.

"Wait, wait, let's not panic," Thrash said, partially for her own sake. She squinted into the distance and caught a bright, glittering flash, almost like a floating discoball. A line of floating discoballs. It took her a moment to place the strange shapes, and then she realized they were signals, the kind used to narrow lanes down to a single road for construction or sometimes—

"A checkpoint." Cresca fiddled with her rings as she stared dead ahead. "A wandslinger checkpoint."

Thrash's mind raced. As the lanes narrowed, the cars ahead of them began to slow. Further up ahead, checkered hats weaved and bobbed between stopped vehicles. When Thrash spotted motorcycles with the same black and white squares along the leyline, that all but confirmed local wandslingers were slowing traffic. Thrash should've known it was only a matter of time before Osmarra tapped the local police.

"Em, how tired are you?" Thrash asked. "Can we go invisible?"

"I—I can try." Em glanced at Saki. "Saki, 'sant me."

"What?"

"Stick a croissant in my mouth so I don't keel over!"

The resulting explosion of pastry flakes almost blinded Thrash. When she opened her eyes, she saw the road race through her hands, Em's seat, and Em—all of which had turned near-translucent except for a faint, rainbow sheen. A gaped-mouth driver one lane over slammed on their breaks. As cars slowed ahead of them, Thrash realized they were seconds away from getting trapped in that gridlock—and possibly rear-ended, since the car behind them could barely see them.

"Hold onto your hats!" Em ordered, yanking the steering wheel to the side and waving her metal wand madly. The convertible leaped up suddenly like it was on a rollercoaster track. Thrash felt momentarily weightless, her stomach suddenly in her chest, as the car U-turned over the heads of fellow drivers. The whoosh of air ruffled a few hats below them. Drivers looked around in confusion at the space where Em's convertible had been.

The invisible car and its invisible passengers shot over to the other side of the road and dove down into the flow of traffic heading away from the police checkpoint.

Thrash felt the tug of the accelerator. Em wasn't slowing down.

"I don't know how much longer I can hold it..." Em said through gritted teeth.

"The wandslingers are getting smaller," Cresca called as they raced away. "I doubt they'd see us now. You can probably let it go."

The spell popped. As their semi-invisibility vanished, Em sagged. The car swerved. Everyone cried out and Em snapped back, getting the car back under control a heartbeat later. An angry driver behind them slammed on their horn.

Saki sheepishly held up another croissant, but Em shook her head. Thrash understood; though they had escaped another trap, she had also lost her appetite.

Em was no stranger to all-nighters.

In fact, it was one of the reasons her dad liked to cite for why she needed to be homeschooled. Her parents thought she worked too long and too hard. Burn out, they called it. Like she was an out-of-control car and if they didn't pull her from school, she would crash.

Look who's not crashing, Em thought as she bit the inside of her cheek to stay alert. Yes, her legs ached, and her head pounded, but that was the price of sweet freedom.

"It's been an hour of backtracking," Thrash said behind her. "Are we sure we should still be heading this way?"

"I'll check the map," Cresca replied. Em heard the rustle of paper in the back seat. A second later, she smelled cigarette smoke and heard Thrash cough.

"Relax, we're not in a library," Cresca said to Thrash as she blew a plume of smoke.

"Careful around the upholstery," Em said. Though the whole point of this trip was to piss off her parents, she wanted them to think she was strong and independent—not reckless. Plus, cigarette smoke smelled awful and seeped into everything.

"Cigarettes smell like death..." Saki said. Em flashed her a smile of appreciation for always reading her mind.

"And don't we need those cigarettes for your knack?" Thrash added.

"I need it more like this." Cresca took another deep inhale. "Plus, I'm just getting the same result. West along 115."

Em wracked her brain for things she might have spotted along the route, but her mind was moving like molasses. Mmmmm, molasses. She would have killed for a stack of pancakes.

"What if we stop there?" Saki pointed at a sign for an upcoming exit that read *Lake Chlala Campgrounds*. Em didn't remember seeing it before, but then again, molasses.

"That might be perfect!" Cresca sat up in her seat, revitalized by the nicotine hitting her blood. "Hopefully they have bathrooms, and it would be free, or at least cheap! We could lay low, check in with our parents, and maybe in a few hours that police barrier will come down and we can hit the road again?"

As Em drove, more signs popped up along the leyline. Charming handprinted ads for the campground enticed campers with proclamations of *Blackberry Picking!* and *Hot Showers!* and *Salt Water Lake!* The last one was a little surprising, but then again there was a prominent salt lake in Calypso. In the 19th century, the Saltar Sea had been cut off from the mountains and the ocean by a greedy, water-hoarding witch.

"Do you think the wandslingers were looking for us?" Thrash asked tentatively.

"I really hope not," Cresca said. "It's bad enough that we've got your mom following us. Also, Em, did you leave your parents a capture yet and ask them to call off the bounty like I told you?"

"Working on it," Em said as her legs broke out in a cold sweat.

"Girl, you've gotta do it when we stop."

Em reassured Cresca she would talk to her parents, but she had little hope they would listen. Em's parents lived in their own world, in an oceanside mansion they constructed to cut themselves off from public scrutiny. Her dad turned down his royal duties to raise her and her mom spent all day tinkering in her lab. Em was their only daughter, the center of their fragile solar system.

Following signs for Lake Chlala, Em steered them off the leyline and onto a dirt road. Em wasn't sure what would horrify her parents more: her stay at a remote campground or her all-night drive. Em bit the inside of her cheek again. She would prove to her parents that she wasn't a princess who needed to be locked away in a castle. She was strong; she could do this.

A few miles down the road they reached a solid wood gate that was padlocked shut with a sign reading *Closed for the Season*.

"That's perfect," Cresca said. "We can hop the fence and we don't have to deal with people recognizing us."

"And I could finally stretch my legs..." Saki added.

As Em reached for the wand, Thrash blurted, "Wait! Before we shoot over that gate, what if this is a trap? Doesn't this seem a little too good to be true that this campground has everything we need, *and* it's closed during peak camping season?"

"I don't taste any danger..." Saki said.

"Cresca? Your knack got us into this mess." Em struggled to

suppress a yawn. "Can you use those cigarettes for something helpful and see what your knack says now?"

"I'm not sure that it works that way," Cresca murmured. "But sure."

In the rearview mirror, Em watched as Cresca savored one last long inhale of her cigarette and then tossed it out the window. Thrash winced in what looked like anticipation of the cigarette burning down the whole campground.

Cresca peered over the side of the car. Thrash unlatched her seatbelt and scooted across the back seat to look over Cresca's shoulder.

"Lake Chlala it is!" Cresca cried.

Em secretly felt relieved. Anything to get to water and sleep. As she guided the car up and over the gate, she noticed that the trip was taking its toll on the car's wand as well. She hadn't mentioned it to the girls, but if they looked closely at the shining wand keeping the convertible afloat, they would notice a dark tarnish creeping up from the base like a growing bruise. Hundreds of miles would do that to a wand, not to mention the stunt they just pulled back on the leyline. Wands could only conduct so much magic before they fried.

That was a problem for Tomorrow-Em.

Today-Em steered the car down a slope. They turned a corner and *bam!* the glittering lake ambushed them. The bright blue brilliance made Em long to turn the convertible back to its original vintage blue beauty.

Em pulled over at the first sign of picnic tables. The moment the car stopped, Saki and Cresca leaped out of the car and ran to the water's edge, orbs in hand. When Em tried to move her stiff legs, the muscles seized and turned to rock.

Tears pricked the edges of her eyes as she watched Cresca and Saki run to the water. Em knew they had spent hours in the cramped car, but she felt just the tiniest bit betrayed—both by her legs and by the girls.

"I don't get it," Thrash said beside her. "It's just water. Anyway, need a hand?"

Em hadn't even noticed Thrash get out of the car, but here she was, standing by Em's door, her hand outstretched.

"I'm good. Thanks."

Em swallowed her tears and heaved herself out of the driver's seat. As she massaged her legs into submission, she wished she could bottle up Thrash's confidence, her quiet strength, and bathe in it instead of salt water.

Welp, that was a weird-ass thing to think. She really needed sleep.

Cresca pulled four towels out of her hat, explaining that she had filched them from the High Moon Motel. Em didn't make it to the end of the story. The moment she laid down on the shore, her eyes shut like anvils dropping. She was *out*.

9

Thrash felt the good sort of exhausted, the kind that came from a day of sunshine and laughter and reading in the sand. The moist heat of Morganshyre made her miss home. People always praised the lack of humidity in Calypso, and now she knew why.

Sweaty and sunburned, Thrash tried to dry some of the dampness with the towel she was sitting on. She almost wished she had kept that *T* necklace her mom had given her, if only for the magical sunscreen. Osmarra gifted it to her less than two weeks ago, but it felt like a lifetime had passed.

As the sun set behind the trees of Lake Chlala, Thrash closed *Song of the Silent Daughter* and saved the last chapter for later. Ironically, the novel was about a fugitive on the run. *So much for escapism.* She stowed the book in her hat and joined the Lunes at the picnic table.

Though it was getting dark, the girls were bright and lively. Cresca laid across the wood bench reading on her orb while Em leaned against her, nestled in her voluminous skirt, scribbling furiously on a note card for the adjacent Good Shit Jar.

Saki emerged from the woods and dumped a pile of branches into a makeshift fire pit.

"If I was a Growth witch, I guess I could just grow these..." Saki wiped her sweatshirt sleeve across her brow. "Do you think I would make a good agricultrix?"

"I dunno," Em said. "Do you like plants?"

Saki's face fell. "Well...no...not really..."

Cresca looked up from her orb. "Does anyone have any experience starting a fire?"

"I've never even gone camping," Thrash admitted. She also wasn't really sure they should be making a huge fire in a closed campground.

"Thrash, do you have any candles in the bottomless chest?" Cresca asked.

"Probably. I'll go check. Do we need anything else?"

"Dessert," Saki said, her expression sober.

Thrash smiled. She was really starting to like Saki. "I'll do my best. Em, can I borrow the wand?"

Em tossed Thrash the car's wand without looking up.

"Good luck finding the car," Em said unenthusiastically. All this because Thrash insisted they park the convertible in the trees and use Em's knack to turn it green. Ah well. They only had to survive another day or two together. Once they made it to NSU and cast the Gifts on each other, this alliance wouldn't matter anymore.

Thrash jogged across the road and into the copse of trees whose pale branches packed sharp green needles. Twilight hid the convertible nicely; Thrash almost walked right past the car. Stepping over bulging roots and the shed bark of the tall, white trees, Thrash gripped Em's wand. *Tap the trunk three times,* Em had explained earlier, *then trace the letters of the ward.*

Thrash tap, tap, tapped. Then she held the wand aloft and spelled out the words P-R-E-C-I-O-U-S E-M-E-R-A-L-D.

Clearly, Em's parents had set up the car's ward.

Red light pulsed from the keyhole of the trunk door, and it popped open a second later. Inside the boot, Osmarra's priceless leviathan bone chest sucked up most of the space. Thrash flipped the silver latches and twisted the proper clasps. With both of her palms on the bottomless chest's lid, she intoned, "Food."

Thrash pulled back her hands as the chest opened with a sound like a maiden's sigh. Inky purple velvet lined the inside of the chest, upon which rested jars of herbs and salt crystals, a few strings of garlic bulbs, and three of her favorite sea salt chocolate bars (that must have been her aunt). Thrash grabbed one of the candy bars and closed the chest.

She placed her hands on the lid again.

"Candles."

The chest opened with another gentle sigh and presented three dozen candles of various shapes and sizes—along with the Gift of Glamour.

"You're not a candle..." Thrash picked up the leather book. The embossed silver script winked at her in the dying light. Thrash still hadn't told the Lunes about the stolen Gift and what was inside it. A good friend would've come clean by now, but Thrash wasn't sure if she was really friends with the Lunes or just a temporary accomplice.

Thrash eased open the cover of the fake book. The five black candles explained why the bottomless chest offered up the Gift, but it was the three pouches and their contents that Thrash hadn't quite shaken since the night she left. The Gifts were supposed to amplify magic. When Thrash thought of amplification craft she thought of bells and drums—not the weird items inside the hollowed-out Gift.

Thrash peered inside the pouches. The gold amulets were still there, as were the baby teeth and the gemstone pins.

Thrash could make guesses about amulets and teeth, but the pins truly baffled her. Then she remembered the clay doll tucked into the back of the book.

She lifted the mini-Thrash from its resting place. The simulacrum was heavier than she remembered, and rougher. Thrash looked more closely at the figure and noticed faint marks in the clay, like someone had used a fingernail to gently press Xs into the clay in various spots—the forehead, the heart, the stomach, the groin, the mouth...

The Gifts are used to oppress witches, Coco had said.

This shit was undeniably creepy, unlike any craft Thrash had seen before. She really should give the Lunes a heads-up about it before they got to NSU, but what would she even say? *Sorry, I forgot to tell you I stole my Gift to piss off my mom, so it's my fault my mom is chasing us?*

Thrash shoved the pins back into the pouch and tucked everything back inside the Gift of Glamour. She lowered it back into the bottomless chest and grabbed an armful of assorted candles.

Then she shut the lid and left the Gift behind.

When Thrash returned, she found Saki precariously toasting sliced bread over a crackling campfire. Beside her was a spread of ingredients including three bruised bananas and the largest jar of peanut butter-and-jelly swirl Thrash had ever seen.

"The best I could do was a chocolate bar," Thrash said, setting it beside the bananas. Saki was so in the zone that she didn't even notice.

Thrash set the candles on the table and Em helped light them. Cresca conjured a flame-like yellow glow on her orb as it played the soothing, low-fi tunes of a playlist Cresca informed them was titled *Lake Chlala is for Luners*. As darkness settled around them, shy stars appeared overhead. Frogs started chatting and bugs grew more daring, darting around the candles. It felt like the woods were finally starting to get comfortable. Gathered around the table with the Lunes, waiting for dinner and listening to music, Thrash felt like she was finally starting to get comfortable too.

The next thing Thrash knew, Saki thrust a mysterious toasted sandwich into her hands. Thrash hadn't had a warm meal since yesterday and eagerly took a bite. The toasted bread, the salty peanut butter, the sweet bananas—plus the unexpected crunch of snack chips Saki snuck in there—it was an explosion of flavor. Especially compared to her mom's bland food.

"Saki, this is genius," Thrash said between bites. "These flavors should not go together, and yet somehow they do and it's delicious."

"Huh." Saki took a bite of her own sandwich, chewing thoughtfully. She swallowed. "I guess it is."

When Saki offered to make Thrash a second sandwich, she agreed without hesitation. It was only later, when they cleaned up and Thrash noted Cresca had only eaten a single spoonful of peanut butter for dinner, that she felt self-conscious about her appetite. Cresca didn't seem to notice; she was leaning her elbows on the picnic table, fidgeting with the compostable spoon.

"I'm bored," Cresca stated, with an undercurrent of *entertain me*. "Thrash, do you still have that tarot deck with you?"

Saki's eyes lit up. "Can you tell our fortunes?"

Before Thrash had a chance to reply to either of them, Em cut in, "It's just superstition. Tarot decks are only accurate if a Sight witch wields them."

"That's true," Thrash said, finally, as she reached into her hat. Her fingertips brushed against the soft cardboard of the worn box. "But with or without magic, it can be a tool for reflection."

"Or entertainment," Cresca added. Thrash set the deck box down on the table. Saki stared at it intently. No one spoke for a long moment.

"I would like to reflect," Saki said. "May I ask a question?"

"Sure, but how in-depth do you want to get? Like, you could draw one card, or I could do a full ten-card reading?"

Saki looked down at her hands as she considered it. She nervously picked at one of her nails. Across the table, Em was tilting one of the candles back and forth, playing with the wax. Cresca yawned. This was probably not whatever action-packed tarot shenanigans Cresca had envisioned.

"One card," Saki said. She pulled her sweatshirt sleeves up and over her hands and wrapped herself in her arms. "I want...certainty."

Thrash slid the cards out of the box and handed them to Saki. "In that case, you should shuffle them yourself. When you feel it's right, stop shuffling, ask your question, and pull the top card."

Saki unlaced her arms and pushed up her sleeves. With care, she shuffled the deck three times and then gripped the cards firmly between her hands.

"What Gift should I pick?" Saki asked the tarot deck.

Cresca sat up and leaned in. Even Em stopped messing with the candle, eyes watching the top of the deck. Of the four tarot suits, three responded to Gifts. Rings could indicate Glamour, roses Growth, eyes Sight. Cats were the wild cards— and the Major Arcana, of course, would paint a more complicated picture.

Saki flipped the card up. An armored skeleton riding a white horse, the sun rising—or setting—behind it. Beneath the horse's hooves it trampled a garden of flowers and human limbs. Below it, a single word: *Death*.

Saki dropped the card to the table as if it burned.

"Death, as a card, isn't actually that bad," Thrash said hurriedly. "It doesn't mean literal death. The card is about transformation. Changes that lead to rebirth and renewal."

"What about Mr. Le Kep's Wheel?" Saki said, referring to a tarot spread that could supposedly predict the time and cause of a person's death. "That's an entire tarot game that revolves around the Death card. Literally."

"It's not the same." Thrash tried her best to sound reassuring.

"It doesn't have to mean anything if you don't want it to," Em told Saki, placing a reassuring hand on her arm. Saki nodded, but she still looked disturbed, eying the card like it might leap up and bite her.

Never one to let a somber moment last, Cresca clapped her hands together.

"I think it's time we play a lighter game. How about Quebesto?"

"What the hell is a Quebesto?" Thrash asked. It sounded like a sandwich that she didn't want to order, but both Saki and Em perked up at the mention of it. No one was coming to Thrash's rescue on this one.

"Thrash, how have you never played Quebesto?" Cresca gushed. "It's, like, an essential party game."

"When your mom's a protectrix, you don't get invited to a lot of high school parties."

"Well, the game's pretty easy. You start by asking someone a question. Like, Em...what do you think is your sexiest body part?"

Em thought for a moment and then said, "Got it."

"Now the rest of us have to pick a tarot card we think *could* be the answer to Em's question, and then she picks the one that feels true." Cresca reached across the table and shuffled the deck. "Everyone, draw three cards."

Thrash looked at her hand. Her options were *Seven of Rings, Two of Flowers,* and *Nine of Cats.* She didn't love her choices, but she ultimately picked the *Two of Flowers,* because...well, who didn't like their eyes? Thrash placed it face down on the table. Cresca and Saki followed suit.

"Then I add the top card of the deck, right?" Em wiggled her fingers over the deck, plucked a card, and added it to the rest of the guesses. She shuffled them and then revealed each card: *The Gardener, Two of Flowers, The Wheel of Fortune,* and *The Snake Charmer.*

"*The Gardener* reminds me of my mom, so that's a point against it. Though I like the flowy dress the woman's wearing, very nice," Em thought out loud. "But the thing is, my sexiest body part, in my humble opinion, is my eyes. And I'm kinda getting eye-vibes from the flowers...so I'm gonna go with *Two of Flowers.*"

"Oh, that was my card," Thrash said. "Do I win?"

"If your card gets chosen, you get to ask the next question," Cresca said.

"Ah, okay, um..." Thrash looked between the Lunes, as if that would give her some sort of hint of what to ask. Then her eyes snagged on Cresca's white hat, and she remembered a nagging question.

"Cresca. Why do you have Coco's hat?"

Cresca's eyes flashed in the candlelight. She touched the cream-colored brim of her hat and smiled. "Submit your cards and maybe you'll find out."

Thrash reached for the deck and drew five cards. She glanced briefly at the illustrations, then peeked over the cards to scrutinize Cresca. You didn't wear the hat of a sister you hated, but things with Coco had been tense. Really tense. Thrash's eyes kept catching on *The Bridge,* in which a woman held up a stone bridge for another to cross. The card symbolized connection, through space and through time, as well as bridge-building and mending. Maybe Coco offered the hat as an olive branch, or maybe Cresca wore it to remember the times when the sisters were closer?

Saki and Em placed their cards down one by one. Cresca added the top card from the Major Arcana deck and shuffled the four cards together. Then Cresca revealed the cards one by one.

Almost immediately, she tapped *The Bridge.*

"Coco gave me her hat before she left." Cresca said it cavalierly, but Thrash could sense it was anything but cavalier. "She told me to keep it safe until she came back. And she never came back."

"I'm sorry, Cresca," Thrash said. "I didn't know."

"It's fine. All it led to was crippling abandonment issues." Cresca chuckled softly to herself. She unfastened the crochet hat and turned it thoughtfully in her hands. "After Coco left to go join the revolution or whatever, it tore my parents apart. I mean, my dad claims my mom already had one foot out the door, but I dunno. I blamed Coco for my mom leaving. Even if I shouldn't have..."

The pain in Cresca's eyes was so genuine that Thrash wanted to reach out and hug her. She might have had a little experience with judging people too harshly herself...

Cresca cleared her throat and picked up *The Bridge.* "Anyway, whose card was it?"

Thrash sheepishly raised her hand.

"Again?!" Cresca cried. "Maybe you really do have a special connection to these cards. This is your mom's deck, right?"

Saki and Em watched Thrash with bright, curious eyes. Thrash shifted uncomfortably on the hard wooden bench.

"They belonged to my other mom." The girls didn't say anything with their mouths, but their eyes all said, *I thought she only had one mom.* "It was, like, right after I moved to Belmar. She passed away."

Murmurs of sympathy. Thrash picked at a splinter of wood on the table. She hated rehashing it. That was one of the few perks of moving and leaving behind her childhood friends—no one knew her family, no one expected explanations.

"What happened?" Cresca asked. Thrash's eyes stayed glued to the table. Maybe it would feel good to talk about it— or maybe it would be painful. She wasn't sure, and then suddenly fingers studded in brilliant rings gently set Mum's tarot deck in front of her. An opportunity to express herself without words.

The girls followed Thrash's lead and drew cards. When everyone had placed a card before her, Thrash added one from the top of the deck and shuffled them all together. Thrash dealt them face-up: *The Triumph, The Brave, Ace of Eyes,* and *The Justice.*

Thrash picked up *The Justice.* It was the obvious choice, though the balance of the scales—the idea of fairness—struck Thrash like an arrow. Duna's death was anything but fair.

"Whose card was it?" Thrash asked. Her pounding heart was all she could hear.

No one replied, which meant the deck had submitted the card. Duna's own deck. A chill ran through Thrash.

"Did The Justice kill your mom? Or cover it up or something?" Em whispered. Thrash almost didn't comprehend what she said, then realized Em meant the Named Witch, not the archetype on the card.

"No, no, I picked it because Mum had the Gift of Sight. She

was a seer. She also had cancer. It's a bad combo. For obvious reasons."

The girls remained silent, but the sort of supportive silence that makes room for someone else. Thrash only saw kindness in their eyes, kindness that she didn't feel like she had earned.

"She saw her death years ago," Thrash said. "Like most Sight magic, there was a chance the future might change, so she didn't tell me or my mom. Duna just kept living life to the fullest, even though if she had changed everything to try to prevent the disease...I don't know. Maybe things would've been different. But by the time she told Osmarra, it was too late."

"I can taste how sad you are," Saki said. "Sharp, like biting a lemon. But salty, like tears."

"Whatever it tastes like, that's messed up," Em said.

"What's really messed up is that sometimes I kind of resent her for dying," Thrash said. She almost smiled, just at the ridiculousness of it all. "I know that books on grief say that's normal, or whatever, but my mum really *got* me. Whereas with Osmarra, I know she loves me...but does she *like* me?"

Thrash shouldn't have uttered it. It felt too real, too serious for a group of teenage girls who pranced around calling themselves the Lunes. But Cresca surprised her, as she often did, by placing a hand on Thrash's.

"It's easy to put someone on a pedestal once they're gone," Cresca said. "Or, you know, condemn them. But for whatever it's worth, *I* like you."

"Thanks." Thrash choked on a swell of emotion as she said it. Saki leaned across the picnic table and placed her hand on top of Cresca's. She stared right into Thrash's soul.

"I like you," Saki said.

Tears pricked at the corners of Thrash's eyes.

Em sighed and scooted forward.

"And obviously I like you too," Em said, adding her hand to the pile. "You're brave as hell, Thrash. No one should have to go through what your family went through."

"Thank you," Thrash said. She wiped away a budding tear with her free hand. What was this, if not friendship? The thought made her feel grateful to the Lunes, and a little guilty for keeping the Gift of Glamour secret.

"Sorry for hijacking Quebesto and making it all sad."

"No need to apologize." Cresca gave her hand a squeeze. "But maybe we should just play Go Fish for now."

After an hour of simple, drama-free card games, Thrash started to grow restless. Her butt was getting sore from sitting on the bench and she couldn't stop thinking about the Gift of Glamour. Specifically, how the Lunes had no idea about the strange craft inside of it. If they were really going to perform the Gifting on each other, wouldn't it be better to arm themselves with knowledge?

Plus, the longer Thrash hid the truth from the Lunes, the more likely it was to blow up in her face. Telling them now would either make or break their fragile friendship. Thrash felt her palms sweating, or maybe it was the heat and humidity, which were still going strong into the evening.

"I need a soak. Who's up for a night swim?" Em clapped her hands together, eyes darting between the girls, ruthlessly enthusiastic.

"A swim could be cleansing for everyone," Cresca said. Her eyes flitted to Thrash.

"I'm good," Thrash said. "I've got a book."

"Your book'll be there tomorrow," Cresca urged. "We're only at Lake Chlala once! Live a little!"

Cresca pulled her tank top up over her head and threw it into the dirt. Thrash had seen the girl pack; she knew for a fact that Cresca didn't have a tank top to waste.

"It's just one little dip in the lake," Em said. "And it's dark. No one can see you."

Thrash's last concern was hiding her fat body in the darkness, but then she realized insecurity could be the perfect excuse to hide behind.

"I know, but I just don't feel comfortable swimming in my underwear," Thrash said. It was partially true. Most of her wardrobe was black, but she loved goofy, loud underwear. It was like a secret gift for herself and no one else. Today's pair: bright red with dancing strips of bacon.

"Your loss!" Cresca cried, careening toward the starry glisten of moonlight on water. "Last one to the lake is a boiled toad!"

Saki and Em tossed their hats onto the table and raced after Cresca, but the moment they all reached the lake their squeals turned to screams of, "It's cold!" "Oh Goddess!" "Why?!"

"I'm gonna get some more candles from the car!" Thrash called in the direction of the lake. She didn't hear much of a reply, but that was fine. She plunged her hand into Em's velvet hat and felt around for the cool metal wand. As soon as her fingers closed around it, she was up on her feet.

Thrash grabbed one of the candles and set off toward the trees. Retrieving the Gift of Glamour would be the easy part. Breaking it to the Lunes was another story.

I should've told you all sooner, but I have the Gift of Glamour with me. When you see what's inside, you'll understand my misgivings... Or maybe she should beg for forgiveness right off the bat: *So, I did something really stupid before we left...*

Heightened by moonlight and adrenaline, the woods felt

creepier at night. Shadows danced in the corners of her vision as Thrash hustled past the pale trees, whose half-sloughed-off bark made trunks look like splintered femurs. She half expected a person or a creature to be lurking behind every trunk.

So when someone actually did emerge from behind the convertible, Thrash had a minor heart attack. She almost dropped her candle, which would have been especially bad as the middle-aged woman walking toward her was wearing a khaki Lake Chlala campground uniform.

"The campground is closed for the season," the woman said. Thrash froze. Should she put her hands up in the air? She felt like she was being arrested as the ranger produced a glowing orb from her pocket.

Where was that orb when Thrash was approaching the car? Something felt off about all of this. Had the woman been waiting for her? In the dark?

"Oh. I'm so sorry, we didn't realize," Thrash said, inching toward Em's convertible. "We can leave. Right now if you want."

"Wait, wait!" As the woman came closer, her dirty-blonde hair darkened to chestnut brown and her wrinkles smoothed. The nose, the cheekbones, the eyebrows all morphed into the familiar, unchanging face Thrash had known all her life.

"Mom?!"

"Don't run. Please. I didn't want to scare you." Osmarra held up her empty hands like she came in peace, but Thrash knew better. A witch was never unarmed. "We need to talk."

10

"Stay away from me," Thrash said, gripping Em's wand and wishing she knew how to use it. Osmarra's finely drawn eyebrows lifted in sympathy—or maybe pity. In the flickering candlelight, it was hard to read her face.

"Theodora..." Osmarra stepped forward and Thrash backed away without thinking. Osmarra sighed that familiar "I'm disappointed in you" sigh that made Thrash die a little inside. "Please don't run. I'm here to help you."

"Just leave me alone." Even to her own ears, Thrash sounded like a petulant child.

"I'm afraid it's too late for that." Osmarra waved a hand at the surrounding woods. "There are wandslingers surrounding us as we speak."

Osmarra folded her arms as she waited for that information to sink in. Thrash stood her ground, but inside she was panicking. Was this it? The end of the line? The part where she returned home with her mom and endured some creepy Gift of Glamour ritual?

"I'm sorry," Osmarra continued, "but your little road trip is at an end."

Thrash's heart sank, but then it snagged on something. "If we're completely trapped, then what are you doing here? Why are you sneaking around as a fake park ranger?"

"It's in everyone's best interest for this to end quietly, without fuss," Osmarra explained. "And I think I know what will change your mind."

Thrash bristled. Her mom was always so presumptuous, but she had to stay calm. She couldn't let it get to her.

"Nothing is going to change my mind," Thrash said.

Osmarra reached for a loose curl that didn't exist to tuck it behind her ear. Thrash knew that tell; her mom was nervous —but why?

"I know you don't want the Gift of Glamour," Osmarra admitted. Hearing her mom say that made something burn in Thrash, who had been trying to get her to understand this exact sentiment for what felt like forever.

"Now you suddenly understand?" Thrash swallowed. "Why now?"

"Because this foolishness has gone on long enough," Osmarra said. "Here, let me be plain. Call off this stunt, and I will give you the Gift of Sight."

"What?" Did Thrash really just hear those words? Did her mom really just offer her the Gift she had always wanted?

"I know that's what this is really about," Osmarra said. She took another small step forward. Thrash couldn't remember how to use her legs. "Just come with me and we'll work it out."

"How do I know this isn't a trap?"

"What can I tell you that will make you trust me?"

Thrash thought of the Gift of Glamour, weighing on her even as it was tucked safely away in the trunk.

"Tell me about the Gifts," Thrash said, her throat suddenly

dry. "I tried to read the Gift of Glamour and all I found inside it was craft. Like, ritual items. And all of it seemed related to me."

"Ah, my ever-curious daughter!" Osmarra laughed off Thrash's concern with a fake enthusiasm she recognized from her mother's interviews with politicians and reporters. Thrash saw right through it, and Osmarra could see that too.

Osmarra dropped the mirth and continued, "Yes, bestowing the Gifts requires a ritual. That shouldn't surprise you."

"But why is it so specific to me?" Thrash insisted. The baby teeth, the clay doppelgänger—it made Thrash squirm, and her mom's forced smile didn't soothe her anxiety. "You want me to trust you and come with you. Then tell me, why do you need a vial of baby teeth and a bunch of pins to give me the Gift of Sight?"

As Osmarra began to speak, Thrash couldn't hear her. Thrash didn't understand at first; had the wind picked up or something? Osmarra's lips were moving, but instead of words, the only sound Thrash heard was a fuzzy sort of silence. Her head felt muddled, like she was waking up, half in a dream—

Thrash didn't realize she was swaying until she stumbled and almost fell face-first into the earth.

"Theo!" Osmarra rushed forward. "Are you okay? I shouldn't have tried, but I knew you wouldn't believe me unless I showed you."

"Showed me what?" Thrash yelped, backing away from her mom. "What was that?"

Osmarra merely drew her thumb and index finger across her mouth, the motion of a zipper closing.

"Does this have to do with the Gifting ritual?" Thrash asked. Osmarra's eyes grew heavy as she nodded. "Did it... mute you or something? So you can't talk about it?"

Osmarra nodded again. The wheels were really spinning

now. The pins and the clay doll—did they cause the muting? What kind of magic was that?

"What else does it mute?" Thrash asked.

Osmarra said nothing.

Thrash could feel the trees and the dark pressing in around them, like the onlookers at her Kindling, tightening. Suffocating. She tried not to panic, aware as she was of the reflective, shatter-able convertible within an arm's reach.

Thrash inhaled sharply.

"Mom...do the Gifts...mute knacks?"

This time, Osmarra hesitated. When she finally gave a single, somber nod, Thrash's heart sank. Sure, she had had her knack for less than a month, but it felt like a part of her, a part she was eager to explore. Why did she have to give up something that felt like a piece of her for the Gift of Sight to work?

Osmarra opened her mouth and tried to speak, but Thrash still couldn't hear her. Whatever wards had been woven into the Gift snatched every word away. A wave of dread rose in Thrash as she pictured the Lunes' knacks snuffed out like candles, the dreariness of a world in which Saki no longer tasted moods and Cresca never tossed cigarettes. Why did it have to work this way?

Osmarra cleared her throat.

"Theodora. I see that expression on your face," Osmarra warned. "Say nothing. To anyone. Just because you're capable of...do *not* say anything."

"People should know about this," Thrash fired back.

"Not from you, they shouldn't," Osmarra said. "You don't understand what's at risk. Do not tell those girls."

"They're my friends."

"Those 'friends' I've never seen before your Kindling? Leave them out of this and accept the Gift of Sight."

It was like her mom had thrown a bucket of ice water on

her—not only had Osmarra known all along that the Gifts muted knacks, but she still wanted to mute her own daughter? Thrash felt like she was wide awake now, seeing Osmarra for what she was: a ruthless, icy protectrix who would never understand her.

"Theodora..." Osmarra said her name like a warning.

Thrash took a step back toward the car and vaulted over the door, landing right in the passenger seat of the convertible. Had she ever driven a car before? No. Had she been watching Em's arm from the backseat, studying her wand movements for three days?

Yes. Yes, she had.

Thrash traced a symbol that reminded her of a treble clef and the convertible rose up into the air, shedding dead leaves and branches.

"The park is surrounded!" Osmarra yelled, grappling for the handle of one of the doors even as the car levitated a good three to four feet off the ground. "All this will do is ruin your future—and mine!"

Thrash didn't know what the future held, but she did know she had to get away from her mom to figure it out for herself. Like a batter winding up for a hit, Thrash gripped the wand tighter and drew three circles in the air—which she hoped translated to "really fast"—and then whipped the tip of the wand forward. The convertible flew. Thrash grabbed the steering wheel.

As trees barreled toward her, Thrash knew she had to keep her eyes straight ahead, but she allowed herself a quick glance in the rearview mirror. Barely illuminated by the car's receding taillights, Osmarra stood still, just watching her drive away.

~

How do I brake?

Thrash drew a blank. A very dangerous blank, as the car was currently careening toward the picnic benches covered in pointed hats and candles. Thrash dodged trees until the image finally came to her, a sort of flick like a conductor might do at the end of a piece. She executed a much wilder version of the move, but it did the trick. The convertible halted.

Thrash caught her breath. Ahead of her, all she could see in the car's headlights was rocky sand. Though she couldn't see the Lunes, she could hear them scrambling out of the water, peppering the air with questions.

Em appeared first in the bright headlights, hand held up to block the blaring light.

"Thrash?" Em said. "I thought you didn't have a license?"

"My mom's here. There are wandslingers with her. We need to grab our stuff and go!"

Em nodded and raced past her, followed by Cresca. Saki squinted into the light, looking a little dazed, and then jogged after the rest of the girls to the tables. The Lunes blew out candles and grabbed the food that no one had put away.

"Forget the food!" Thrash called. "Just grab your hats. We've gotta—"

"*HALT!*" a male voice boomed through the surrounding hills. A wandslinger, most likely, using a wand to magnify his voice. "*STAND DOWN. STEP AWAY FROM THE CAR.*"

The Lunes froze, trading unsure looks. Were they really surrounded?

Only one way to find out.

"Get in the car!" Thrash yelled. She lowered the car down and the Lunes leaped inside. As soon as Thrash counted three heads, she jerked the car back into the air and wound the wand not three but five times. After the final frantic circle, Thrash unleashed the magic from the wand.

The car shot like lightning across the lake. The force threw Thrash back into her seat. Wind and water—water?—whipped her face and Thrash realized that rushing sound beneath the car was their wake as they zoomed across the water.

"Slow down!" Em screamed between clenched teeth. "It's gonna blow the wand!"

Blow the wand? Thrash didn't know exactly what that meant, but she could guess.

White knuckling the wand, Thrash reversed two circles and then flicked the wand. The car slowed from I-can't-straighten-my-neck fast to regular fast. Thrash had to resist the urge to whoop.

"*HALT!*" the voice ordered. "*BY ORDER OF THE MORGANSHYRE PROTECTORATE, STAND DOWN.*"

Thrash squinted at the darkness ahead. At the end of the lake, just before the trees climbed the ridge, moonlight glinted off dark metal that looked an awful lot like the hovering motorcycles of—

"Wandslingers," Saki breathed. A wall of wandslingers waiting for them.

"We'll deal with them when we get there," Thrash replied.

"If we get there," Cresca snapped, "because *you don't know how to drive.*"

"Haven't crashed yet!"

"She's right," Em said. "Keep doing what you're doing, Thrash."

Easier said than done. As they approached the wand-slingers, a wall of shimmering red symbols wrapped around the lake. Thrash recognized the wards from that one driver's ed course she took last summer.

Cresca leaned forward and hissed, "How are we supposed to get around stop wards?"

If the car passed through the wards, they would sever the

connection between the wand and the magic it channeled, causing the car to plummet. Not great, but what other options did they have? Osmarra said the whole park was surrounded. Then again, could Thrash trust her mom? It would be just like her to exaggerate, to use her words, or her magic, to lie—

"*HALT THE VEHICLE!*" the voice boomed. They were running out of lake, seconds from hitting the looming wall of magic.

Instead of slowing down the car, Thrash continued to charge forward.

"It was nice knowing you girls," Cresca declared dramatically, flopping back into her seat. Saki and Em braced for impact, wrapping their arms around each other.

Thrash shut her eyes, bracing herself for the wards to strip the wand of its connection, for the car to nosedive and crash into the shore. Instead, she didn't feel or hear anything. When her eyes fluttered open, the wards were behind them. The car glided straight through the wandslingers like they were made of dust and moonlight.

Someone—Cresca—pounded the back of Thrash's seat in victory.

"Glamour!" Cresca cried. "It wasn't real! Holy shit, I thought we were goners!"

"Don't forget about trees!" Em cried from the backseat. The distant hills were rushing toward them, the woods becoming less distant by the second. It was now or never. Thrash prayed that tracing the same symbol for "up" would work.

However, she wouldn't need prayers today. Em placed her hand over Thrash's and jerked the wand through the pattern. The car leaped up into the sky just in time. Branches scraped against the underbody like nails on a chalkboard, but the trees failed to snag them.

The girls cheered in the backseat as the car crested the

ridge. Thrash allowed herself a moment to shove her beating heart back down into her chest. They had escaped—they were still free!

"Do you hear that?" Saki's whisper cut through the glee. As the car dipped down the other side of the valley, a light flashed in the rearview mirror. One by one, wandslingers appeared behind them, their wands bursting with blinding white light as their floating motorcycles rushed down the slope after them.

"*HALT!*" the voice boomed. At the edge of the woods, the convertible found the leyline.

"Nice try, glamour!" Cresca called back at the trees.

In response, a bright red bolt hit the car. Thrash almost dropped the wand, which burned hot. The convertible dipped dangerously toward the cement and then righted itself. The wand cooled.

"*THAT WAS A WARNING! HALT THE VEHICLE!*"

"I guess they're real!" Em said.

"And they're gaining on us!" Cresca cried. "What do we do?"

"Where's my hat?" That was Saki. "Has anyone seen my hat?!"

Thrash's head was starting to spin. She looked to either side of the road and all she could see were patches of farmland. Maybe she could lose the wandslingers in the stalks of one of the taller crops? They needed some sort of cover if they were going to hide.

"Do we have any weapons?" Cresca asked.

"We don't want to hurt them!"

"Yeah, but we need some way to slow them down."

Thrash bit her lip. "There might be some weapons in the bottomless chest?"

"The trunk is locked, and the wand is busy," Em said.

Suddenly, a leg appeared in Thrash's peripheral vision. Cresca's leg. Bending herself like a contortionist, Cresca twisted between the seats, over the wand, and landed in the front passenger seat.

"You're a weapon," Cresca said, staring straight at Thrash. Thrash kept her eyes on the road—well, the lack of road.

"What?"

"Let me handle the steering wheel and Em can use the wand from the backseat. You climb in the back and use your knack."

"On what?!"

"On the wandslingers!"

"That's not how it works. I need a reflective surface or something."

"You don't know what you need," Cresca replied. She leaned in closer, her enchanted silver hair brushing Thrash's arm. "Maybe your knack will work if you focus—it's worth a shot."

"This isn't going to work," Thrash murmured, but she proceeded to disentangle her legs from the old wheel well and its obsolete pedals.

"Not with that attitude it isn't!"

"I'll do my best." Thrash stood up awkwardly in her chair. "Keep an eye out for somewhere to hide. Our best strategy is still to disappear."

Cresca grabbed the wheel as Thrash angled herself between the seats. Ignoring Saki's proffered hand, Thrash tumbled into the back, landing on the seat between the girls. Meanwhile, Cresca slid effortlessly over to the driver's side.

"You're a witch, bitch!" Cresca called behind her. "Start acting like it!"

Thrash wanted to roll her eyes, but at the same time Cresca's belief in her gave her an undeniable surge of confidence. One leg at a time, Thrash stood up on the back seat. Her legs wobbled. Balancing in a moving car was a feat of magic alone.

Luckily, she wasn't alone. Saki hugged one of her legs and Em followed her lead, bolstering Thrash so she could stand up to full height.

"We've got you," Em said.

Thrash raised her arms, as if in surrender, as she peered into the darkness. She didn't want to hurt the wandslingers, but what else could she do? Before she could make out much of anything, a dozen blinding white wand-beams shifted and focused on her.

"*WHAT ARE YOU DOING?*" There was a hint of uncertainty in the wandslinger's voice. "*STAND DOWN!*"

Oof, those lights ruined her night vision. Thrash dropped her gaze to the ground. She expected to see grass, but there was asphalt underneath them. They were on a leyline now! So much for the "lose 'em in the fields plan," which she had failed to tell Cresca anyway.

"Thrash!" Em said, snapping her out of it. "Do something!"

Asphalt wasn't particularly reflective, but maybe it didn't have to be. Maybe what mattered was the willpower behind her knack. Thrash had only read a few books on Magic Theory, but she knew that some philosophers thought magic all boiled down to force of will.

And Thrash had plenty of that.

She pictured Osmarra approaching her in the woods, her features rearranging themselves because she didn't even trust Thrash not to bolt. She didn't trust Thrash with anything, whether it was choosing her own Gift or taking care of her own body. It was insulting, and it made her miss Duna. She wanted her Mum. It was all so *unfair*.

"*STAND DOWN!*"

No, Thrash thought, raising her palms. *I'm done standing down.*

Thrash slammed her hands together. The asphalt erupted like two tectonic plates crashing. Huge sheets of cement clashed, forming a giant rocky barrier between the car and its pursuers. As the gray wall went up, it cut off the sound of shouting humans and the blinding white beams of their wands.

Thrash dropped to her knees as the Lunes sped away, leaving a minor mountain range in their wake.

INTERLUDE

Tempest followed Osmarra as she examined Thrash's asphalt abomination for the hundredth time, determined to find some new revelation in one of its jagged niches. Only Tempest's ironclad professionalism stopped him from yawning. The wandslingers that had failed to catch the girls were busy blocking off roads and holding back nosy reporters, but it was impossible to prevent their orbs from capturing the aftermath of Thrash's knack—and speculating about it.

It wouldn't be long before the full story got out. The High Circle was fully aware a Gift of Glamour was missing, and as of last night, there were a dozen wand-wielding typicals who could confirm that Osmarra's daughter had escaped with it. Protectrix from neighboring cities had been arriving all morning, clad in black coats upon black horses, cougars, and bison. One hardy familiar took the shape of a buffalo-wolf. A little gauche, if you asked Tempest.

"Can you believe she did this?" Osmarra muttered, not for the first time that morning.

"She will be very powerful someday," Tempest replied carefully. If witches were tools for magic, then Thrash was a wild, dangerous tool. Good for destroying roads. Bad, most would say, for civilized society.

"I just don't understand it," Osmarra said.

"Thrash?" Tempest joked. Osmarra *almost* smiled. Almost.

"I meant her little stunt, with the car and those girls." Osmarra sighed and rubbed her temples. "Where is she going? What does she want, if not the Gift of Sight?"

"Well, that's why the Council is bringing *her* in, isn't it?" Tempest said. "It's certainly not for her sense of humor."

"Or for those birds."

Tempest brayed in delight. "Oh, how I despise them! This will be a treat."

"I'm glad somebody's happy about it."

Osmarra stared off toward the eastern horizon, her face clouding over. There was something else bothering Osmarra, beyond Thrash's getaway, beyond the High Circle calling in the National Protectrix.

"I can't get this one thought out of my head," Osmarra said.

"Tell me."

Without meeting Tempest's eyes, Osmarra whispered, "*Duna would know.* That's what I keep thinking. That if Duna were here, *she* could get through to Theo. She could stop this." Osmarra sighed. "How can I do this without her?"

In the lead-up to Duna's death, Osmarra stayed strong through everything Duna foretold—the collapse on the staircase, the Growth witch who could not stir her, the stillness as Duna took her last breath just before midnight. For Thrash, Osmarra locked her grief away, but she could only hold her broken world together for so long. In the weeks after Duna's death, Osmarra would wait until Thrash was asleep and then slip into the stables, crying into fistfuls of Tempest's mane. *"How am I supposed to go on without her?"*

"Duna is still with you," Tempest said. He knew from experience that it was one of the few notions that could give Osmarra an ounce of comfort.

"I know," Osmarra whispered, fingertips tracing the asphalt wall that Thrash had thrown up between them.

At the same time, Tempest sensed something disturbing the clouds above. The Named Witch approached.

"Time to get it together," Tempest warned. Osmarra didn't need to be told; she had already glamoured away any hints of tears. Hands folded behind her back, Osmarra lifted her chin to the skies as a massive black falcon broke through the clouds, its talons trailing pale mist as they ripped through the pall. When the familiar landed on the leyline, the ground shuddered.

"Show off," Tempest murmured.

"Play nice," Osmarra replied.

"I'm always nice."

The bird crouched, splaying its huge wings and revealing The Justice on its back. The Named Witch released her legs from a harness on the familiar's back and landed, boots first, on the leyline. As far as Tempest had seen, she always wore her hair in the same severe bun, with huge black sunglasses that made her face unreadable.

Osmarra bowed deeply as The Justice approached, her dark blue trench coat dusting the ground. "An honor and a blessing, Justice."

The Justice tipped the brim of her leather hat in reply. "An honor and a blessing, Protectrix."

Behind her, the falcon shrank from ten feet tall to two. It

shook off the harness and flew over to The Justice, landing on her shoulder with a smug look.

"Raging Tempest Shapes The Land," the falcon said, dipping its head in respect.

"Always a pleasure...Blade? Is it?" Tempest refused to learn the names of The Justice's *four* familiars. Tempest sensed the other three birds circling in the air above, waiting for a sign from their mistress.

The bird didn't move, didn't blink, for an agonizing moment.

"Blade's Edge Finds Blood," it finally chirped.

"Of course! It has been too long!" Tempest cried. The bird didn't reply. It took a special kind of familiar to assume the shape of a bird.

"Let's get on with cleaning up this mess," The Justice said, dismissing the falcon with a wave of her hand. Blade took one last accusing look at Tempest, as if *he* had been the one to dismiss the bird, and then flew up to join the other three falcons circling overhead.

"I wouldn't call it a mess..." Osmarra interjected.

The Justice's head snapped toward Osmarra, her black sunglasses unreadable and unnerving.

"You had the suspects surrounded and they still got away."

Tempest saw Osmarra's forehead crinkle at the use of "suspects." That implied a crime. Osmarra wouldn't be able to shield Thrash from the consequences of her choices for much longer.

"From what I understand, you also have a personal connection to the case?"

Osmarra lifted her chin higher. "Yes. My daughter is with those girls."

"She stole the Gift of Glamour," The Justice said. Osmarra swallowed. "The High Circle is denying it, but you've seen the reporters. Our sources also say someone tipped off the MLM. The Magic Liberation Movement is calling on *your daughter* to show the Gift to the world. Whether or not she has heard their pleas, protesters are rallying around it. That, Protectrix, I would call a mess."

Osmarra looked pale as The Justice raised her arm and made a fist.

"Fetch the hat," The Justice ordered, and the four black falcons dove for the saddlebags, shoving and pecking midair. Tempest cringed; he found the familiars a little *desperate*, the way the birds jostled and competed for her attention.

Finally, one of the familiars—not Blade, so it had to be either Strike or Flood or whatever that other one was named—emerged with a bright pink witch's hat clutched in its talons. The bird dropped the hat into The Justice's hand.

"You may be interested to hear that we found warproot in this hat," The Justice said. "Possession is a misdemeanor. But burning it, *that* is a felony."

"They're just teenagers," Osmarra said, her voice strained.

The Justice peeled off one of her leather gloves and touched the pink hat with her bare hand. Ah, yes, her Sight worked best with "materials." The Justice nodded faintly as she held the hat and peered into a future that Osmarra and Tempest could only guess at.

"Now, that wasn't so hard," The Justice said, re-gloving her hand. "They're going to New Salem University."

Osmarra glanced at Tempest, who was just as surprised. Strange choice for someone who had just turned down the Gift of Sight.

"At this point, the goal is containment," The Justice continued. "We retrieve the Gift and squash all talk of 'muting' like we did in '88."

"What about Theodora?" Osmarra asked.

The Justice gestured toward the wall of broken asphalt. "Your daughter's magic is destructive and untamed. We need to capture her and Gift her. Understood?"

Heeling like a dog did not become Osmarra. As her mind raced through her options, Tempest pictured Thrash standing in the back of that car, wielding the kind of magic that the Thirteen States wasn't so fond of anymore. This was why Tempest considered "government" one of humanity's most questionable creations. A hundred years ago, Thrash might have been considered a prodigy. Humans were so mercurial.

"Time is of the essence," Osmarra finally said.

"We will find them at the Garnet Caverns, where we will capture the girls as long as everyone follows my command." The Justice wrinkled her nose. "There will be an obstacle, but I cannot see it with clarity. Not related to the girls, at least not directly, or I would have seen it."

Osmarra nodded but that wasn't enough for The Justice, who leaned in and said, "I need *everyone* staying on book."

"I understand," Osmarra replied, her smiled forced.

"And who knows," The Justice added. "Follow my instructions, get this situation under control, and maybe I can make a recommendation to the High Circle."

Tempest's ears twitched. Some color, and some hope, returned to Osmarra's face. This could be their path to a Name, to power and renown for Osmarra that could tether Tempest to this plane for generations. Centuries clinging to an earthly body had a steep price, one that only powerful names could pay.

The Justice threw back her head and called to the sky: "Who wants to make me proud today?"

One of the falcons opened its beak and gave an ear-splitting call. The rest followed suit, all flapping wings and puffing chests, pecking at each other in some immature contest to run a simple errand. Then again, that was essentially what Osmarra and Tempest were signing up for too. Tempest just hoped it was worth it.

"Find the girls," The Justice said, and her four black falcons took off like fireworks.

11

Saki could not sleep.

While Em drove and Thrash and Cresca whispered in the back seat, Saki clutched the Good Shit Jar, replaying that night over and over again. The loop started with Thrash arriving behind the wheel of Em's convertible and ended with the frantic cold dash from the picnic tables to the car. Saki's feet still hurt from running barefoot over twigs and rocks, but that pain was dull compared to the anguish she felt remembering how, in the chaos, she grabbed the jar.

You can't do anything right. Saki pulled her legs to her chest, willing herself not to cry. *Where was your danger taste when there was actual danger?*

The answer was that Saki had been distracted. From the moment she drew *Death*, she had been fixated on what the card could mean for her. Her mind had been on Gifts when it should have been present.

All you had to do was grab your hat, and you couldn't even do that.

The loop began again. The events, inevitable. Saki hugged her legs tighter when Cresca's voice rose above the din.

"But I don't have a plan for *this*," Cresca said to Thrash in an agitated tone.

Desperate to be anywhere but her own head, Saki listened in on the conversation behind her.

"We can't give up," Thrash whispered.

"They know we're coming," Cresca hissed back.

"Why would they assume we're going to NSU?"

"I don't know! But I'm pretty sure we've lost the element of surprise. I just think maybe we should turn ourselves in and apologize or something..."

"An apology won't get you a Gift, or stop Em's parents from holding her back," Thrash said. "We might not have the perfect plan for going forward, but we can't go back."

Cresca said nothing. Or maybe she whispered something too low to hear.

Saki replayed their whispers in her head to block out her own voice. It did the trick. One of her last thoughts before she slipped under the fog of sleep was that Thrash always sounded so confident, so certain... How?

Saki dipped in and out of sleep, but the moment the sun came up she was fully awake and fully exhausted. Saki squinted down at the jar, her shame swelling again.

Minutes or hours later, Cresca yawned and stretched. Saki tensed as Cresca gave her a little wave and started checking her orb. It wasn't long before Thrash was rubbing her eyes and sitting up too.

"Good morning!" Em called. "After a night of semi-peaceful driving, we're somewhere along the border that runs between North Hecatanee and South Hecatanee. I can happily report no sightings of Thrash's deranged mom."

"Takes someone with deranged parents to know deranged parents," Thrash said with a yawn.

"You wound me like this? Before I've even had breakfast?"

"The truth hurts."

As Em and Thrash tittered, Saki peered at the dense trees along the leyline. What made her lean forward in her seat was a strange black vine she spotted climbing up the trees. In some areas, the vines crept up thick trunks like black, bulging veins; in others, they blanketed vast swaths of trees like a suffocating black canopy.

"What is that?" Saki whispered aloud.

"That's zuku, an invasive species," Em replied. "It's slowly strangling the forests. Fun fact: the Hecatanees, together, employ more Growth witches than any other state to fight the zuku. Unfortunately, it's basically resistant to magic at this point—"

"This is fascinating," Cresca interrupted, "But I'm dying for a pastry. Saki, would you 'sant me?"

Saki stiffened. Cresca felt it—their arms were touching—and leaned forward to look her in the eye. Saki couldn't bear the weight of her gaze. Her guilt was strangling her like the black zuku.

"Uh, are you okay?" Thrash asked.

"I lost my hat," Saki blurted. "We have no food. And no warproot. I'm sorry. I'm so, so sorry."

Her cheeks burned hotter than that one time she swallowed a whole spoon of wasabi.

Thrash folded forward and rubbed her temple, disappearing beneath a cloud of magenta hair. She muttered, "What else could *possibly go wrong?*"

Saki could answer that. As she opened her mouth to reply,

Cresca reached across Thrash and gave Saki's shoulder a firm squeeze.

"We're gonna be fine," Cresca said. "We're literally only one state away from Wyckton. I think we can handle a little hunger."

As if on cue, Em's convertible bucked like an untamed unicorn. Saki gripped the Good Shit Jar closer to her chest as Em cursed under her breath and waved the wand.

The car came to a full and sudden halt that threw the girls forward. Thankfully, it was early, and there weren't many cars on the leyline. A magic-channeling motorcycle swerved around them. The angry driver turned to flip them off, his silver helmet glinting like armor. A black flag mounted on the back of the motorcycle looked chillingly familiar, like a modern-day version of her tarot card. *Death.*

What was the universe trying to tell her? Saki was at a loss.

"Don't do this to me you COWARD," Em screamed at the failing wand. Well, at least Saki wasn't the most disappointing member of the team anymore. Now it was the wand. "Don't you dare burn out on me, you mother—"

"Em!" Cresca said, literally clapping her hands to snap her out of it. "Keep it together."

After a few more starts and jumps, the car evened out. Everyone breathed a sigh of relief until they realized they were cruising the leyline on a subtle downward trajectory. Em tried the wand again, and Saki noticed the silver metal had turned the color of burned caramel from top to bottom. The convertible continued sinking.

"Hey, Em?" Thrash said. "If we're going down, could you aim us to the side of the road?"

"I can't believe this!" Em swore and threw the wand to the floor as she steered the car toward a soft patch of ground carpeted by zuku. "This shit better not swallow my car."

The car scraped the pavement with a teeth-clenching screech. Saki actually saw the tip of the wand spark as it channeled one final burst of magic and died. Em swerved off the leyline just in time for the convertible to slide to a stop in the grass along the road.

No one moved for a long moment.

"So...what now?" Cresca asked. It wouldn't be long before the occasional passing car or familiar turned into normal midday traffic. They might as well give themselves up if they didn't get moving.

"We need to push the car into the trees," Thrash said.

Everyone hopped out and got behind the convertible. All four of them pushed at the same time, but it barely budged. The car weighed too much.

They moved on to Plan B: covering the car with zuku. It took longer than they expected to hack a patch of the weed off the forest floor and haul it over Em's convertible. In the end, it still looked conspicuous, and Em was more frustrated than ever.

"I need a moment," Em said. There were two kinds of storming off with Em—the "follow me" kind and the "stay away" kind. Em's shoulders were up to her ears, her jaw clenched. Definitely "stay away" signals.

Cresca traipsed off into the woods next, declaring, "Bathroom break!"

That left Saki and Thrash.

"Maybe we should check the bottomless trunk for a wand?" Thrash suggested.

"Sure..." Saki walked with Thrash to the trunk of the car.

"Oh, wait, I just remembered we need the wand to unlock the trunk." Thrash groaned. "This is so much worse than I thought."

Worse because of me, Saki thought. *I am the worst.*

"I'm sorry," Saki said. "I only had one job."

Thrash frowned and looked up at her. "What do you mean you had a job?"

"My one job was to keep track of my hat and I couldn't even do that. I'm bad at everything."

Thrash's brows furrowed deeper.

"That's not true," Thrash said. "You're generous, smart, observant, and creative too. That sandwich you made at the campgrounds? I never could've put those ingredients together and made something so delicious. That's just one example, but you're good at so many things!"

"Thanks..." Saki said. It wasn't true, but it was nice of Thrash to say.

Something moved in the forest. Saki's head snapped up and she squinted into the tangled trees. The clawing zuku created an eerie false twilight in the woods. What was out there? Saki imagined a creature with lots of fangs prowling the forest, but it was only Cresca who emerged from the trees.

"Think Em's got it out of her system yet?" Cresca asked no one in particular. Saki shrugged. Today was just a shrug of a day. "Let's go get our firecracker back!"

Saki followed Thrash and Cresca deeper into the woods. There was a taste to the air that Saki couldn't quite place, like an overripe fruit about to spoil on the vine. Was it her knack, or the scent of zuku?

Another unexpected rustle stopped Saki in her tracks. She whirled around just in time to see a bird take off from a branch, escaping the dark forest in a few flaps of its powerful black wings. The image of *Death* and Em's creepy description of the zuku must be putting her on edge.

It was far too easy to picture the dark vines swallowing all of them.

Thrash saw the clearing first, bright with sunlight and untouched by zuku. Then she spotted Em, sitting on an old stump and frowning at her orb. A strange combination of relief and impatience swept over her. Thrash was uncertain about a lot of things—the Gifts, what to tell the Lunes about them, how she felt about her knack, what she'd choose at NSU—but the one thing she knew for sure was that they had to get out of this weed-choked forest and stay ahead of Osmarra. Once they were back on the road, Thrash could wrestle with her complicated feelings about the Gifts.

"I picked up a capture for a craft station to the south," Em said without looking up. "Their ad says they sell wands."

"That's great news!" Cresca's pleading eyes looked to Thrash for affirmation. Saki arrived in the clearing last, dragging her feet.

"I'm not thrilled by the idea of showing our faces..." Thrash said, but what was the alternative? Her best plan so far was to break into the trunk of the car. At best, it was hard. At worst, impossible. "Is there anything else around?"

"The craft station's part of some tourist trap." Em sighed and tossed her orb back into her hat. "But I don't know. They probably don't have the right kind of wand. We're probably just screwed."

An uneasy silence settled over the girls as they stood in the clearing. It was one thing for Cresca to panic but coming from Em it truly sounded like the death knell.

"This isn't how it ends," Thrash finally managed. "We'll get a wand and get back on the road."

Cresca nodded, Thrash's words breathing a second wind into her. Cresca glanced back and forth between Em and Saki like a flustered mother hen.

"Em, remember that kid who sat behind you in ninth grade who kept sticking tape and candle wax and stuff in your hair?" Cresca asked.

"Olzar. Yeah, I remember him." Em ran a hand through her short hair. "Mr. Lestran said he was 'just flirting with me.'"

"And when you cut off all your magnificent hair—which, by the way, still super cute, don't change a thing—that jerk still didn't stop. It seemed pretty hopeless. *You* felt hopeless. But then I got my hands on an instruction manual..."

"...for how to enchant magic chalk." Em glowed just a bit brighter.

"I read the book and figured it out," Saki chimed in. "It wasn't hard to make the chalk stop copying what Mr. Lestran was saying and write what we wanted instead."

"I'll never forget the moment Olzar saw that blackboard," Cresca said.

A hint of wicked glee touched Em's lips. "He ran *so fast* out of that classroom."

The Lunes all laughed.

"Wait, what did it write?" Thrash asked.

Cresca didn't hear her.

"Middle fingers up!" Cresca called, defiantly flipping off the sky. Saki and Em both laughed and joined her, proudly bearing their crescent moon tattoos on hands glittering with various enchanted rings. Thrash stood there, acutely aware of her ring-less and tattoo-less hands and unsure what to do with them.

A reinvigorated Cresca looped her arm through Em's and tugged her off the stump. As they walked toward the trees, Thrash fell into step beside Saki and asked, "What did the chalk write on the blackboard?"

Saki shrugged. "It wouldn't make sense out of context."

Thrash shoved her hands into her pockets as Cresca led the way back to the car.

The creeping zuku grasped at Thrash's tennis shoes as she followed behind the other girls, bringing up the rear. Cresca chattered nonstop in a sweet but annoying attempt to keep spirits high. Thrash knew Cresca was only reliving the Lunes' glory days to keep the girls' spirits high, but it made her feel invisible.

The bigger you are, the louder you must be. That's what one of the buttons on Thrash's hat read. It was part of why she dyed her hair magenta and kept her face free of makeup and enchantments. This was her true, loud self and she wouldn't let anyone else—not even Osmarra—erase it.

"Thrash, did you hear me?" Cresca said. When had she started walking backward to face Thrash? "I was saying that you have a knack—har har—for dressing like a cat burglar. Like when you showed up to my house in head to toe black?"

"But she always wears black," Saki pointed out. "That's why the joke wasn't funny."

Em snorted.

Thrash wasn't really in a mood to defend her wardrobe, so instead, she asked, "So, how much does one of these wands cost?"

"Brace yourselves," Em said. "You need a platinum wand to channel enough magic to power a car. They cost like ten thousand dollars."

"Holy House of Curses!" Cresca cried.

"Yeah, my parents are going to kill me. That wand should've had at least a year left in it." Em's eyes looked ancient and tired behind her wire glasses. "The good news is that platinum isn't our only option. Silver is cheaper, but it burns out faster. It should last for a week of driving so long as we stick to the leylines instead of off-roading."

"And how much does a silver wand cost?" Thrash asked.

"Probably around four hundred."

No one needed to say what they all knew: they still couldn't afford it.

Without any fanfare, Cresca stopped and picked up a stray branch. Thrash caught up to her as she tossed it in the air. It landed on the forest floor with a soft thud. The tip pointed in roughly the same direction they had been heading.

"That's a good sign," Thrash said. "Em, what sort of tourist trap are we looking for? Are we talking like World's Largest Candle or like a museum for something that doesn't deserve a museum?"

"Some caves or something." Em checked her orb. "A very cute, very low-budget capture calls them the Garnet Caverns. They're supposedly cursed."

"Cursed?" Thrash wasn't superstitious—she knew curses were just a money-grubbing scheme, a way to sell trinkets and make easy money off humans who wished magic could be harnessed to deal with annoying bosses or cheating spouses. But at the same time, the dark woods had already put Thrash on edge, with its trees shrouded in zuku. Why did the caves have to be cursed?

"New plan!" Cresca declared. "And it's only two words: *gem heist*."

Thrash laughed. "What?"

"It's called the Garnet Caverns for a reason," Cresca said. "So, we only need like an extra hundred dollars, right? We sneak into the cave, break off some garnets—boom. We're rich."

"Because the craft station will totally just accept suspicious gemstones as payment?"

"Details!" Cresca said, throwing back her mane of silver hair. "This will be my greatest heist since I stole Saki's confiscated orb off Mrs. Nelson's desk while her back was turned!"

Saki and Em both chuckled at the memory. Intentionally or not, Cresca picked up the pace and returned to lead the front of the pack. Now that Thrash had grown used to the golden glow of Cresca's attention, she missed it when it was gone, or it shone on someone else.

For the first time, Thrash found herself wondering what would happen after this trip was over. Was she a real member of the group now? Or was she a supporting character, like Olzar or Mrs. Nelson, necessary for Cresca's current caper, but doomed to become a footnote in a future story?

When all this was said and done, would the Lunes just go back to being the Lunes? Without Thrash?

12

Three miles away sounded reasonable to Thrash when Cresca checked the map for the distance to the craft station. Thrash didn't have much experience turning miles into minutes, but how long could it take?

The answer, thanks to an uneven forest floor tangled with roots and zuku, turned out to be an hour and a half of trudgery. And bugs. Lots, and lots, of bugs.

"Really makes me miss having a car," Cresca commented, her pace slowing. The terrain wasn't ideal for flip-flops, and the oppressive heat didn't help either. Meanwhile, Thrash and Em lingered toward the back, trading who was last.

"Hey, Em? How many people can you fit on that magic cane?" Cresca called back.

"Only one," Em said, pausing to catch her breath, "so don't get any ideas."

"Maybe you should use the cane?" Saki suggested in her direct, but gentle way.

"I'm good."

With a burst of energy, Em pushed forward and caught up

to Saki. But as Thrash watched Em walk, her gait uneven and her hair soaked through with sweat from the exertion, "good" was not how Em looked.

"I wish I had a familiar," Cresca mused. "What form do you think mine would take?"

"Unicorn," they all answered at once.

Cresca huffed about it for a few minutes, though Thrash sensed she was secretly pleased. Most girls dreamed of getting their knacks and receiving Gifts, but Cresca seemed to have this romantic notion of magic that went beyond a teenager's normal fixation on it.

"Actually, Thrash, that reminds me," Cresca said. "I had a question about your mom."

"My favorite topic of conversation."

"I'm sorry, it's just been bugging me. When we were at the lake, I was wondering...what was Osmarra doing just lurking by the car? That's where you found her, right?"

"Yeah, I was getting more candles." Thrash felt her pulse quicken. She was very aware that she still hadn't told the Lunes about the Gift of Glamour.

"What I don't get is that you literally walked right into her hands," Cresca continued. "And then she didn't do anything. That's so weird."

"She wanted to talk."

"But, like, about *what?*"

A bead of sweat rolled down Thrash's back. She was so damn hot, from the hiking and the humidity. Her brain felt fuzzy. Meanwhile, Cresca waited patiently, not a hint of suspicion in her eyes, only a yearning to understand Thrash at a level that no one ever delved.

What was she supposed to say? *My mom offered me the Gift I've always wanted, but I turned her down because of a gut feeling that maybe she was lying and also maybe Gifts aren't all they're cracked up to be?*

Shame glued her mouth shut. Maybe she was overreacting to the muting. Would the Lunes even care about losing their knacks in exchange for real magic? Cresca certainly wouldn't. For a flickering moment, Thrash wondered if she shouldn't have turned down her mom's offer.

But what the girls wouldn't understand, because they didn't know Osmarra like Thrash did, was that Osmarra lied every day to get what she wanted and called it diplomacy. Her mother was still hiding something about the Gifts. Thrash was sure of it.

"*Oh Goddess,*" Em groaned. "I can already hear the lecture I'm getting from *my* mom when this is over..."

The conversation moved on and Cresca let it go, which convinced Thrash, yet again, that Cresca was a better friend than she deserved.

Thrash saw the movement through the trees first, followed by the wings of a twenty-foot-tall wooden bat.

For craft stations, especially ones in rural patches of the Thirteen States, survival depended on grabbing the attention of drivers along the leyline. Thrash loved an enchanted sign, from tacky dancing witch hats to cat-shaped balloons that meowed incessantly, but the giant bat beckoning weary travelers was in a class of its own. It glittered in the sun, painted a sparkling red that matched an adjacent sign for the Garnet Caverns.

The station, in contrast, looked squat and unremarkable beside the bat. Posters that read *Garnet Caverns Tickets Sold Here* fought for attention against windows piled with sun-bleached souvenirs and essential herbs. Displays for cheap curses and travel charms crowded the entrance, along with a dozen posters...of Em's face.

Oh Goddess. It would be impossible for anyone entering the craft station to miss the *TROUBLE* posters—or the number of zeroes behind the reward for Em's capture.

"Emmmm," Cresca groaned. "Have you *still* not sent your parents a capture asking them to call off the bounty?"

"Yes, I mean, sort of," Em sputtered, her cheeks burning. "I did, but that doesn't mean they listened necessarily. I mean, apparently."

Cresca gave Em some suspicious side-eye, but let it drop.

"I think we may need to revise the plan," Thrash muttered. There was no way anyone within ten feet of the craft station wouldn't recognize Em.

Cresca cracked her knuckles and knelt down in the dirt. She picked up a twig and tossed it into the air with a little spin. It landed with its tip pointing toward the craft station.

"Em, you hang back and be the lookout. Otherwise, same plan. The wands are usually kept behind the counter with the other high-ticket items." Cresca took off her hat and pulled out a light pink sweatshirt. She tied it around her waist. "While you both buy a bunch of food and distract the cashier, Thrash'll knock something over and I'll use the diversion to slip one of the wands into the sleeve of my sweatshirt. Sound good to everyone? Saki?"

Saki stared off into the trees. Her eyes refocused on Cresca. "Oh. Sure. Whatever you say."

"Anything else you want to add?"

"No," Saki said with a quick glance back at the woods. "Just tell me what to do and I'll do it."

"Let's start with disguises," Cresca said, clapping her hands together. "Thrash, you go first."

"Me?" Oh boy. Em rubbed her hands together and wiggled her fingers in anticipation. Seeing no reasonable way out of it, Thrash stepped forward.

Em clenched her fists, staring at Thrash's head with unblinking eyes. A second later, with a light *pop!* Thrash's hair turned a forgettable shade of brown not unlike her natural hair color. Two seconds later, Cresca was unfastening Thrash's hat and shoving it into Em's.

"Our hats are pretty recognizable," Cresca explained as one of Thrash's homemade buttons shot off her hat and into the woods. Hats within hats were unstable, everyone knew that. "Em, I'm gonna put my hat and Thrash's into yours. Cool?"

"Sure." Em shut her eyes in concentration. Saki's straight black hair disappeared, replaced a few seconds later by blonde locks. Did nothing look bad on her? Only Saki could wear the same NSU sweatshirt for four days straight and still turn heads wherever she went.

"Cresca?" Em asked, turning to her. "You ready?"

Cresca smiled, but her eyes held a far-off look. Absent-mindedly, she twirled one of her rings, a lonely amethyst on a silver band. Then her gaze sharpened, and she ceased fiddling.

"Actually, I have a better idea." Cresca turned away slightly, shielding her face as she gently slid three rings off her left hand.

Cresca's silver hair vanished in an instant, replaced by tight close curls that shaped her skull like a fabulous black swim cap. The style was almost vintage, like how classy champagne-guzzling witches wore their hair at the turn of the last century.

Cresca tucked the rings into the pockets of her shorts and whirled around. Now she had freckles! And a nose! Well, she had always had a nose, but her unremarkable illusion-nose was gone, replaced by a broad, friendly nose that just had so much more personality.

At the last moment, Cresca slid one more ring off her hand. The change was slight, as it was more about the absence of a few lumps and bumps, a few pounds in her stomach and her thighs. Something turned sour in Thrash's stomach at the thought that Cresca was naturally thin but still felt the need to enchant herself just a little thinner.

If Cresca thinks she's too fat…what does she think of me?

"Well, there's no going back now," Cresca said. She ran a single hand over her head, feeling her short hair. "If any of you take a capture of me, I will throw your orb out the car window. Let's get going, witches."

Thrash had an entire backstory plotted out, and she rehearsed it as she crossed the parking lot with Cresca and Saki. *Why yes, people think we look like those renegade teenagers, but we're actually a Wildergirl Troop from Morganshyre earning our camping badge.*

Thrash was actually pretty proud of her idea to pose as a troop of scouts, which she felt covered all their bases. An ill-fated camping trip could easily explain why the girls had tromped out of the woods sans transportation and hats, sleep-deprived and yearning to buy snacks.

Glass doors slathered in mirror-paint were an easy, cheap way to expose illusions on a budget, making them the go-to for craft stations in the middle of nowhere. In the reflective paint, Thrash's new brown hair caught her eye. Odd that her hair still shone brown in the mirror, which dispelled illusions. Did that mean Em's knack wasn't Glamour magic, as Thrash had assumed, but something else? Could Em's knack be transforming and changing things beyond what Glamour could achieve?

The bell above the door clanged, jolting Thrash back into the present. *Showtime.* Hands stuffed into her pockets, she strolled into the craft station, walking at what felt like half speed as her heart beat like a hummingbird's. She veered toward the aisle of packaged food, Saki and Cresca on her heels.

As Thrash picked out semi-healthy bags of vegetable chips and protein-rich nut clusters, she glanced at the cash register. Wands lined the wall behind the counter, guarded by a layer of glass and a teenager roughly their age. The willowy teen sat hunched on a stool, engrossed in a romance novel. This kid seemed so out of it that Thrash wasn't even sure they needed a distraction to steal the wand. Could they have hit a patch of good luck for once?

Thrash, Saki, and Cresca pretended to peruse the shelves for another minute or two and then marched armfuls of snacks toward the register. Last-minute knickknacks and charms crowded the counter, vying for their attention under a sign that read, *We do not accept blood contracts in lieu of payment.* A display of floating ice cream bars pirouetting beside the counter made Thrash's mouth water. Goddess, it was so hot, even inside the store.

The clerk closed the book, placing the cover—two mermen kissing passionately against a stormy sky—face down on the counter. A name tag on their jean jacket read *TAKODA* and beneath that *THEY/THEM.* As they hopped off the stool and stood up straight, Thrash saw they were wearing a red shirt emblazoned with the Garnet Caverns logo and text that read *ASK ME ABOUT THE GRAZZLESNATCH.*

"What is a grazzlesnatch?" Saki asked immediately.

"It's a legend that my grandparents made up to scare white people away." Takoda casually flipped their long, black braid over their shoulder and started ringing up snacks. "It didn't work. But at least now we make money off it."

"What's the legend?" Thrash asked to keep the cashier talking.

They cleared their throat. "Well, the caves below the store have these veins of 'garnet,' but really it should be called fool's garnet because it's worthless."

Takoda motioned behind the counter toward an entrance Thrash hadn't even noticed, a set of rickety wooden stairs descending into the earth from the craft station. Thrash thought of caves as wide, gaping mouths with stalactite teeth; she had never pictured a hole in the ground and a handful of hand-painted steps as a cave entrance.

"The grazzlesnatch is part-bear, part-wolverine. Its claws are as long as my arm and made of solid diamond." Takoda dragged a finger across their throat. "One swipe of a grazzlesnatch claw and you're dead. Then it takes its prey and smears their blood along the walls of its lair, thus the veins of red gems."

"Your grandparents sound...creative," Thrash said. Cresca gently elbowed Thrash, as if to remind her to stay on task.

"Right?" Takoda said. "Tickets are twenty bucks for adults, sixteen for students."

"Wow, that's such a good deal—" Thrash knocked over a standee of brochures for the Garnet Caverns, spilling them back behind the counter. "Oh Goddess, I'm so sorry!"

Takoda shrugged and ducked down to gather up the mess. Now was Cresca's chance—but she didn't rush behind the counter. Cresca shook her head and mouthed something Thrash couldn't make out. When Thrash still didn't get it, Cresca rolled her eyes and pointed at the wands.

Ah, the real reason Cresca had nudged Thrash: the wands were locked behind unbreakable glass. The braided pattern was unmistakable, a product of skilled Growth witches who rewove glass at its most basic form into intricate, shimmering lattices.

What do we do now?

"Y'know, you look familiar..." Takoda said as they shot back up from behind the counter and straightened the pile of brochures.

"Our troop comes here every year for a camping trip," Thrash said, fresh sweat breaking out on her forehead. "You've probably seen us around."

"Is this you?" In the blink of an eye, Takoda had pulled out their orb, channeled a news stream—and now Thrash was staring right at a capture of herself.

"Uhhhhh...."

"No persecutin' way," Takoda whispered. "Y'all are those girls who are all *ditch the Gifts!*"

Thrash was speechless. She had heard that phrase before, from Coco's flyers. Who was applying it to them? As Thrash fumbled for words, Cresca, cool as a floating ice cream bar, said, "I don't think that's us."

Takoda put away their orb and rolled up the sleeve of their jean jacket. On the inside of their wrist was a small black tattoo. Twin candles, both equal height and shining bright. The symbol of the Magic Liberation Movement.

"Don't worry, I can keep your secret. I was literally supposed to go to a solidarity march this afternoon in Chaptown, but I got stuck working, obviously."

Takoda pulled out a hand-drawn sign from behind the counter and showed it off proudly. It read *Native Magic is the Original Gift* in letters made of small multicolored circles, almost like the beads in the chokers witches wore.

"Wait, so people think our road trip is a protest?" Thrash said. "And it's causing other people to protest?"

"Isn't that why you stole the Gift of Glamour? Which, by the way, is *such* a badass way to stick it to the High Circle."

Thrash felt faint and sick all at once. Did her mom leak that information about the Gift of Glamour? Or did the press figure it out somehow? It didn't really matter. The secret was out. Thrash couldn't even look at Cresca.

Thrash finally said, "It's actually pretty complicated—"

"Oh, we have time," Cresca said, her voice ice. "Feel free to explain it. For all of us."

"Actually, I think we should go," Saki said, her eyes fixed on the entrance. A shadow flitted past the front door like a bird in flight.

"Wait, before you go..." Takoda grabbed one of the free maps of the Garnet Caverns and smoothed it on the counter. Uncapping a pen with their teeth, they marked an *X* on the map and then added an offshoot to one of the tunnels. "If you need somewhere to hide from The Justice, we have some booze and snacks stashed in the Caverns. And there's actually an exit to the caves, but we obviously don't advertise that. I tried to give you an idea of where it is."

For a moment, Thrash forgot about Cresca's hurt feelings. *The Justice* was chasing them? Had Osmarra recruited Thrash's idol, the witch that Thrash dreamed of growing up to be, the unstoppable seer and hunter of murderers...to hunt *them* down?

"Oh! I just realized—do you need help finding the Brotherhood?"

"What's that?" Thrash asked. At the same time, Saki nudged her and pointed at the front door.

A huge black bird, a hawk or a falcon or something, perched on the handle of the door and peered at them as if it could see through the mirror paint. The bird had an intelligent glint in its eye, like that of a familiar, and the moment Thrash thought *bird familiar,* she knew Takoda was right. The bird opened its wings and shot up into the sky.

"Em is outside. We need to move," Cresca said.

Thrash grabbed Takoda's map and shoved it in her pocket. "Thank you for everything, Takoda. And I'm sorry, but we need a wand."

Thrash pried open the metal door on the bottom of the floating ice cream display, exposing the wand beneath. Without thinking twice, Thrash plunged her hand into the compartment and yanked the wand out. Suspended ice cream bars dropped all over the counter and floor.

"I'm sorry!" Thrash yelled, emptying her pockets and tossing the last of her crumpled bills on the counter. Saki and Cresca were already halfway out the door.

"It was an honor to be robbed by you!" Takoda called after them.

Thrash burst out into the bright parking lot, ready to run, but her feet had barely hit the gravel when she tripped over Saki. Thankfully, Cresca caught Thrash by the arm and stopped her from face-planting. She straightened up slowly and got her bearings, but she didn't like what she saw—a dozen National Protectrix mounted on black familiars circled the parking lot, their wands trained on Thrash, Cresca, and Saki.

13

"H ALT!" the voice boomed. It was the voice Thrash heard in her dreams ever since their narrow escape at the lake. The difference now was that she saw the protectrix who said it, a male witch with his wand pressed up against his throat.

The other difference, of course, was that they were truly and undeniably surrounded.

Thrash scanned the circle of uniformed witches atop black horses, deer, and mountain lions. Apart from one snarling buffalo-wolf, the familiars were as unreadable as their riders. The protectrix stood like a wall between Thrash and escape, and no expression was as studiously blank as Osmarra's. She sat atop Tempest, her hands white knuckling Tempest's reins. She was the only witch without a stun wand in hand.

"STAND DOWN!" the male witch bellowed.

"Do we not look like we're standing down?" Cresca snapped back.

Thrash gritted her teeth. She wasn't ready for this road trip to be over yet. She still needed time to figure out what to do about the Gifts.

Thrash scanned the dark trees beyond the wandslingers. As tempting as it was to turn tail and run for the caverns to escape, Thrash couldn't leave without Em. The girl was impulsive, but hopefully she was level-headed enough to stay hidden in the trees. For now, no sign of her was a good sign.

One of the protectrix trotted toward the girls on a black horse. It wasn't Osmarra who broke rank and approached them but a leather-clad witch wearing a cowboy hat the color of midnight. When she gripped the brim and tilted it back, Thrash found herself looking into the huge dark sunglasses of one of the greatest witches alive.

The Justice.

The Named Witch slid effortlessly off the back of her black horse. She was *tall*—had Thrash's books mentioned that? The woman was practically the height of her horse, which, by the way, had changed instantly from a horse to a falcon in the time between The Justice dismounting the familiar and her boots hitting the ground. Tempest once said something *very* rude about those birds, but Thrash forgot what it was as she watched the powerful beat of the familiars' wings overhead.

Thrash felt both star-struck and intimidated as The Justice walked inevitably toward her, her sweeping blue coat dusting the ground. Her four black familiars circled above the clearing, climbing and diving in mesmerizing patterns. The tension was so thick that Saki could probably taste it.

The Justice stopped a stone's throw away and waited. Or at least, that's what Thrash assumed she was doing; the sunglasses conveniently eclipsed all the features that might give her thoughts away.

"An honor and a blessing," Thrash finally said, bowing her

head. The etiquette had come to her suddenly, instilled by Osmarra years ago. The Justice tipped her hat in return.

"An honor and a blessing, Thrash," the woman said. "Tales of your knack are...intriguing."

"Thank you," Thrash said, but she was still wary. You didn't call in two dozen protectrix from surrounding states to commend someone.

"The Universities are intrigued, too, though none too happy that you spurned the Gift your mother chose for you—and then stole it."

"I—"

"You remind me of myself at your age," The Justice said. Thrash sputtered as a blush crept up her neck. Was The Justice truly comparing herself to *Thrash*?

"You have so much power, Thrash Blumfeld-Wright. You will be a Named Witch someday—I have seen it."

Thrash's heart leaped. She couldn't help it. As a girl, she had always dreamed of being The Justice when she grew up. It was a dream, she realized, that she was probably throwing away right now. And for what? A knack and some quality time with a group of girls who might go back to ignoring her as soon as the school year started?

The Justice smiled.

"The High Circle sees potential in you, Thrash. Though your actions have put your future in danger, there is still time to turn this around."

"There is?"

The Justice clasped her hands behind her back and began to pace. Above her, the falcons seemed more frenetic, bobbing and weaving in the air.

"For the first time in the history of the Thirteen States, the Circles both High and Low have agreed to grant you any Gift you desire."

Cresca gasped behind Thrash and grabbed her hand. Thrash's head spun. This was what she had wanted all along... wasn't it? She dared a glance at Osmarra. Her mother's face betrayed nothing.

"This is the path forward," The Justice urged. "This is the path to your brightest future."

"And what about my friends?" Thrash asked.

The Justice paused. "What about them?"

"Does this offer stand for them too? Do they also get to choose their Gifts?"

"Mmmm." The Justice scratched her chin. Thrash baked in the sun, wishing she had a hat or a fan or, better yet, one of those floating ice cream bars. She realized, with a small start, that she had almost totally forgotten about the nickel wand gripped in her first.

The Named Witch held out her arm and one of her familiars dove for her gauntlet. At the last moment, the black falcon opened its powerful wings and glided into place on The Justice's forearm, its huge talons sinking into the leather. *Leather that was once flesh,* Thrash thought with a shiver.

The bird had something clutched in its beak—a small plastic button with pink text that Thrash knew read *I Love Big Books.* Thrash died a little inside as The Justice removed the leather glove from her free hand and plucked the button from her familiar's beak.

The Justice held the button for a long, breathless moment, then regloved her bare hand.

"Yes, your friends may choose their own Gifts as well," The Justice said with so little emotion that it chilled Thrash. Had The Justice just peered into the future to determine exactly what to say to get her to comply?

Thrash did *not* like that. It felt eerie, in the same way that the Gifts muting knacks just felt wrong.

Thrash's hands itched to pull a tarot card. When she looked to Cresca and Saki, their eyes urged her to say yes. Beyond them, in the window of the craft station, Thrash saw Takoda pressing an orb up against the glass, capturing the confrontation. Were they channeling this for the whole world to see?

The Justice's boot tapped impatiently. "Of course, if you choose to throw this opportunity away, you're not just throwing away a Gift of your choice. You are throwing away any Gift, ever. No Historically Magical University. No future."

Thrash swallowed and stole a glance at her mom, who continued to maintain her unreadable facade. The last time they had met in the woods, Osmarra urged Thrash to take the same deal. The knack-muting ritual gave Thrash the same bad feeling she had now, a warning that stirred deep inside of her.

The sun beat down. Were the wandslingers hot in their black double-breasted coats? *Focus, Thrash.* As her mind raced to find a way out of this situation, her eyes roved the parking lot and landed on a purple truck with huge metal spikes studding its grill.

Madame Wiki.

As if on cue, Em crashed through the bushes. She stumbled a few feet and tripped on the gravel of the parking lot, landing on her hands and knees. Before Thrash could even blink, Rongo emerged in all of her camouflage-clad glory. She scooped Em up by the back of her shirt like she was grabbing a kitten by the scruff. Thrash glimpsed red angry scratches along Rongo's forearms.

"Nice try," Rongo grunted. Em's eyes blazed with fury.

"Ah, the obstacle," The Justice said. "Bounty hunter. Ji'ishland?"

"I—yes. Rongo, hardworking freelancer, at your service." Rongo bowed but continued inching toward her truck. "Don't mind me. I know half the country's looking for that missing

Gift of Glamour, but I'm only here for the girl with the royal parents—"

"Hand the girl over to me."

The Justice's command was so stark that it startled Thrash and stopped Rongo right in her tracks.

"Looks like you've got plenty of girls to me," Rongo said. "I just need this one. And I've gone through a lot of trouble to get her."

The Justice made some sort of hand signal and the protectrix stepped forward as one, the circle around the girls and Rongo tightening. Rongo chuckled, but there was a nervous edge to it.

"Turn the girl over to us and we'll ensure you receive your bounty," The Justice said.

"After you gnats screwed me outta the reward last time?" Rongo's eyes darted to Osmarra. "I learned my lesson. I'll haul her back to her parents and collect the money myself, thanks."

"You are a private contractor who hunts under a license granted by the Low Circle," the Justice said. "A license I can revoke."

"I don't respond well to threats." The bounty hunter said it with a shrug that emphasized the hefty staff resting on her shoulder. Though the protectrix were armed, their wands only delivered enough of a punch to stun an average-sized human, and even then there was the added complication that law enforcement had to justify, legally, any use of brute force. Sure, they also had their Gifts on their side, but when it came to channeling magic into raw blasts, Rongo was the only one whose weapon was truly deadly.

"In defying me, you defy the law," The Justice stated. A few familiars stamped their hooves in support. "Do you know how many years you'll spend in Realignment for defying a Named Witch?"

"I know my rights as a bounty hunter," Rongo replied coolly. "You might be able to confuse and intimidate regular folks, but I know the law forward and back, and Ji'ishland's laws are on my side. Legally, I'm defying squat."

A trace of a smile twitched on The Justice's lips. She pushed her sunglasses up the bridge of her nose.

"Let me speak a language you understand: you won't get your payday if you lose her, and in thirty seconds, if you don't hand her over to me, she gets away."

"What a convenient vision." Rongo tsk'd and pulled Em closer. "You witches are always playing mind games."

Thrash paled. *Mind games.* That was what was so unsettling about The Justice, only she couldn't put a finger on it until now. Sure, The Justice had claimed she'd seen Thrash as a powerful witch—but had she truly looked into Thrash's future, or was she enticing Thrash to do her bidding by feeding her exactly what she needed to hear?

As if hearing Thrash's thoughts, The Justice suddenly turned toward her. Thrash couldn't see beyond those mirrored sunglasses, but she could feel The Justice's furious stare. Was Thrash changing The Justice's precious prized outcome right now? Behind those lenses, was the Named Witch watching a thousand different futures all collapsing at once?

The Justice swiveled, birdlike, back to Rongo. "Listen to me, bounty hunter. We're both about to lose them. I've *seen* it."

Rongo shrugged. "And I've seen my mom hanging up her apron and retiring from her cafe. I've seen me and my wife visiting twice a year and drinking a few umbrella drinks along the way. That sugary shit is expensive."

The Justice raised a gauntleted fist and the protectrix tensed, wands at the ready. Rongo hefted the metal staff off her shoulder and thumped it against the ground. The earth shook, the gravel of the parking lot dancing and chattering all around them.

"Last chance to hand her over," The Justice warned.

"You know, it wasn't personal, at first," Rongo said, eyes narrowed and muscles tensed. "But now...now I've decided I just don't like you."

Rongo lifted her staff, but then she faltered. Her staff was gone. Visibly gone, at least. A faint rainbow sheen outlined the weapon, but Rongo didn't notice that. Not yet.

Rongo growled at The Justice, and in her momentary confusion, accidentally let go of Em—and that was all that Em needed. Without a sound, Rongo's prized fugitive vanished.

Em ran for her life, but Rongo was a hunter. The moment Em's foot hit the gravel, Rongo zeroed in on the footprints of her prey. Rongo's grip tightened around her invisible staff, and she raised her weapon, taking aim—

One of the protectrix blasted first. Rongo's wrist snapped back, and she dropped the staff.

"Forget the girls!" The Justice ordered. "Subdue the bounty hunter!"

Rongo dropped to her knees, trying to find her invisible staff, and the protectrix swarmed the bounty hunter. Stunning shots rippled through the air like bolts of lightning, but it was protectrix who were suddenly falling from horses, clutching their shoulders and sides in pain. That's when Thrash noticed that the magic bolts were ricocheting off Rongo. Off her enchanted camo jacket, specifically.

Em, or a glimmer of Em, hurtled toward the girls. Despite the chaos, this could be their moment to escape. Thrash felt the craft station calling to her.

But what about The Justice? Curiously, the Named Witch had barely moved. She just stood and watched Thrash, waiting patiently to see what she would do next.

If there was such a thing as "the point of no return," Thrash wondered if this was it. Could her future really hinge on a single moment? Was her life just a seesaw with "Named Witch" on one end and "failure" on the other?

Run, or stay.

Knack, or Gift.

The Justice turned away, back toward Rongo, who was punching wildly at anyone who came near.

The last thing Thrash heard her say was, "Let them go. There will be one more chance."

Screw that, Thrash thought. Rongo was right, it was all mind games with The Justice. Thrash didn't care what The Justice had supposedly seen—she was never going to make a deal with someone so calculating and cruel. Grabbing Saki's arm and tugging Cresca's hand, she ran for the craft station and didn't look back.

14

Cresca was *so* confused. Had someone enchanted Thrash? Is that why she was pulling the girls toward the craft station and away from The Justice, the Named Witch who had just offered them not only an out, but *everything they wanted?*

"Um, why are we running?" Cresca asked. No one stopped to answer. Thrash was too busy kicking down the front door as Em's semi-invisible outline rocketed past them, propelled by pure adrenaline and a determination to put as much distance as possible between her and the madwoman Coco married.

Cresca tried again: "Seriously, what are we doing?" She tried to catch Saki's arm, but Saki was too busy following Thrash like a shadow. Cresca recognized that look of admiration on her friend's face; Saki was swept up in Thrash's current, like she once had been in Cresca's.

Is this what happens when I take off my rings? The thought stung. Cresca had forgotten how terrible it was to be ordinary. To be ignored. To be *typical.*

Thrash didn't need beauty to be powerful. Hell, she didn't even need a Gift to be magical.

As Cresca jogged toward the craft station, the rest of the girls ahead of her, a bolt of shimmering red magic hit Saki square in the back. Saki's knees buckled and she collapsed in a heap inches from the entrance. Stunned from head to toe, the only sound she made was the crunch of her body hitting the gravel.

Cresca ducked and glanced back at the chaos. The protectrix were firing stun wands at Rongo. One of the bolts must have ricocheted off Rongo's jacket, but that didn't mean the gnats wouldn't turn their wands on them next. Beside Cresca, Saki whimpered, face down in the gravel. Someone had to help her up, and Thrash and Em were already inside the store, oblivious.

Cresca made a fist with her naked hand.

Enough of the pity party; she had to protect her girls.

Cresca maneuvered one arm under Saki's shoulder and dragged her limp body through the door. Her long legs were like two anchors trailing behind her. Saki moaned, her voice strained and unintelligible. Cresca hoped this wasn't hurting her; stunned didn't mean unable to feel pain.

"Thrash! Em! Can I get a hand?" Cresca yelled. Two heads turned—three, if she counted the cashier, who was still annoyingly clutching their orb and capturing all of this like it was their own personal soap opera. "Saki got hit by a stun wand."

As Em reappeared in full color, Thrash rushed over and ducked under Saki's other arm. Saki tried to vocalize something, but it came out as a gurgled mess. A wave of fury washed over Cresca. How had she let this happen to one of her own?

"My cane!" Em gasped, rooting around in her hat. Thrash's hat shot out and she just barely managed to grab it. Em snapped the metal hover-wand together and tapped the head of it. The end flipped up, and the cane hovered parallel to the ground.

The three of them helped Saki onto the cane. Doubled over, her face obscured by hair so blonde it was almost white, she was the picture of an old, hunched crone on a broomstick.

As Cresca guided Saki toward the caves, she caught Thrash's eye and whispered, "Thrash, what are we doing? I don't even know if we can get Saki down those steps."

"We have to get away," Thrash said. "I'll explain it more when we're safe."

"Safe, like Saki?" Cresca quipped. "I'm confused. Didn't The Justice just offer us exactly what we wanted? Explain *that* to me. Please."

"Trust me, we don't wanna take that deal." Thrash couldn't quite meet Cresca's gaze. "The Gifts aren't what you think they are."

Takoda gasped, still capturing everything.

"Nothing is what I think it is. Apparently." Cresca bit her lip. What else was she going to do, though? Turn back around, let the gnats arrest her, and take the fall for all of this alone?

"Please, Cresca," Thrash urged. Em was already waiting at the cave entrance, waving them forward. Cresca could still hear the fighting outside. Amid the muffled shouts and thumps, Rongo's bellowing voice rose above the din. What if the protectrix couldn't subdue the bounty hunter? What if Em was still in danger of capture?

"Fine," Cresca said. "Let's go disappear into some haunted caves."

At least there might be booze.

Cresca ducked her head as she scrambled down the steps of the cramped tunnel. As she supported part of Saki's weight and guided the cane down the incline, she almost lost her balance on the rocky steps. To her relief, Saki didn't plummet down the steps. Actually, she seemed to have stopped moving all together, even when Cresca nudged the hover-cane forward.

"I've got Saki," Em said. "I'm in a better position to steer her from below."

"Are you sure?"

"I can handle it." There was just enough space in the narrow tunnel for Em to peer around Saki and pass Cresca's hat to her. "You should get your orb out. There isn't much light down here."

"Good idea." Cresca scooped up her orb, which shined at her touch like it was happy to see her.

At the top of the stairs, Thrash's voice boomed, "Move back!"

Cresca hurried down the manmade stairs after Em and Saki. As Cresca raced down the uneven steps, one of her flip-flops slipped. She reached out for balance, and her hand missed the guiding rope and landed on a glittering red streak of rock instead. The dazzling red crystals ran through the rock, winking at her as she moved.

As Cresca caught her breath, she peered up the stone stairs and saw Thrash hovering between steps. Hands outstretched, Thrash faced the glow of the craft station.

"Takoda! Put your orb down and move back!" Thrash called.

The earth started shaking all around them. Cresca gripped the rope with both hands and watched the ceiling above the portal crumble. Rubble piled up around the cavern entrance until the rocks finally strangled one last gasp of light.

Thrash waited until she was sure every rock had stilled. Then, finally, her arms dropped.

Now *that* was a knack. None of this branch-tossing nonsense. Cresca remembered finding Thrash in the library bathroom, her raw magic so startling, her hesitancy to embrace it so *curious*. And now look at her! She was controlling cave-ins with spooky power and precision.

What was that, if not magic?

The steps descended for what felt like two or three stories. A rope marked the main path, and Cresca followed it until the tunnel finally opened up into a large cavern. By that point, Saki was able to stand without the cane and walk with only a slight trembling in her legs. She could talk again but didn't seem to want to.

"So...what's the plan?" Cresca asked, feeling flippant. Her head ached from squinting in the dark and the cold, dry air gave her goosebumps. Did tourists really endure this? There better be some spectacular stalactites or stalagmites or whatever along the way.

"We find the car," Thrash replied.

Cresca bit down several sarcastic retorts as Thrash double-checked the map and led them toward the left-most of three branching tunnels. As Cresca followed behind Thrash's bobbing head, she noticed cave dust in Thrash's poofy hair. Cresca almost reached out to fix it, but she didn't.

Instead, she said, "Hey, Em, how far do you think we can drive with a nickel wand?"

"...A day."

"Seriously?" Thrash groaned.

"It's a wand that makes ice pops dance!" Em said. "What did you expect?"

Cresca sighed, but what she really wanted was to shake some sense into Thrash, like, *Of course this plan was half-baked! We ran into the caves without discussing anything!*

"Saki, how are you doing?" Cresca asked gently.

"I think my shoe's untied." Saki paused by the side of the path and tried to bend down, but her thighs immediately started shaking with effort. She wobbled dangerously.

"I've got you." Cresca kneeled at Saki's feet and laced up her sneakers. As casually as she could, Cresca asked, "How did it feel? Are you okay?"

Saki shrugged. Cresca nodded and waited. She knew Saki's rhythms, knew she needed time.

"My muscles are sore," Saki said. Then it all came pouring out of her: "I feel like my entire body had a charley horse. And I'm worried I won't know how to enchant the ice cream wand to drive a car. The chalk trick was so long ago."

"Girl, you literally won a prize freshman year for memorizing the most digits of pi," Cresca said. "I think you're being too hard on yourself."

"It's not only that..." Saki slumped. "When The Justice said we could choose our Gifts, I started wondering... What if I don't want a Gift?"

"No Gift? Like, at all?"

Cresca didn't know what to say. Why was everyone suddenly ready to throw their Gifts away? Cresca was still acutely aware that her dad didn't believe in her knack and her grandma hated magic. Cresca's family hadn't had a witch since her maternal great-great-grandmother, one of thousands of magical West Afrakan refugees. When the Great Igidan Dragon awakened in 1866, Cresca's great-great-grandma was driven out by her own community, who turned on its witches and blamed them for the dragon's awakening. It was practically tradition in Cresca's family to blame magic for their misfortunes.

What Cresca's family failed to grasp was that in the Thirteen States, magic could turn your luck around. Good jobs were magical jobs, with names that ended in "trix." Accepting The Justice's offer was the only way Cresca could guarantee herself a Gift, and all the doors that Gift opened.

Nothing in life is guaranteed. Her dad was fond of saying that, always while making direct eye contact with Cresca like she was one of his sunball players. But as annoying as it was to hear her dad's voice in her head, maybe he had a point. Cresca was getting ahead of herself. Maybe Thrash was right, and nothing was what it seemed.

"Is it that crazy to not want a Gift?" Saki whispered.

"No, I'm sorry, I was just trying to imagine what you'd do after graduation, if not go to one of the HMUs?"

"I don't know," Saki said, head in hands. "That's the problem."

Two hours later, Cresca was tired of tripping over loose rocks and ducking around grasping stalactites. Poor Em had spent the last half hour out of breath and leaning heavily on Saki for support—*Saki*, who wasn't doing so hot herself. Cresca had never seen the Lunes look so worse for wear. Meanwhile, Thrash consumed herself with the map, carefully scrutinizing it at every turn to avoid conversation. If Thrash had her way, they would never talk about what happened.

Cresca wasn't a "wait around forever" sorta person. As Thrash paused at a fork in the road, Cresca snatched the map out of her hands.

"Maybe we need a moment to rest?" Cresca suggested, carefully avoiding naming any names. Cresca knew that Em was stubborn; the only way to get through to her was to strike at the right time. Whenever Cresca found that chance, she was going to have a long, brutal conversation with Em about lying to their faces about scrying her parents. The same sort of conversation Thrash deserved too.

"I don't need to rest," Em said.

"Well, I need a moment," Cresca said, trying to rally and keep it light. "Anyone want to do some cave yoga with me? My calves are gonna kill me tomorrow after all those steps."

Then, out of nowhere, Em's legs buckled. Thrash and Cresca both rushed in, arms out, to steady Em.

"Em, seriously, we can take a second," Thrash said.

"We need to get out of these caves..." Saki said as she helped Em to a suitable rock.

"I know." Thrash rotated the map. "The directions made it look like a straight line once we got off the path. Do you think it's weird that we haven't found the alcohol yet?"

Cresca was in the middle of stretching her hamstrings when she realized Thrash was actually looking at her, waiting for an answer.

"Why are you asking me? You're the one with the map."

"You're the one with the knack," Thrash replied.

"Ah," Cresca said, abandoning her attempts at cheer. "That's why you're finally talking to me."

"What do you mean 'finally talking to you?' I've been talking to you."

Cresca was tired of this passive-aggressive dance and decide to just cough it up: "You still owe me an explanation. The Justice offered us everything we want, and I still have zero clue why you turned it down."

"I know it's going to sound crazy..." Thrash unfastened her hat. "Here, let me get the Gift of Glamour—"

"I don't want to see the book. I want to hear it. From you."

Thrash sighed. "The Gifts aren't what they seem. I opened the book on the night of my Kindling, and it wasn't a book. There's a box inside filled with ritual items, like a vial of my baby teeth and a clay doll shaped like me."

Em and Saki both sat up straighter.

"I asked my mom about it when she jumped me in the woods, but she couldn't talk about it. It was like she had been literally muted. What I've pieced together is that the Gifts grant us Glamour or Growth or Sight, but they also *mute* our knacks and prevent us from talking about it."

Cresca's first thought was ...*and?* It didn't seem like a terrible price to pay, but she sensed how Em paled, how Saki swayed for a moment.

"I wish you told me sooner," Cresca replied, trying to stay calm. "And I wish you consulted us before making this decision all by yourself. What if I don't even want my knack?"

"Cresca, no—"

"You don't get it. *Your* knack is a superpower. Em's is useful and Saki's is unique. But mine? I'm like a human dowsing rod, except even less effective, because I still need a stick and it doesn't even work half the time."

"If you had seen the stuff inside the Gift of Glamour...it's creepy, Cresca."

"All witches go through it."

"That doesn't mean it's okay."

"Well, I'm the one who should decide if it's okay for me," Cresca retorted. "What if I wanted to accept The Justice's offer?"

"I don't think we can trust The Justice," Thrash said quietly.

"I don't think we can trust *you!*" Cresca fired back. Thrash's mouth clapped shut. "No wonder you've been so worried about Osmarra this whole time—you knew you stole that book and she was coming for you. But you didn't bother to tell us. You lied."

"Sorry that I didn't run every decision past you." Thrash's sarcastic voice failed to mask the hurt painted plain across her face. "It was *so* unreasonable of me not to immediately trust a bunch of strangers who only talked to me for the first time a week ago."

Cresca stepped back, mentally and physically. Her theraprix always told her to stop and take a big breath when dealing with her anger toward Coco. Maybe that was just what you told an eleven-year-old with intense separation anxiety and mild episodes of kleptomania, but Cresca found it worked. She inhaled deep and exhaled long, letting her anger wash out of her.

"We're in this together," Cresca replied once she had calmed herself down. "And we have to trust each other."

"Sure," Thrash said. She sounded anything but sure.

"No more big decisions without us," Cresca continued. "And no more relying on my knack. All it's done is get us into trouble."

Thrash frowned. "That's not true..."

Cresca started counting the times off on her fingers: "The lake with the wandslingers, the craft station with the NatPo..."

"It's still probably more reliable than this map," Thrash huffed, turning it upside down as if that would help. "We're seriously lost—"

"I think I found a way out..." Saki said. She held up a broken glass beer bottle, her eyes glued to the cave floor.

Thrash blinked. "What? When?"

"While you were arguing." Saki shrugged. "I saw the bottle

and wandered down one of the paths. It's a small opening, but I think we can fit through."

"See? We don't even need my knack!" Cresca joked, but it was a joke that lingered, a joke that started sounding more like truth as the girls retraced Saki's steps. Why was she so sure that the buzz in her bones was a knack? Maybe it masked some deadly disease or was an early warning that she smoked too many damn cigarettes. She should really try harder to quit.

Saki led them to the hole in the rocks. A beam of light broke through the cavern wall, illuminating a dozen empty beer bottles littering the ground. Great, they didn't even have free booze to look forward to.

One by one, the girls scaled the rocks and squeezed through the gap. Cresca crawled through and emerged in the woods, her eyes squinting as they adjusted to the bright light of day. Zuku clung to the tree branches overhead, swaying in the breeze as if nothing had changed since they left the forest, even though *everything* had changed. She remembered her rings and dug them out of the pocket of her shorts, slipping them back on her fingers, her armor restored.

Cresca let the other girls take the lead in finding the car. Listening for the sound of drifting radios and the telltale whoosh of speeding cars, they found their way back to the leyline. Using Em's map and her memory for mile markers, they followed the road, confident they'd get to the zuku-covered car in a few miles.

To Cresca, it was proof that they didn't need her knack.

Hell, they didn't need Cresca.

~

As the girls walked the forest floor in silence, eyes peeled for any sign of wandslingers or protectrix, Cresca began wondering what their play was at this point. The girls were obviously on the radar of the country's most powerful witches. If the whole country was swept up in their road trip due to the MLM's interference, how would they sneak into NSU? That plan was shot.

As the sun dipped in the sky, Em stopped suddenly. She pushed her glasses up her nose and leaned in to study the map. Cresca didn't like the look of that...

"It should be here," Em muttered. "I hate to ask this, but could you all push this mound of zuku aside?"

Cresca bent down and grabbed a handful of the tough black vines. What was a little more dirt under her nails? With a yank, the blanket of zuku shifted easily—too easily. This was indeed the zuku that they had chopped and laid over the car to conceal it, but there was no car underneath. Only a trail in the dirt, like someone or something had dragged a very heavy object into the trees.

The car was *gone*.

15

It was mid-afternoon, but the sky was darkening faster than Thrash's mood. Guilt nagged at her as she slogged through the woods, zuku grasping at her black sneakers. She was following the dirt tracks because...what else was she going to do? Thrash had dragged Cresca, Saki, and Em into this mess. The least she could do was get them out of it before they resented her forever, and to do that, they needed to find the car.

But then what? They were only one state away from Wyckton, but what was the point of arriving at New Salem University if they (or at least Thrash) didn't want a Gift anymore? The purpose of the Historically Magical Universities was to train witches to use their Gifts. If Thrash didn't have a Gift, where did that leave her?

Above the treetops, thunder boomed.

"Is that normal?" Cresca asked.

"The Hecatanees have thunderstorms all summer," Em explained, pausing to catch her breath. An hour ago, Saki begged Em to use the hover-cane, but Em insisted on tripping over tree roots with the rest of them.

"It rains? In the *summer*?" Cresca shook her head. "Now I've seen it all."

Em paused and opened her arms, welcoming the first drops of rain as they trickled down from the treetops. She sighed, long and sweet.

"It's not a saltwater soak," Em said, "but it's something."

As the girls all paused to catch their breath, Cresca saw her orb glowing with a new capture and stepped away to listen to it. When she returned a few minutes later, her face was ashen.

"I'm grounded for the rest of my life," Cresca said. "The media is going crazy, especially about Thrash, and not just because of the road trip. Look at this..."

Cresca summoned up one of the local Hecatanee news streams on her orb. The mist in the glass cleared, revealing a grave-faced reporter standing before a pile of rubble. Thrash wasn't sure exactly what they were looking at until she noticed, in the background, a craft station sign shaped like a giant glittering red bat.

"For nearly four decades, the Garnet Caverns have been a beloved local tourist attraction and a craft station for weary travelers along Leyline 17." The reporter turned and motioned toward the wreckage. "That is, until four teenagers caused a dangerous cave-in that destroyed this family business..."

Thrash's hand flew to her mouth.

"I didn't know sealing the entrance would destroy the store," Thrash said. No one else said anything, though Saki gave her a sympathetic look. Had Takoda gotten out unharmed? Thrash's heart ached at the thought of the building collapsing around them.

The reporter continued, "The High Circle reports it was the knack of teenager Thrash Blumfeld-Wright that caused the collapse of the building, and that these young witches are, in fact, the same fugitives fleeing across states lines with a stolen Gift of Glamour in their possession. The precise motive behind what many are calling an MLM stunt is unclear."

The reporter's image dissipated into an older capture, one of the Lunes soundlessly smiling and laughing on a picnic blanket. Their faces then faded into a capture of Thrash, taken by Osmarra on her 15th birthday. Thrash cringed looking at her own double-chin as she blew out the candles on her birthday cake, her bent head exposing black roots in sore need of a touch-up. The unflattering footage, clearly provided by Osmarra, felt like an act of war.

Everyone wordlessly drifted apart, pulling orbs out of hats and pockets. Thrash dreaded checking hers and stalled for a second, unintentionally overhearing Saki's mom. "We are *very* disappointed in you, young lady..." Out of the corner of Thrash's eyes, Saki's shoulders slumped.

Thrash's orb gave three white pulses when she cupped it in her palm. She summoned up the most recent capture from her mom.

Osmarra's face looked pale, even within the eerie glow of the orb. Her mom must not have checked her glamours recently, because dark bags had crept under her eyes.

"Theo—I mean, Thrash, please, listen to me." Osmarra's voice sounded strained. She glanced around before continuing, "You need to surrender yourself and hand the Gift over. Do not tell anyone you've looked inside. I can only protect you from the consequences of your own actions for so long."

Yeah, because this is entirely on me, not on you *for refusing to listen to me.* Thrash dismissed the capture and didn't bother to listen to the rest. She wandered back over to the Lunes. The mood, like the weather, was overcast and gloomy.

"Is it fair to say we're all in trouble?" Thrash asked.

Before anyone could answer, a tree branch rustled overhead. Thrash's gaze snapped up to the sky. A dark bird took flight. No one moved for a long moment.

"Too small to be a familiar," Saki whispered. She smacked her lips. "There was a faint taste when the birds were watching us at the craft station. I don't taste anything now."

"I hate those birds," Cresca whined. "How can a witch have four familiars? Is that legal?"

"When you graduate from an HMU, there's a ceremony that summons unbonded familiars," Thrash said, grateful to talk about anything but the mess they were in. Thrash had three biographies of The Justice on her bookshelf back home, and she had scoured her memories all afternoon for any useful details that might give them an advantage the next time they faced the Named Witch. "The spirits are attracted to power, so they only pick the top witches. They say that The Justice was so powerful that the familiars actually *fought* to be hers."

"Coolcoolcool," Em said. "Just another reason we're doomed."

"All I'm hearing is that we should've taken her up on her offer," Cresca said sweetly, her comment a thinly veiled "told you so" that wounded Thrash.

"I'm not scared of The Justice," Thrash replied.

"I'm not *scared*. But I'm also not *stupid*."

From behind them, Saki whispered, "Please don't fight."

"We're not fighting," both Thrash and Cresca snapped with such force that Saki winced.

Thrash tried to tell herself that this was just Cresca blowing off steam, that Cresca had to be glib and a little mean to make herself feel better...but how well did Thrash really know her? If—or, more realistically, *when*—The Justice caught up to them, would Cresca immediately trade them to the Named Witch?

The further the girls probed into the woods, the thicker the zuku grew. Branches bowed under the weight of vines draped like thick curtains. It wasn't long before the forest floor disappeared entirely under the robust weed. Thrash knelt down to examine the trail and felt a twist of dread in her stomach. The zuku wasn't even ruffled by a two-ton car being dragged over it.

They'd lost the trail.

"What now?" Cresca asked. It sounded like a challenge.

"You could use your knack," Thrash suggested.

"I'm giving it a break."

"You're 'giving it a break?'" Thrash felt her temper bubbling just beneath the surface but tried desperately to channel ice instead of fire. "Cresca. I get that you don't want to rely on your knack, but we need to find the car, and we have no idea where to go from here."

Cresca examined her painted nails, unchipped thanks to one of her enchanted rings, no doubt. With an eerie, calculated calm, Cresca said, "Maybe this is the end of the line."

Em stepped between Thrash and Cresca like a referee hopping onto the field.

"Can we pause this for a second?" Em hissed. "Listen. Do you hear that?"

Everyone froze and listened. Thrash did her best to shut her frustration away, but she only heard dripping rain and distant bird song—at first. Beneath the normal forest sounds, vines creaked and mud squelched. Something was moving out there, but by the time Thrash caught a glimpse of a big black shape emerging from the shrouds of zuku, it was too late.

"GRAZZLESNATCH!" Saki cried as a huge beast thundered out of the zuku, all claws and teeth and beady black eyes. Saki grabbed Em's hand and they dashed off into the trees. Thrash and Cresca held still, frozen in place.

A bear. It was just a black bear running toward them, not a grazzlesnatch, but that wasn't super comforting either. Only a few feet from Thrash and Cresca, the bear planted its paws and roared.

Cresca whimpered and dropped to the ground. At first, Thrash thought she had fainted, but then Cresca hissed, "Pretend to be a cub!"

Thrash didn't curl up into a ball. Something didn't seem quite right about this bear. The way it charged and halted felt so *intentional*. And its black fur was a shade too black, a coat so dark no light escaped. If Thrash had to name the color, she'd call it "abyss black." Thrash recognized that color—and the look in the bear's eyes, as if it were assessing Thrash just like she was assessing it.

"We're witches!" Thrash called. She raised her hands to show she didn't have a wand. Cresca looked up at her like she was insane. "We're lost and trying to find our car. Can you help us?"

The bear growled. It didn't back down. Thrash decided not to back down either, even when it pulled back its lips into a full, threatening snarl. She was pretty sure familiars couldn't hurt humans. It was part of the bond—part of the deal.

"Please," Thrash said. "We just need our car."

"Leave this place," the bear warned, its voice deep as a ravine.

I knew it! Victory flooded her, even though she knew this was no time to celebrate. The bear wasn't exactly on her side.

Yet.

"We didn't mean to trespass," Thrash continued. The bear stopped growling—that seemed like a good sign. "We're just trying to find out who took our car. Someone literally dragged it off the side of the leyline into these woods. It's a blue—um, green convertible. Have you—?"

The bear cut her off with another teeth-rattling roar. Thrash shrank back. She caught a glimpse of Em and Saki watching from a copse of trees, close enough that they were within earshot but could run at a moment's notice.

"Get out of my forest!" the bear bellowed.

Thrash hesitated. This just didn't make sense. Familiars didn't stomp around forests laying claim to them—they wanted mortal power. There had to be a witch tied to this, in some way.

"Let's do what the nice bear says," Cresca murmured from the ground.

The bear sniffed the air. After wrinkling its nose for a long, tense moment, it heaved a displeased sigh. Thrash was so fixated on the bear that she didn't even hear the squelch of muddy footsteps approaching.

"Oh my Goddess, Surge. Stand down! You're terrifying them!"

A young man jogged up to the bear, emerging from the zuku like an Olympic runner in short shorts and a tank top. He smiled apologetically and ran a hand back through his damp jet-black hair, the gesture emphasizing his beefy arms. Cresca got slowly to her feet and clutched Thrash's arm.

"Intruders..." the bear snarled, but the familiar sounded less sure.

"We didn't mean to alarm your familiar," Thrash said. She eyed the boy's wispy moustache, trying to gauge his age. He looked too young to have graduated from a university. Maybe a few years older than her.

"Ha! He's not my familiar. We're just brothers." The bear huffed as the boy approached Thrash and held out his hand. "Rok. Rok Wu. It sounds like we have your car."

~

Rok led them deeper into the soggy woods, chattering all the way about how the Brotherhood was a hidden community of "anarchists and rebels." Apparently, they'd found the car, assumed it was abandoned, and dragged it to their camp to scrap it for parts. Thrash also learned Rok never got bug bites, he loved sunball, but he hated swimming, and he missed his dog, Boomer. Rok had the energy of a Labrador retriever that had downed four coffees.

"You wanna ride Surge?" Rok asked Em, still clearly struggling at the back of the pack. Em's eyes narrowed. Thrash couldn't understand Em's reluctance—she would've killed to ride a bear!

"I'm good," she answered. "How much further do we have to go?"

"Check it!" Rok exclaimed, pointing ahead.

To an unassuming hiker, maybe the zuku just looked a little wilder here, growing so dense it formed lattices that wrapped around trees. But Thrash saw it for what it really was: a fortress of black vines bolstered by the forest. Thrash assumed it was the work of a Growth witch until Surge ambled right through the glamour, the vines winking briefly out of existence.

"He's just grumpy because he lives for a good scare," Rok explained with a shrug. "Usually, we let guests go first."

The Lunes traded looks, hesitant to lead the charge, so Thrash stepped forward. She wasn't gonna let a little glamour magic intimidate her.

Thrash plunged through the zuku, wincing on reflex even though she didn't feel a thing. She emerged on a dirt path at the edge of a sprawling garden. Patches of crops waved at her in the breeze, from barley reaching as high as her shoulder to carrot tops just peeking out from the ground. She felt the rain caressing her cheeks and looked up to see a vast gray sky.

From this side of the illusion, Thrash watched as the girls passed through a doorway cut into the forest growth one by one. The wall of zuku surrounding this oasis was very real; it was only the portal that had been cloaked from view.

"This is the edge of our land," Rok said, waving them down the dirt trail. Thrash noticed that despite the rain, the dirt path stayed dry. "But the heart of the Brotherhood is up ahead."

Rok led them toward a cluster of trees which, as they grew nearer, Thrash could see had been coaxed by magic into structures. At the base of the trees, three large wooden domes provided shelter. Mismatched quilts and sheets hung between branches and provided shade and protection. Thrash also spied smoke wafting from metal torches ringing the perimeter of the camp. Thrash sniffed the air, but she didn't smell fire. It was more like sage, almost.

Rok chirped, "That herbaceous scent is warproot," and Thrash almost choked on her own inhale.

As they neared the village center, Thrash heard the sound of drums. The stillness was broken by a chicken running across their path. A few seconds later, two kids ran after it, shouting, "Sorry!" and "'Scuse us!" The path widened and they came upon a drum circle sitting in a clearing, people of all ages and colors making music and enjoying each other's company.

At least, that's what she thought was happening. Then she noticed how the misty rain shifted with the rhythm. The beat of the drums was somehow gathering water into streams and guiding it into buckets.

What was this place?

"Welcome to the Brotherhood! A haven for witches who shun the Gifts," Rok declared. He called them witches, but Thrash didn't see any of them wearing beaded collars. "Don't forget to look up."

Thrash craned her head, her eyes climbing up tree trunks

and rope ladders until she landed on dozens of wooden bungalows sculpted out of the trees, complete with windows and balconies.

"You're saying none of this was crafted using the Gift of Growth?" Thrash asked. "Or Glamour?"

Rok beamed and nodded. Thrash's jaw was officially on the floor.

"I'm in love," Cresca said, but she wasn't looking around the camp. Rok met her eyes and Cresca instantly looked away. Flirting 101. Thrash wanted to barf.

"I'd give you the grand tour, but Chihto is waiting for us in the Longhouse. It's our meeting hall and also where we cook and eat our meals."

"Who's Chihto?" Saki asked. She and Em were subtly leaning on each other, a reminder of the long, fraught day they'd already endured.

"Did I not mention Chihto yet? Oh, brother." Rok hit his forehead playfully and Cresca giggled. "He's the guy who founded the Brotherhood and built most of this. If we had a leader or a chief—which we don't, cuz it's fundamentally against what we stand for—he would be it."

They skirted the edge of the courtyard, passing a witch with flowing gray hair wielding a feather like a wand. She was sculpting an old log into something new using the feather to guide the magic. A few feet from her, two gossiping boys Rok's age weaved their fingers in the air and mended clothes. The boys' conversation died down to a hush and the artist's curious eyes followed them as they passed. Thrash couldn't help but wonder...how often did the Brotherhood welcome new people?

"To our left is the Bathhouse," Rok continued. "And this is the Longhouse."

The entry of the large domed building was marked by a

curtain of mismatched beads. Rok pulled them aside and gestured for them to enter.

"How hippie chic," Cresca commented as she ducked past the beads.

"That's Chihto for you," Rok chuckled.

It was darker and hotter inside the Longhouse, but it smelled delicious. Smoke and animal fat clung to the air as woodland creatures (RIP) roasted on spits over a glowing red pit in the center of the building. Long wooden tables circled the fire, arranged in messy rings. Wooden stools were strewn about as if abandoned the moment the last meal concluded.

Thrash half expected to find the Brotherhood's non-leader leader sitting on a throne at the end of the hall, but instead she spied a man with a braid of salt-and-pepper hair down his back, staring into the flames of the pit. He was built like a willow tree and when he looked up at their approach, his smile didn't meet his eyes. His brown complexion and the soft fire-light made it hard to tell his age, but he looked somewhere around fifty. Parent-aged.

"Rok, I see we have guests?"

"They're the girls I was telling you about," Rok chimed. "The Justice offered them Gifts and they turned them down. Everyone's talking about it outside."

Chihto's fuzzy eyebrows shot up to his forehead. "Ah, yes. Rok tells me half the country is spellbound by you, the other half is hunting you."

"And which half are you in?" Thrash asked.

"We are the Brotherhood of Lone Wolves," Chihto said, giving each of them a long look. Did he hear how ridiculous that sounded? Or was it just her? Silly name aside, it didn't escape her that Chihto didn't answer her question.

Chihto gestured to the chairs. "Please, have a seat with me. Allow me to explain. Rok, have you offered our guests a drink?"

"Ale, water, or moonshine?" Rok asked with a wink.

"Water will do," Chihto said. "Thank you."

"But I want to try that moonshine later," Cresca added, twirling a strand of silver hair around her finger. *If there was a later.*

Rok ducked out the beaded curtain. Thrash had half a mind to stay standing, but that would be weird. Instead, she grabbed a stool along with the rest of the Lunes. Chihto pulled up a chair, joining the circle. What did he see when he looked at them? Were they a symbol of rebellion, as Takoda imagined? Or were they walking bags of cash, four fugitives whom he could turn over to the government for a hefty sum?

"You must be Chihto. I'm Cresca, and that's Thrash, Em, and Saki. We're sorry to intrude. This seems like a really special place you have here."

Bless that girl and her ability to strike up a conversation with anyone. Rok reappeared, handing each of them a repurposed wine bottle filled with fresh water. Thrash didn't realize how thirsty she was until the cold water hit her throat. She drank half the bottle right then and there.

"We are a haven for all magic," Chihto explained. "Here, you will find witches who have rejected the Gifts. We have dozens of students of Hash magic, which was practiced on this very soil hundreds of years ago. All Seven Schools of Magic are welcome. We even have a talented practitioner of Oudon magic."

"That sounds really impressive," Thrash said. "But the real reason we're here is because you have our car?"

"A misunderstanding. Our magical talents are many, but we still must scavenge certain things. We patrol the leylines every morning. You see, people will dump anything by the side of the road."

"We didn't dump it," Thrash said. "We were having car

trouble and we went to get help. We just want our car back and we'll be on our way."

Chihto sighed.

"I'm afraid that's not entirely possible." Chihto's words sent a chill through Thrash. "You've never heard of the Brotherhood for a reason. We're on no maps, and we want to keep it that way."

"You can't keep us here," Thrash said. "We have parents. Families."

"No, no, we're not going to keep you here forever. We just can't have you leaving before you understand the value of the Brotherhood, and why its secrecy is worth preserving."

"So, we're your prisoners," Thrash growled.

"Honored guests," Chihto insisted. "I have a community to protect, and we've barely gotten to know one another. Think of it as a chance to rest. It looks like you girls need it."

Chihto tilted his head toward Em, who was slumped forward on her stool, dead asleep. It pained Thrash to admit it, but maybe they did need a break. Maybe this mix-up was a blessing in disguise.

"Whatever you need—fresh clothes, a wash, meals—we're happy to provide it."

Chihto raised his bottle. Cresca and Saki joined him but Thrash hesitated. If they had to earn Chihto's trust, so be it, but how many hours did they have until The Justice tracked them down? Chihto could burn all the warproot he wanted —Thrash wasn't convinced it would stop The Justice from finding this commune.

Chihto might not see it yet, but these witches were better off without Thrash and the Lunes. Or at least Thrash.

With a sigh, she raised her drink. They clinked the bottles, the merry sound easing the tension clinging to the room.

Chihto smiled, a single turquoise tooth flashing among the rest.

16

Em woke up warm but disoriented.

A tub. She was in a metal tub, filled with lukewarm salt water, in what must be the Bathhouse, though she had no memory of being escorted here or shedding her outer garments. Em glanced down at her legs, bare under the water. Her gut clenched at the thought of one of the girls seeing her scaly legs as they helped her undress.

Em sat up and took a long, deep breath in—and coughed. The moist air was hotter, and maybe even wetter, than the saltwater bath.

"She lives!" Cresca cried. Em turned her head toward the sound of splashing water. Over the lip of the tub, she saw that her metal basin perched on the edge of a hot spring. Steaming water bubbled up from the depths of a winding pool dotted with dark, smooth stones. It was the ideal spring, so perfect it belonged on a nature calendar—which is why Em was pretty sure someone had designed it. There was magic at work here, for sure.

Cresca and Saki waded over to her, their long hair tied up

into practical topknots. As far as Em could see, they were the only ones in the dark, hazy Bathhouse.

"How are you feeling?" Saki asked Em. How *was* she feeling? It was something Em didn't pause to consider nearly often enough. Em wiggled her toes and stretched her neck. Her head felt clear, though her vision was blurry. She could just make out the outline of a wolf painted on the far wall.

"Have either one of you seen my glasses?"

"They're over by your orb and your hat," Cresca said. "I'll get them."

As Cresca paddled over to the other side of the steaming pool, Saki leaned in and whispered, "Do you remember the meeting with Chihto?"

"Not...really..."

"You fell asleep and almost tipped off your stool. You didn't wake up, even when we moved you here."

Em groaned. The thought of her limbs splayed, drool crawling down her chin, made her face burn with indignation. This was her parents' worst nightmare, all their warnings about all-nighters and burnout come true.

"I'm sorry," Saki whispered.

"Don't be. It's not your fault," Em said, probably not with enough conviction, but her racing mind had already moved on. It was all slowly coming back to her—the missing car, the bear, the tents and treehouses. Her parents would kill her if she lost their vintage convertible to a gang of wolf-worshipping vagrants.

Em squinted into the haze. "Hey, where's Thrash?"

"Off with Chihto." Saki glanced furtively around the Bathhouse, as if Thrash might walk in any moment. "She said she'd bathe later. Something about her underwear being too embarrassing."

"And no one wanted to go skinny dipping!" Cresca called

from across the room, where their belongings rested in wooden cubbies that looked like bird feeders. Or maybe that was just Em's mediocre vision.

"Would you toss me my orb?" Em asked. She couldn't make out any of the shapes that Cresca held, but she could see the white glow of her orb.

"Actually, Em..." Cresca bit her lip. She was still gripping Em's orb. "I wanted to talk to you about that."

"About what?" Em couldn't keep the creeping edge of panic out of her voice.

"Your parents," Cresca said. "I checked your orb while you were out. You said you were going to scry them, but you never called them off."

Em shot up out of the bath. Water splashed over the edge, slapping the stone floor.

"You went through my captures while I was unconscious?!"

"I know! I have a problem! I shouldn't touch people's stuff!" Cresca set Em's glasses and hat on the floor and backed away, but she didn't relinquish the orb. "But Em, you lied to us."

Em splashed out of the tub. For a brief, blissful moment, her rage burned away her self-consciousness. She wanted to rip her hair out—no, she wanted to rip Cresca's hair out. She wanted to cut that fake silver bun right off her head—

"You told me *multiple times* that you talked to your parents," Cresca said.

"Those messages are private." Em picked her glasses up off the floor and slid them back in place. "Now give me my shit back."

Em tried to grab her orb out of Cresca's hands, but Cresca surprised her by swerving toward the hot springs and leaping into the pool. As Cresca backed away from the edge, she swirled her hand around the orb and the fog cleared within the crystal.

"*Please, Em, just talk to us.*" Em could see the tears in her mom's hazel eyes as she appeared in the orb. "*We'll give you whatever you want—a later curfew, a new car—we'll even cancel the bounty if you just tell us you're okay.*"

Cresca dismissed the capture and let the secret air out. Em swallowed, the sound like a gavel coming down.

"I missed that capture," Em said, but the excuse sounded weak, even to her own ears. She couldn't bear to look at Saki and see her reaction.

"How about this one? It's from two days ago."

Em's mom and dad appeared this time, their heads tilted toward each other as they jockeyed for space.

"*Em, this is your dad. We're so worried about you. Are you taking care of yourself? Please just scry us or send us a capture and we'll call off the search.*"

Cresca conjured up yet another capture.

"*Em, where are you?*" her mom pleaded. Then her dad cut in, "*Young lady, if you don't reply to this message, there will be serious consequences.*"

"That one was sent while we were at the Sunny Bucket," Cresca said as Em's parents faded into the orb's mist. "Are you telling me you didn't see it?"

"I don't know!"

Cresca narrowed her eyes. "Em, you are the most curious and observant person I know. Are you really going to tell me that you ignored all of these messages from your parents? Actually, don't answer that. Tell me this: why didn't you call them off?"

Em hesitated. How to explain that contacting them felt like surrendering? That for the first time in her life, she had tasted freedom, and that she feared her parents would demand it back? Over the past week, Em had expanded, like her knack, beyond a neat little box. She could never fit inside it again.

Instead of all that, Em murmured, "They wouldn't listen."

"From these messages, it sounds like *you* were the one who wouldn't listen," Cresca fired back. "And to some extent, I get it —we're all kinda running from our problems, aren't we? But it sounds like your parents are willing to compromise—so why aren't you?"

Cresca climbed out of the pool via a set of stone steps. Em dared a glance at Saki, who had sunk deeper into the pool, the water up to her ears. At the cubbies, Cresca silently grabbed her hat and pulled out three crumpled High Moon Motel towels. Em had seen Cresca get angry before, but never like this. A chill passed through her.

"I'm sorry," Em said.

"If you're really sorry, then stop being stubborn," Cresca snapped. She wrapped a towel around Em's orb and thrust the bundle at Em. It hit her square in the gut. "And call off your parents."

Cresca wrapped one of the other towels around herself and opened the door to the courtyard. Bright sunlight blinded Em for a moment, then the door slammed shut.

With Cresca gone, Em's wounded pride seemed to fill up the surrounding space. Em felt suffocated; she needed fresh air. Even though her underwear wasn't dry, she pulled on her skirt and threw on the first shirt she found in her hat.

Saki paddled over to the edge of the water.

"Are you okay?" Saki whispered, inching closer.

"I just need some space." At home, Em's parents were always hovering, and now the girls were hovering too. Though the anger had subsided, there still some piece of emotional shrapnel wedged in her chest.

Why can't you face your parents? it whispered.

Why are you so weak?

The Brotherhood reminded Thrash of a summer camp she attended when she was twelve. Desperate for her to make friends, her moms enrolled her in a Wildergirl Troop and shipped her off to the woods for two weeks. She cried when they arrived at the camp and the only thing that would make her stop was a promise from Duna that if she hated it after the first night, she could come home. Duna allowed Thrash to pack her tarot cards and told her to draw a card if she felt nervous or scared.

Even though summer camp was everything Thrash told herself she hated, she ended up loving it. Those two weeks were magical—swimming in crystal-clear rivers and exploring pristine trails by day, huddling around the campfire, telling spooky stories and making messy s'mores at night. She had been loath to admit it, but her moms had been right. There was something about the woods—and maybe the open road—that brought people together. Or maybe these places just stripped away all the glamour, as it were.

Thrash admired the Brotherhood, but she didn't know what Chihto wanted, and it made her nervous. This wasn't actually summer camp and adults didn't necessarily have her best interests at heart. What Thrash should be doing right now was finding the car.

Out of the corner of her eye, Thrash noticed a basin of rain-water. The surface sloshed as if an invisible hand rocked the bucket. A reflection of her nervous energy?

"Stop," Thrash whispered at the water. She held out her hand and kept it steady. A few seconds later, the water quieted.

When Thrash looked up, Chihto approached like a cautious

cat, his arms clasped behind his back. He looked older in the daylight, his gray hair almost white and sprouting out of odd places. Shadows lurked under his eyes. He gave her one of his sad smiles.

"You have some natural magic, I see." Chihto's eyes darted to the water.

"Knacks are natural magic?"

Chihto nodded. "I started this community to explore natural magic. There's more to magic than the Gifts, you know. Are the Seven Schools of Magic still taught in schools?"

"Yeah. We learned about them in middle school." If a few paragraphs in a textbook counted as "learning." Most of what Thrash remembered were dismissive descriptions of the rest of the world's magic that painted them as primitive and weak.

"Well, I don't mean to lecture, but I think the more you see of the Brotherhood, the more you'll realize this place is more welcoming than any school or university."

Thrash squinted at Chihto. He wore jean shorts, an old loose tee, and a plain necklace strung with black beads. Thrash noticed a fair amount of dirt under his nails, but at the same time, she hadn't seen him doing any manual labor around the camp. What was *his* natural magic? She couldn't figure out how to categorize him.

"Are you afraid of heights?" Chihto asked.

"No..."

"Good." Chihto's eyes twinkled. "I wanted to show you our library."

Thrash's pulse quickened as she followed Chihto through the camp. She had a soft spot for libraries, after all. Chihto stopped at the base of a thick tree, where a black banner painted with a white *H* hung from the lowest branch.

"Everything here has an address of sorts. A number for how high up it is, and a letter for which tree to climb."

"So organized for anarchists," Thrash commented.

"Only took me about thirty years to figure it out." Chihto chuckled. "I was your age when I started this place. It was just me and my friends at the time. And a lot of drugs. It was the seventies."

Thrash nodded, feeling faintly scandalized but trying to maintain a mature facade. Is this what it felt like to be taken seriously by adults? The Justice negotiated with her like an equal, and Chihto didn't talk down to her because of her age. Osmarra could learn something from them.

"As you can see, we've grown quite a bit. Almost eighty people call the Brotherhood home. Rok could tell you the exact number at any given time."

Intriguing, Thrash thought as she followed Chihto up a rope ladder. Looking down from her new vantage point, Thrash searched for a hint of chrome around the camp as Chihto explained how the ladders became solid wooden supports in the higher tiers.

The library "pod," as Thrash had come to think of the tree bungalows, was sparse but cozy. Gleaming wood shelves packed with books wrapped around the oval room. A handful of scrappy, handsewn beanbag chairs were the only furniture. Like the rest of the Brotherhood, it was a strange mix of polished magic and repurposed castoffs.

"You won't find these books in any library," Chihto said, beaming at the shelves. The turquoise tooth winked at her. "It's taken me decades and a good chunk of my trust fund, but I'm building the largest collection of alternative magical litera-ture in the Thirteen States. You'll notice a few journals by yours truly as well. I encourage everyone who stays with us to write down their story and add it to the collection."

It was a lot to absorb—the books, the theories, even the

trust fund. Chihto was loaded? That explained a lot about this slice of utopia. Money, like magic, made life easier.

"Tell me your story," Chihto said, gesturing toward the beanbags. What Thrash really wanted was to hear *his* story, but maybe the best way to get some information was to give some information. Thrash sank into one of the beanbags, which promptly entombed her. It smelled like old, unwashed jeans.

"I ran away from home because my mom wanted to force the Gift of Glamour on me," Thrash explained. "I probably wouldn't have left on my own, but Cresca, who you met earlier, came to me with this plan to steal our own Gifts. It seemed like a solid plan until I looked inside the Gift of Glamour."

Chihto leaned in, elbows draped over knobby knees.

"I had second thoughts," Thrash said. "To say the least."

Chihto nodded thoughtfully. "Knacks can be powerful, but unpredictable. The kind of magic the High Circle wants to stamp out."

Thrash swallowed. "And they use the Gifts to do the stamping, right?" It felt so strange to say it out loud, to discuss this dark truth with someone else.

"Ah, so you *have* figured it out." Chihto gave her another bittersweet smile. "Did they try to feed you the lie that the Gifts only mute knacks?"

This felt *so* weird. Like Chihto was peering into her brain. "Yes."

"The Gifts mute *all magic*," Chihto explained. "All but one path. There was a set of Oudon pins, no? That is a way to close off magic. Take the Gift of Growth—it snuffs out everything that isn't related to healing and horticulture, but that which remains grows stronger."

Thrash found herself nodding numbly.

"Magic is easier to control when there are only three paths," Chihto continued. "Originally, the Gifts consolidated and strengthened magic—but they also erased the magical traditions of indigenous witches and non-Europan refugees."

Chihto touched his beaded necklace, lost, for a moment, in thought.

"Of course, much of what we still use today was stolen from those traditions. Native magic coaxed spirits into flesh, made them what the colonizers call familiars. The Gifts cut off magic, while using Fae wards and Oudon to do it."

Chihto released his necklace and folded his hands together. As they sat in uncomfortable silence, Thrash thought of the beaded chokers witches wore, so obviously lifted from Native jewelry if she had ever thought to look closely. Her stomach turned. The world was a much uglier place than she had realized.

"The Gifts mute magic," Thrash repeated. She felt like she was trying to find her footing again amidst this new tide of information. She thought of the rush of power she felt when she shattered Rongo's window and escaped, or when she threw up that mountain of asphalt and saved her friends from the wandslingers. Then she tried to picture that magic being ripped away. The absence. The gaping wound.

Chihto rested his chin on his hands. He looked at her with pity.

"There's nothing for you at New Salem University." Chihto's gaze grew so intense Thrash had to look away. *Had she mentioned NSU?* "However, there's a place here for you and your friends. If you want to stay."

Thrash's heart beat faster. There was undeniable appeal to what Chihto wanted to achieve here, to his vision. As her eyes wandered the shelves of the little library, she thought of the library book in her hat. That book had come a long way from the Belmar Library. It was weird to think that if she stayed here, she would never return it.

"The world out there doesn't want you," Chihto said.

Thrash swallowed. She knew that she couldn't run forever, but she also struggled to see herself hiding in this zuku-cloaked fortress forever. Could she stand a lifetime of hiding, of making herself invisible?

"Where's our car?" Thrash finally asked.

Chihto's face fell.

"Stay for dinner," he said. "That will really give you a sense of the community we have here."

I'm sure it will. Chihto stood up and offered Thrash a hand getting out of her beanbag. Staying here was a tempting thought, but as Thrash stared at the lonely library, she had to wonder: what was the point of recording your story if no one ever read it?

At least, no one who could make a difference.

"You're a lone wolf, Thrash. Like us," Chihto said. "Think about it."

Cresca angrily flipped through streams on her orb. She was a people person, but she was pretty over people right now. Everyone always joked that a cross-country road trip was the way to find out if you really liked your friends. Add in the stress of a national witch-hunt and bounty hunter in pursuit, and any reasonable girl would need a break.

"Hey, Cresca? Right?" Rok waved at her and jogged over, his floppy black hair flip-flopping in the breeze. Despite Cresca's vow of isolation, she smiled as he neared.

Earlier, pre-Bathhouse, Cresca caught Thrash scowling at her as she flirted with Rok. *You catch more pixies with rosewater than hemlock,* Cresca thought. If they wanted the car back, they needed to be *likeable.* Yes, Rok was easy on the eyes, but what Thrash failed to see was that he could be a valuable ally.

"How was your bath?" Rok asked. "Enjoy having the hot springs all to yourselves?"

Cresca tucked her orb back in her hat and did a cat-like stretch. She could play along. She knew his type.

"You didn't miss much. Everyone kept their clothes on. It was a damn shame, really."

"Downright tragic."

Cresca smiled. "So, what do you guys do for fun around here?"

"We mostly chill. But I could show you the best spot for chilling?"

"Sure. Lead the way."

Rok guided Cresca past several dangling rope ladders until he stopped before the sturdiest, thickest trunk of the pack. A black banner with a white letter *A* hung from the lowest branch. A metal hut that looked like the junkyard cousin of the egg-shaped treehouses sat at the foot of the tree. Rok grinned and opened the door with a flourish.

"It's not so different from a car, really." Rok plucked a wand off the wall. The inside of the pod was sparse, but thankfully someone had hammered in a few aluminum handrails to the walls. Cresca felt a thrum in her bones, but she chose to ignore it. Not like her knack ever told her anything concrete anyway.

With a flick of Rok's wrist, they started levitating. Cresca gripped one of the rails.

"Don't worry, we're sort of on a track, a groove carved into the tree. We won't fly off into space."

"Or plummet to our deaths?"

"No plummeting," Rok said. "I swear on my dog, Boomer, the goodest good boy who ever lived."

They reached the treetops in less than a minute. Rok waved the wand and the scrappy vehicle halted at a wooden platform. He offered Cresca his hand. She took it.

The Roost looked like it belonged at the top of a pirate ship, but the wooden deck wasn't what took Cresca's breath away—that was the view. Beneath the gray sky, Cresca could see miles of forest in every direction, with as many shades of green as the ocean had blues.

"I spend a lot of time up here," Rok said, breaking the silence.

"It's incredible," Cresca admitted. She spotted a break in the quilt of trees where the leyline ran, a literal lifeline of magic and their one way out of here. "But it also makes me feel a little...trapped."

"Not the intention, I swear. And, for what it's worth, I disagree with Chihto about keeping your car from you. People should only stay at the Brotherhood if they want to stay."

"How did you end up here? If you don't mind my asking."

"The short version is I choked during the knack assessment." Rok said it with a shrug. "It was already an uphill battle to convince my parents to send someone from NSU to test me, and then on the day of the demonstration, I couldn't do it."

"Wow."

"Yeah." Rok clapped his hands together cheerily. "I was a sunball player in high school, so I poured my frustration over missing out on a Gift into that for a while. But then I tore my ACL and all the colleges passed on me. I thought my life was over."

Cresca just nodded and listened.

"I was really angry for a while. I didn't know who I was without sunball, and I didn't know what to do about my knack. One day, I just left. I hitchhiked around the south for months until I eventually heard about this place, and here I am."

"Did Chihto help you figure out your knack?"

You could say that.

Cresca startled. That hadn't been her thought—well, not exactly. She heard it, in her voice, in her head—but she most definitely hadn't thought it. Rok's dark eyes twinkled when she finally got it together enough to look at him.

"Are you kidding me?" Cresca breathed, almost giddy as she fit the puzzle pieces together. It seemed like Rok and Chihto had been in sync ever since they arrived. *Was that because...?*

My knack. It was so weird to hear Rok's thoughts in her own voice. *Give it a try. Try thinking a reply to me.*

Um... Cresca searched his eyes. *Did you hear that? Blink twice if you hear this.*

Rok blinked twice. Cresca couldn't believe it.

"Also, I've gotta come clean..." Rok said. "I've heard some of your thoughts. Unintentionally, I swear. I can hear thoughts from several miles away if I concentrate, but if I'm next to someone, looking right into their eyes...sometimes things accidentally slip through."

Cresca narrowed her eyes at him. *And?*

Yes, you're my type. No, we're not the Magic Liberation Movement. We're totally independent and not interested in starting trouble. Your sister sounds rad, though.

Okay, wow, Cresca thought. *Sounds like* a lot *slipped through.*

Rok chuckled. *Sorry. It's just what's been on your mind around me.*

What else had Cresca been thinking about? Her adrenaline spiked right as Rok ran a hand back through his hair and said, *Also, if it's not too bold...I don't think you need to steal a Gift. You just need to develop your magic and figure out what form it wants to take.*

I don't know, Cresca thought bluntly. It was hard to censor your thoughts, she was finding.

Did you know in Europa, they don't even have Gifts?

Well, sure, but everyone knew that Europa's witches were less advanced as a result. In Cresca's mind, Europa was a dangerous continent plagued by vampires and Fae, where typicals feared what they couldn't understand.

Oof. That sounded a little racist.

That was *a little racist,* Rok interjected.

"Okay, how do I eject you from my thoughts?"

They both laughed, Rok apologizing profusely, out loud, and then their giggling simmered back down into companionable silence. Cresca took in the view, replaying Rok's words, trying her best to keep an open mind and really consider them.

"Do you think you could see yourself staying here?" Rok asked gently.

"I don't know. My dad would kill me." Cresca couldn't imagine totally abandoning her family, not after Coco had left them, even though the idea of "chilling" at the Brotherhood had its appeal. The pressure to get a Gift, to land a good job, to make good money—none of that mattered here. The July 1st Gift deadline—hell, all of high school—felt like a muted memory beneath the gray sky.

"I have a stupid question," Cresca said.

"Fire away."

"Can a Gift *give* you magic? If you don't already have it? I've always wondered about that."

"Nope. You've either got it, or you don't." Rok shrugged. He made it sound so simple, but the words kept ringing inside Cresca, going off like an alarm. *You've either got it, or you don't.*

That was the question, wasn't it?

Did she have magic...or not?

Saki sat braiding her wet hair on a log in the courtyard, unsure why everyone wanted to be alone right now. Should she be comforting Em? Should she be chasing down Cresca? Should she be searching for Thrash to tell her that the Bathhouse was free?

Saki sighed. She didn't know what to do with herself. Frustrated suddenly with her lopsided braid, Saki tore out the hair tie and undid the plait.

Then she caught a whiff of something *delicious*.

Curiosity buoyed her mood. Saki stood up and let the savory smell of smoking meat guide her.

Around the back of the Longhouse, a stout boy a few years older than her leaned on a shovel, wiping his brow with a bright yellow bandana. He shoved it into the pocket of his apron as Saki approached cautiously, eying the smoke drifting up from a patch of freshly turned dirt.

"Is that smell coming from the ground?" Saki asked him.

"Yup," the young man grunted.

Saki sniffed again.

"It smells like an oven. Like you buried a pig in a bed of charcoal with onions, garlic, carrots, and...potatoes?"

The guy stopped rubbing his face and looked up at Saki. When his hands came away, traces of ash smudged his face.

"Yeah," he said. "That's right. Chihto had me slaughter an entire pig and rearrange the whole persecuting Longhouse and now I'm two hours behind schedule. Do you know how hard it is to organize anarchists? We're un-organizable people!"

Saki laughed. When was the last time she had laughed? It

had been a long day for her, too, filled with bickering friends and high tempers. It felt so *good* to laugh.

The guy smiled back at her, his shoulders uncoiling. He stood up a little straighter and offered out his hand for a shake. "I'm Basil, but people call me Baz."

"I'm Saki, and everyone calls me Saki."

They shook hands and Saki's fingers came away smudged with ash, but she didn't mind. Baz gave her an apologetic shrug.

"So, Saki, what's your deal?"

"My deal?" Saki twirled a strand of hair around her finger, thinking about how she spent the last thirty minutes braiding and unbraiding her hair. "I have no deal."

"I could use a hand in the kitchen."

"I don't really know how to cook..." Before she got her knack, Saki mostly ate junk food. In a family with five kids, you ate whatever you were served—until the morning when Saki woke up, sat down at the overcrowded kitchen table, and took a bite of corn flakes. Flavors both good and bad exploded in her mouth. She would never forget how the corn flakes came alive —the crunch, the perfect balance of sugar and salt, the depth of that cornmeal. The cow's milk tasted like grass and suffering. She had avoided it ever since.

"You'll figure it out. That's how we do it here—trial and error." Baz waved her through one of the doors into the Longhouse. Saki couldn't help her curiosity. She followed after him.

Mouth-watering smells welcomed Saki into the kitchen. Colorful light poured through a kaleidoscopic ceiling of salvaged glass. Two people roughly Saki's age hunched over wood cutting boards, slicing their way through mountains of vegetables in a rainbow of colors.

Baz hefted a metal pot toward a sink and started filling it with water.

"We're behind on cooking barley for the suicide soup," Baz explained. Saki must have looked puzzled because he immediately added, "It's what we call a soup that you kinda put a little of everything into...because it'd be suicide to eat it. At least, that's the joke. Not very funny, actually."

"It has everything in it?" Saki asked. How overwhelming.

"Just take it one step at a time. We'll start by washing the grain until the water runs clear. Then we add three parts water to one part barley and bring to a boil. Oh, and salt. We'll add a handful of salt to the water, but after it's done, we also salt to taste. Do you know what 'salt to taste' means?"

"I'm not sure."

"It's like a gut instinct, for food," Baz explained. "You taste your cooking and salt it to the level you think tastes right, instead of following a recipe."

Saki nodded, just so Baz knew she had heard him. Her stomach twisted as she thought of choosing a Gift just to satisfy her parents, of striving to get into NSU just because Cousin Dai had been accepted. Everyone was following a recipe, but maybe Saki didn't need instructions. Maybe what she actually needed was to salt to taste?

Baz set down the pot with a clang that startled Saki from her thoughts.

"Actually, step one is fetching the barley from storage. Let me show you where we keep the grain."

Baz ducked through a beaded curtain that separated the kitchen from the dining hall. Saki felt like a VIP as she stepped into the Longhouse with Baz. The other girls didn't even know where she was! Why was that thought so freeing?

Beyond the tables and the central charcoal pit, a stack of

barrels and crates filled up almost a quarter of the Longhouse. There were way more containers than Saki remembered.

Baz cleared his throat, eying the far end of the hall. "Our storage is actually a little out of control. Wait here and I'll find the barley."

Saki nodded, watching as Baz scooted around the bulk of the food, careful not to disturb the boxes. An unfamiliar scent tickled her nose, like pepper and sweat. Like...discomfort. The smell of trying to hide something, tinged with a fear of discovery, maybe. What was stored inside those barrels?

Baz rolled a large barrel around the edge of the room, but as he passed the towering stack, the barley clipped the edge of the stack with a clang that didn't sound like wood striking wood. Baz cursed and rolled the barrel back, giving the crates a bigger berth.

Was that metallic clang the sound of a car?

17

Thrash woke up from the best nap of her life.

It might have been the long day, the Bathhouse, or maybe just the magic of sleeping in a real bed, but when Thrash sat up and stretched, she finally felt ready to face dinner and snoop around for the car. Sure, the treehouse was much smaller than her room back home, but *the privacy*. Thrash didn't have to fear Saki kicking her in her sleep or Osmarra barging in. That felt downright luxurious.

As Thrash changed her clothes and finger-brushed her hair, she heard someone tap on the window. After everything she had witnessed of "natural" magic, from rhythmic spells that propelled dirt off dishes to a kid who could control fire with his hands, she wouldn't have batted an eye if she found Chihto dancing on air outside her window.

Thrash touched the green glass, crafted, like so many things here, out of discarded wine bottles.

"Open," Thrash said to the window, as per Chihto's demonstration earlier. When she removed her hand, the window dissolved by some magic she didn't understand. As she leaned forward to peer into the black night, a shadow dashed inside.

The black shape stretched and grew. Thrash gasped and stepped back, putting as much distance as she could between herself and whatever *that* was. She fumbled for the only weapon she could find—her library book. She wound her arm back, ready to throw the book and run.

"Calm yourself, wild one," the creature said. It craned its neck and Thrash saw a flash of sharp black beak. The edges of inky feathers caught the weak light of Thrash's orb.

"You're one of The Justice's familiars," Thrash stated, even though the falcon-shaped creature grew to almost twice her size. It shuffled over to the door, blocking her only escape, because there was no way she was squeezing out that window.

"Observant," it said.

"What do you want?"

"We have an offer," the bird snapped. "A deal."

As much as Thrash wanted to spit in the spirit's face and tell it to scram, a rational voice in the back of her mind urged her to hear it out. The Justice only sent her familiar because she thought Thrash could be reasoned with. That meant the Named Witch might be near—and might be extending an olive branch.

"I'm listening."

"Come to NSU alone," the bird said. "Accept the Gift of Sight and apologize for your mistakes before the eyes of the nation."

Thrash paled. There it was again: the Gift of Sight, being dangled before her like a gold-plated carrot when it was actually a noose. She didn't want to mute her natural magic, but The Justice already knew that.

"And what do I get out of it?" asked Thrash.

The familiar perked up. Thrash had a feeling it wanted to deliver good news back to its master.

"Acceptance to NSU," the bird said eagerly. It let those words sink in: *automatic acceptance to the most competitive and prestigious Historically Magical University in the nation.* "The Justice will drop all grievances surrounding you and the other girls. Your companions will return home and may apply for a Gift if they demonstrate a knack. Their actions will not be held against them."

So, in essence, take one for the team and the rest of the girls go free. Thrash swallowed. Deep down, she knew it was the right thing to do for them. After all, Thrash had been the unexpected wrench in their road trip. It was Thrash who stole the Gift of Glamour without telling them and her mom who chased them down and turned it into a national spectacle. Without Thrash, the trip never would have gotten this out of hand—and even if it had, Cresca probably would have turned back sooner if it weren't for Thrash pushing them all to go forward. Every way she looked at it, this was her fault.

"But we must emphasize: only if you come alone. If the other girls come with you, this offer no longer stands."

Thrash considered it, but she couldn't shake the suspicion that she was playing right into The Justice's hands. Had The Justice seen the outcome she wanted—but only if Thrash didn't have the Lunes with her?

"And if I refuse?"

The bird ruffled its feathers, puffing up until it towered over Thrash. It was hard to miss the message.

"No more 'secret' camp practicing forbidden magic," the familiar said, its clipped voice tinged with disdain. "No more second chances. Everyone faces justice."

The bird flapped its powerful wings. Thrash closed her eyes to shield them from the gust, which ruffled the sheets and knocked open her library book, sending pages flipping. When Thrash opened her eyes, the familiar was gone.

Thrash followed the sound of music and laughter to dinner. Strings of glass lights, magically shaped as bears and wolves, draped between trees and glowed red and yellow. By the entrance of the Longhouse, a makeshift band jammed to what could loosely be called a beat for a small crowd waving drinks and dancing along. Watching from the edge of the crowd, Thrash counted three acoustic guitars, a flute, a conga drum, and way too many harmonicas for anyone's taste.

In the fringes of her vision, Thrash caught a dark shape moving toward her. Her whole body tensed, prepared to run if it was one of The Justice's familiars here to take her by force, but it was only Surge. The black bear lumbered up beside her.

"Didn't mean to scare you," the bear huffed.

"You didn't," Thrash lied.

They both stood in silence, feeling a thousand miles away from the revelry before them. Thrash wasn't sure how to strike up a conversation with a familiar. Tempest usually started talking, and talking, and talking...

Surge rumbled, "Every day you're here is a threat to this community."

"Always thinking of security?" Thrash said it lightly, but the bear's head hung low. "You know I'd hit the road if I could, but Chihto—*your* witch or whatever—is the one who won't let us go."

"He's not my master."

"But you're his familiar?"

Surge didn't answer. *Disgruntled bear,* Thrash thought with a sigh. As her eyes wandered the courtyard, she spotted Chihto by the Longhouse. He filled mugs from a cask of golden beer, a true man of the people.

"He is very powerful," the familiar finally said. If bears could shrug, he probably would have. "As are you."

Chihto flagged down someone else to take over his post. Oh, great, he was jogging this way. Thrash smiled at him as he approached, but inwardly she cringed. Did he really expect her to abandon everything to join the Brotherhood and, what, party in the woods forever?

"Thrash! Can I get you something to drink?"

"I'm good," Thrash replied. Her smile felt like a grimace. What she wanted was to find the Lunes, but as she turned to escape, she practically slammed into Rok.

"Wait until you try this food!" Rok cried. He licked his fingers and then wiped them on his tunic like a napkin. Thrash made a mental note to never touch him again. "The pork is amazing."

"This way to the food," Chihto said. He steered Thrash away from Surge, who watched her go with black unblinking eyes. Rok followed them like a loyal hound as they wound through the crowd and through the Longhouse door. When Thrash opened her mouth to protest, she inhaled the delicious smell of dinner and almost blacked out with desire.

Chihto placed a wooden plate in Thrash's hand and told her, "Help yourself!"

"But don't go too crazy," Rok added with a wink. Thrash narrowed her eyes, wondering if his comment was aimed at her weight. In the end, she chose to let it go. Her silence made her point for her, and Rok's smile melted away into an embarrassed blush.

Belmar's Winter Solstice feast might have been ten times as large, but the food at that community potluck could not compare. Thrash piled her plate with pork that practically fell apart in her hands and skewers of vegetables charred to perfection. As she worked her way down the line toward a table with fresh bread and steaming bowls, the last person she expected to find serving soup out of the cauldron was Saki.

Face flushed, Saki had never looked more alive. Her eyes shone bright as the blue bandana that held back her hair, and Thrash noticed she had also ditched her NSU sweatshirt for a fresh shirt and an apron. When she recognized Thrash, Saki smiled wide as the moon.

"Thrash! I made this soup!" Saki exclaimed. She scooped her concoction into a fresh, untouched bowl for Thrash. "You have to try it!"

"Like, right now?" Unlike Osmarra, Thrash couldn't lie to a person's face, at least not without giving away her true feelings. The soup smelled good, but Thrash prayed it tasted delicious as she took a cautious sip, Saki staring expectantly.

"Oh my Goddess..." Thrash said, meeting Saki's gaze. "This is honestly the best soup I've ever tasted. I didn't even know soup could taste this good. It's got so much...I don't know..."

"Depth of flavor?" Saki beamed. "Can you believe this is the first soup I've ever made?"

"Only because I know you have perfect taste."

As Saki eagerly ladled soup into bowls for Chihto and Rok, Thrash couldn't help but notice how tall Saki stood. She was even heckling strangers to come closer and sample her creation. She looked confident; proud.

"Now that you've got the lay of the land, I'll leave you girls to talk amongst yourselves," Chihto commented. As he backed away, he nodded toward Saki and added, "Your friend seems at home here."

That's exactly what had Thrash so worried.

∽

Thrash convinced Saki to take a break and eat some food herself; after all, people were perfectly capable of serving themselves soup. They found Cresca, Em, and Rok sitting at one of the long tables, Em regaling Rok about their escape into the Garnet Caverns. Thrash pulled up one of the stump-like chairs.

"Welcome, ladies," Rok said by way of greeting. Cresca giggled. *Was it too late to take her plate of food back to the tree-house?* "Ah, here comes the chef!"

Em jumped up from her stool and knocked into Saki with a high-velocity hug.

"SAKI, YOUR FOOD IS AMAZING!" Em cried.

"Your soup is the best damn thing I've ever tasted!" Cresca jumped up and joined the hug. Saki's face turned bright red, squeezed between a Cresca and Em sandwich.

Thrash hesitated. *Should she join them?* But she waited just a moment too long, and in that moment Rok got up and wrapped his arms around Saki. Now it felt weird.

When everyone had gotten their touchy-feelies out and settled back down at the table, the small talk gradually faded as they dug into their food. Thrash closed her eyes and savored a flavorful bite of slow-roasted pork. Glamoured cauliflower could never compare.

Meanwhile, Cresca pushed her food around her desolate plate.

"I thought you were practically vegan?" Thrash joked, nudging Cresca and pointing at the pork.

"Huh?" Cresca's head snapped up from her plate, a slight spark of annoyance behind her eyes.

"You said you were practically vegan. At the Sunny Bucket?"

Cresca looked at Thrash blankly. Thrash wanted to disappear and instead settled for murmuring something about getting a glass of water. When she returned to the table with a bottle, Em clapped her hands.

"Now that you're back, I actually have some good news. I called my parents." Em's eyes darted to Rok. "That's *their* car you have, by the way."

"And?" Cresca leaned in encouragingly. Thrash glanced back and forth between them. What had she missed this time?

"Well, to catch Rok up, my parents wanted to homeschool me and delay my Gift for a year because they *claimed* I was pushing myself too hard. To prove I wasn't some fragile flower I stole their car and hit the road. They hired a bounty hunter. You know how it is…"

"And?!" Cresca urged.

"Annnnnd there was a lot of crying and apologizing over the orb. I agreed to no more all-nighters doing homework, no Gift for now, and I'll even go to their overpriced theraprix—but I get to stay in school."

Cresca *shrieked* and leaped up from the table to hug Em.

"You were right, Cresca," Em said. "They were surprisingly cool about it. They're just glad I'm safe and talking to them. And they're gonna cancel the bounty."

"That's huge!" Thrash said.

Cresca vibrated with glee. "That is *incredible,* Em! I knew you could do it!"

Wow. Em's parents forgave her, just like that. Thrash knew she should be happy and relieved, but she felt sort of sour. As everyone around her congratulated Em on bravely reaching out to her parents, Thrash just smiled politely. She picked up the bottle of water and took a swig.

The water *burned*. Thrash choked as she swallowed it down and slammed the glass onto the table.

Rok swallowed down a laugh. "I see you poured yourself some moonshine."

"Not intentionally," Thrash muttered, burning with humiliation.

"Oh, have some *fun,* Thrash!" Cresca's head bobbed to the music that seeped through the Longhouse walls. "When life gives you moonshine, drink it!"

Thrash's temper flared, fanned by Cresca's patronizing tone. The bottle of moonshine cracked. Before she could get her knack under control, the glass shattered.

Thankfully, the shards didn't fly far—though they did shut everyone up. It looked like someone had taken a baseball bat to the bottle, which was about how Thrash felt about this evening.

"Not *that* much fun," Cresca joked. Thrash cringed inside as the rest of the table nervously chuckled along. "Anyone wanna hit the dance floor with me?"

"Dancing sounds great!" Em hopped up from her chair.

"Don't worry about the broken glass," Rok told Thrash as Cresca tugged him toward the music. "Unless you think you can mend it."

Thrash had no idea what that meant. Reading her puzzled look, Rok added, "Your knack might not be as destructive as you think. Give it a try. Maybe you can reassemble what you've broken."

Thrash frowned, not because it was a bad idea, but because she *definitely* hadn't told Rok about her knack. And it didn't take much guessing to figure out who had spilled.

"We can explore our magic tomorrow," Cresca whined. "Right now we want to *dance.*"

Rok gave Thrash one last apologetic look before allowing Cresca and Em to drag him to the dance floor. Thrash watched them disappear through the courtyard door, feeling like she already needed another nap.

Saki scooted closer to the table, her posture all business.

"Thrash," Saki whispered. "I found the car."

"Wait—what? Really?" Thrash's heart pounded, but Saki's eyes widened in warning. Thrash dropped her voice and asked, "Do the other girls know?"

"Why do you think they're distracting Rok right now?" Saki smiled. Cresca and Em's cunning left Thrash genuinely impressed.

"So, where is it?"

"It's actually in this room." Saki kept completely still but gestured toward the far end of the room with her eyes. "Those crates that are roped off? That's the car. They glamoured it to look like a bunch of barrels and stuff."

"You're kidding."

"I am not." Saki looked grave. "Also, Rok can sort of read minds. Be careful what you think around him."

Seriously? Thrash felt a headache coming on. "We need to get out of here."

Saki wilted. "Are you sure we shouldn't lay low for a few more days? We were thinking it might be good to have some time to think about what we do next..."

Thrash nodded numbly. Of course there was no urgency to drive away, to leave—everyone loved it here. Em was back in her parents' good graces, Saki had a new culinary passion to explore, and Cresca was cozying up with Rok. They didn't need the car.

They didn't need Thrash.

Saki caught the eye of a stout young man in an apron and a lemon bandana. He gestured her back toward the fire pit and the tables heaped with food.

"I should go help," Saki said. "Baz wants me to swap back in so someone else can take a break."

"No worries," Thrash lied. *Lies, lies, lies.* She thought of a tarot card, The Snake Charmer, with its scantily clad flutist surrounded by piles of food and treasure. An unearned feast, not unlike this one.

Thrash stared at the shards of the shattered bottle. The dark glass reminded her of the falcon's black feathers. If The Justice sent one familiar to strike a deal with Thrash, why not send a bird to every girl and make an offer? Was Cresca—were all of them—biding their time, waiting to trade Thrash for whatever The Justice promised?

She sighed and swept the glass carefully onto her plate. *One-way ticket to the trash.* Thrash didn't share Rok's optimism about her knack. She knew, deep down, that her magic wasn't one of mending.

Thrash would never be the person who could bring the pieces back together.

The night after the feast, Cresca woke up from the worst sleep of her life.

When she swallowed, it felt like two pieces of sandpaper sliding in her throat. Her head pounded. Her skull felt three sizes too small. *Thank Goddess for rings,* Cresca thought as she slipped them on one by one. Enchanted hair meant no bed head, at least.

By her pillow, Cresca's orb shined with the soft white light of a new capture. She swirled her hands over the mist and Coco's agitated face appeared.

"Hey, sis, I'm calling. Just like you wanted me to. I wanted to warn you that Dad is *furious*, with me *and* you, and I haven't heard from Rongo for two days—"

Cresca waved her hand and dismissed the message. There was no way she was dealing with her sister until after she had a piece of toast and a glass of water in her stomach. As Cresca rolled out of bed and down the ladder, she prayed that the Brotherhood had a magical cure for hangovers. She didn't feel nauseous yet, but she knew from experience that she couldn't truly count on that until she had some carbs in her stomach.

Cresca smiled, remembering Thrash's horrified face last night when she accidentally downed a mouthful of hooch. It delighted her to no end to picture Thrash—usually so mature and composed—experiencing the teenage rites of passage that were in Cresca's rearview mirror. There was Thrash's first game of Quebesto, Thrash's first sip of moonshine...hell, this was probably Thrash's first road trip.

How many more firsts did they have left?

Cresca swatted the Longhouse's beaded curtain aside. There was no food in sight apart from the smell of smoked meat still clinging to the dark. She was about to go snooping in the adjoined kitchen when Chihto ducked through the doorway. He looked grim, yesterday's shirt rumpled.

"Thrash is gone," Chihto said without preamble. "And so is the car."

"Wait, what?" Suddenly, Cresca's stomach didn't feel fine. Chihto waved her out to the courtyard, and she practically tripped over herself following him. "And no one stopped her?"

"Someone helped her," Chihto said. "Surge? I know you're there."

Cresca blinked and the black bear appeared, shimmering for a moment like a dissipating mirage.

A wave of wooziness hit Cresca. Suddenly, she was nine years old, running into Coco's room on a Saturday morning and finding the room pillaged. Her sister thought she could erase herself right out of Cresca's life, but anyone who had ever picked up a pencil knew that erasers didn't do shit. The marks never fully vanished.

"I won't apologize," Surge said. "She wanted to go."

The reality hit Cresca like a glass of ice water to the face. Despite her efforts to build a coven around her, Thrash had left Cresca, just like Coco. Fury filled her veins. Did friendship— did *sisterhood*—mean nothing?

Let Thrash have the car, Cresca decided. Let her have whatever it was she wanted.

Cresca was *done*.

18

On the one hand, Thrash knew this was crazy.

Here she was, driving Em's car, wide awake thanks to the adrenaline buzzing in her veins. She felt like a criminal fleeing the scene of the crime as she soared down the empty leyline. Every time Thrash glanced at the black sky, it seemed a little lighter. Dawn had to be an hour or two away.

Post-dinner socializing went later into the night than Thrash had wanted, but then getting Surge on board with her plan had been surprisingly easy, especially when she told him that one of The Justice's birds slipped through his cloaking magic and protective wards. Surge already wanted the girls gone; all he had to do was unveil the car and Thrash, The Justice's highest profile target, would travel as far from the Brotherhood as possible.

Surge lifted the glamour without ruffling his fur. The familiar even enchanted the nickel wand, the one Thrash had grabbed from the ice cream display at the Garnet Caverns, and then escorted her out of the camp. With the black bear by her side, the one or two people they passed as they left the Brotherhood didn't even bat an eye.

But what would the girls think when they woke up and Thrash was gone? She pictured Saki's shoulders slumping and Em cursing her to the moon and back. When she tried to imagine Cresca's reaction, all she saw was a wall of blinding white fury.

Thrash couldn't dwell on the Lunes. She already had enough eating at her; no need to add doubt to the mix. Instead, she focused on the words of The Justice's familiar: *Come to NSU alone. Accept the Gift of Sight. Apologize for your mistakes before the nation.*

Yes, this was crazy. But it was also the right thing to do. Thrash had had plenty of time to mull it over last night, watching the Lunes dancing and laughing under the stars.

Only one future needs to be ruined, Thrash told herself. The other girls could live the lives they wanted—but only if Thrash distanced herself from them, which is exactly what she planned to do when she arrived at the university. She would set the record straight; she would claim that the Lunes were unwitting victims, that in stealing the Gift of Glamour and inciting some sort of anti-Gift rebellion she had acted entirely alone.

Up ahead, the headlights of Em's car revealed a wooden sign painted with flying fish and mayflowers. Thrash's heart leaped. Beneath a gold chalice read three simple words: *Wyckton Welcomes You.*

Despite countless obstacles, Thrash had finally made it to the eastern coast of the Thirteen States.

As the mile markers along the leyline started climbing, Thrash remembered that her turnoff was coming up soon. It would redirect her toward the coast, branching off east to the port city of New Salem, which had to be only a few more hours away.

But then the headlights died, and so did the flutter of hope in Thrash's chest. She cursed under her breath and toggled the ancient metal knob that she was 85 percent sure controlled the lights. When they didn't flicker back to life, Thrash tried the dashboard buttons, but their unfamiliar symbols might as well have been hieroglyphics.

"You've gotta be joking," she muttered. As Thrash fiddled with the car's controls, she soared past her exit. By the time she realized it, she wasn't sure if she should turn around or find a new route.

An extra set of hands would've been really nice right about now. Balancing the finicky nickel wand in one hand and using her elbow to steer, Thrash unfolded Cresca's map. It had so many *lines*. In Thrash's humble opinion, this map needed some editing.

As she squinted at the map, leaning in to examine the dense tangle of roads, the wind reared up. It tore the map from her right hand and the paper slapped her in the face. For a heartbeat, she was blind.

Thrash didn't remember swerving, but she would never forget the sound. Like a thousand soda cans all being crushed at once, the car slammed into one of the trees with a bone-rattling *crunch*.

Thrash flew forward, her seatbelt cutting into her like a knife. Her head snapped forward, but something cushioned the impact, a flashing red glyph that appeared for a moment and stopped her momentum with a sharp sting like a belly flop.

Thrash dropped the wand, stunned by her sudden stillness. A second later, metal groaned, and the back of the convertible sank like a drowning ship. Stars filled Thrash's vision from the tilted driver's seat.

Slowly, Thrash emerged from her daze. She unbuckled her stiff seatbelt and fished for the wand under her seat. Her neck spasmed in protest. Cautiously, she tried moving her head from side to side, then twisting her body until she could finally reach it.

Everything ached, but at least she was only battered and not broken. She couldn't say the same for the car. The front of it, at least, was totaled. Thrash tried the steering wheel. It had locked in place.

"Please," she whispered, a prayer as she held the wand aloft. Maybe, if she could just back the car out of the tree... maybe she could fix it? Thrash traced the proper patterns, but instead of levitating the car, the metal vibrated like a broken washing machine. The craft station wand burned in her hand and Thrash dropped it. The car stopped buzzing.

The message was clear: no amount of magic would make this car move.

Thrash convinced herself if she just kept moving, like a shark, she would stay alive.

What now? What next?

She could still walk to New Salem University, but it would take her a day, maybe two. As she did the math, Thrash realized there was at least one night of camping in her future, and she was not prepared.

She paced back and forth along the length of the car. She had to get moving. It wouldn't be long before a friendly driver spotted the wreck and stopped to lend a hand—or called the local wandslingers to handle it instead.

"Where do I get camping gear?" Thrash murmured, working through it as she paced. "And food?"

Thrash gave a little gasp as a plan clicked into place. At the boot of the car, Thrash pulled out the cheap wand and tapped the trunk three times. She spelled out P-R-E-C-I-O-U-S E-M-E-R-A-L-D and the door popped open. To her great relief, the bottomless chest was there, untouched by the Brotherhood. She wanted to collapse against its smooth ivory and cry.

Instead, Thrash soldiered onward. She flipped the silver latches and turned the clasps in the correct order. Squaring her shoulders, she placed both of her hands on the lid.

"*Food,*" Thrash intoned. She stepped back as the chest opened with a weary sigh. On the bed of purple velvet, she found the two remaining chocolate bars and a few craft supplies that were *technically* edible, salts and herbs and the like. Thrash took the candy.

She chewed her lip.

"What the hell." Thrash flipped the lid shut. She placed both hands on the bottomless chest and said, "*Camping.*"

The chest hesitated for a moment and then threw back its maw. Inside, Thrash found a pack of matches, a mug that read *Gifted AND Glamorous*, a magical hot pad, and a set of practical white sheets for a twin bed. Not exactly a sleeping bag, but she'd take it. As she slipped the matches into her hat, the puzzle pieces all came together—these were the dorm supplies her family and friends (well, Osmarra's friends) had given her for her Kindling.

When Thrash tried to put the hot pad in her hat, she hit a wall. Her hat was full, and she didn't even have the sheets in it yet. Reluctantly, she closed the chest and laid out all of her supplies and belongings one by one.

At least half of her hat had been stuffed with clothing. Thrash pulled out two pairs of black jeans, three black shirts and two tanks, the black jumpsuit (why?), a pair of sleep pants, and a Belmar High School sweatshirt. Thrash grabbed the sweatshirt—it could be a pillow. Then she removed her orb, her toiletry bag, Mum's tarot cards, and the library book.

With her arm elbow deep in the hat, Thrash's fingers brushed glass. She frowned as she tugged out the Good Shit Jar. It would definitely not be making the cut.

In went the sheets, the hot pad, the sweatshirt. Thrash shoved her orb and the matches into the pockets of her jeans, ate a chocolate bar (for morale), then stashed the remaining bar in the hat. Something about ditching her clothes on the side of the road just felt so savage. This was a version of herself she didn't like to see in the mirror—intense, calculating, cold. A girl who broke mirrors and glass bottles but couldn't fix them. A lone wolf, as Chihto had called her.

Thrash had room for one more large item in the hat. It was between an extra pair of jeans, the library book, and the Good Shit Jar. What was it about the jar that so annoyed her? Was it her paranoia, her fear, about what Saki and Em had written? Possibly about *her?*

Thrash twisted the lid off the jar and plucked out one of the folded slips of paper. She had no idea who had written it, but it read, *Quebesto on the picnic benches with my witches.* Thrash snorted. Okay, maybe she did have an idea who wrote that one.

She picked out another.

Thrash standing up to The Justice!!! Badass!!

She blushed. Was that one written by Saki? By Em? Did it matter? Thrash wanted to read more of the memories, but it felt wrong to indulge in them after she had left the girls behind. She realized she had been holding onto a pathetic scrap of hope this entire time that, when all of this was over, the girls would still be her friends.

What have I done?

No. There was no time to dwell on the Lunes, or the brightening sky, or the miles she would have to walk alone. Thrash put the Good Shit Jar in her hat.

"Sorry, *Song of the Silent Daughter*." Thrash traced her fingers over the plastic cover of the library book. It was a shame to leave it behind, especially with only a page or two left.

Thrash flipped to the end of the book, skimming the last few paragraphs. On the final page, someone had defaced Belmar Library property with a handwritten note—and this time she recognized the handwriting.

"Mum?" Thrash's voice cracked. She almost dropped the book.

Right there on the final page was a note written in Duna's tidy cursive, the letter dated with today's date. Could this be real? As Thrash devoured the words, tears filled her eyes.

> Theodora,
>
> I know this letter comes as a shock. I wish I was still there to guide you, but you have faced so much and been so brave.
>
> Osmarra loves you. I know it may not always seem that way, but she only wants what is best for you. I cannot make you accept that any more than I can order you to accept the Gift of Glamour, but remember that it is within every person's power to accept the gifts they are given.
>
> I am so proud of you. I love you.
>
> Mum

Sobbing, Thrash clutched the book to her chest and sank to the ground.

She cried because Duna's note was such an unexpected gift.

She cried because she wished the note was longer.

She cried because she heard her mother's voice every time she reread the words,

I love you.

What had she done?

What was the point of attending a Historically Magical University if she lost Osmarra, the only parent she had left? Sure, her mom had been misguided at first, but she wanted what was best for Thrash. Osmarra was invested in her daughter and believed in her potential, which was more than most people.

Thrash buried her head in her hands and groaned. Her mother's unconditional love was not the only love she had thrown away. The Lunes had only ever welcomed her and offered her friendship. Why did she struggle to accept it?

In some ways, Thrash noted with a snotty laugh, she was acting like Osmarra. She treated the Lunes exactly how she hated to be treated by her mom, holding the girls at arm's length as if she were superior, assuming she knew what was best for them without their input. Though Thrash despised how Osmarra sucked up to the Council, here Thrash was, playing by their rules. She was ready to drive to NSU and hand herself over to them on a silver platter for a chance at a diploma and success down the line.

Yes, Thrash had truly, royally broken something good. Not with her knack, but with her actions. She knew she was a breaker—but could she also be a mender? Could she put the pieces back together?

Carefully, Thrash tore the page with Duna's note out of the library book. She rolled it up and put it in the safest place she could think of—the Good Shit Jar. Thrash fastened her hat and peeled herself up off the ground. She approached the dark river of asphalt and crossed to the other side. The side that would take her back to her friends.

Then she stuck out her thumb and waited for the sun to get on with it.

Today was Sunday, she realized. A lazy, summer Sunday, which probably was why few cars and fewer familiars passed by her on the side of the road. Hitchhiking back to the Lunes was proving more difficult that she had hoped, even with the crashed convertible causing hovering cars to slow and rubberneck.

At first, Thrash thought it was a trick of the eye, but an approaching purple station wagon appeared around the bend and slowed on her side of the road. Thrash squinted into the morning sun, wishing she had Cresca's sunglasses. She could just make out the silhouettes of a family of four inside.

As she stepped toward the car, hoping a family would help her, she spooked the driver. The car sped off. As it retreated, Thrash caught a glimpse of her reflection in the windows. Her eyes were bloodshot from all the crying, her clothes stained with grass and dirt from the crash. Thrash wouldn't have offered herself a ride either.

Thrash dragged herself back to her post beside the leyline. How many more strangers would she scare off before she got a ride back to the Brotherhood? With a sigh, she resumed waving at cars as they inevitably passed her by.

Then she saw something she couldn't quite believe. The blur of a black familiar rounded the bend in the road, galloping so fast Thrash couldn't even make out its shape. Thrash barely had time to suck in a breath of air before the bear halted beside her.

It was Surge, and atop his back sat Cresca, Saki, and Em, hair blown wild from the ride and arms looped around each other's torsos. Three witches on a familiar with fur so black it ate sunlight. A portrait of a coven.

"You came," Thrash said, words spilling out in a breathless rush. Fresh tears stung her eyes. "I didn't think you would come."

"Don't think I wasn't tempted." Cresca made no move to get down off the bear.

"I don't know what to say..."

Cresca scoffed. "You could start with explaining why you abandoned us?"

"I— The Justice told me I had to come to NSU alone."

"Girl, you literally told me yesterday not to trust a thing that witch said."

Thrash struggled to find the right words. When Cresca put it like that...it did seem pretty foolish to trust the word of The Justice.

"I wasn't thinking clearly," Thrash finally said. "I don't know, you all seemed so happy at the Brotherhood, and I knew our original plan was blown anyway. When The Justice promised me a way out that would spare you all, I took it."

Cresca didn't even nod. She just waited. Thrash sighed.

"I know I messed up."

"Not for the first time," Cresca huffed. "I still don't understand why you didn't tell us about the Gift of Glamour?"

"Because I barely knew any of you yet!" Thrash cried. She scanned the other girls. Saki's head tilted sympathetically; Em looked straight-up guilty. "I didn't know *how* to tell you, Cresca, and...I think a part of me was scared you'd call off the trip. I've never had an experience like this before. Friends like this before." Thrash swallowed. "All I do is break things."

The dam holding back her tears broke, and they ran down her cheeks. Cresca's frown softened, but she still held firm to Surge's back.

"You know, when Surge offered to take us to you, I wasn't sure I wanted to follow you," Cresca said. "Without you, we wouldn't even be here."

"I'm sorry."

"No, I mean without you showing up at my house, we never would've left on this road trip."

Thrash rubbed her eyes, trying to see Cresca clearly through the salty blur. She murmured, "I doubt that."

"I know you do. And that's a damn shame, because from the moment I saw you break that mirror in the library, I knew you were gutsy." Cresca's eyes were warmer than Thrash deserved. "Even when that means stealing a car and taking off without us. Which was very rude."

"I'm so sorry." Thrash rubbed her eyes violently, feeling ridiculous and exposed and alone—until a pair of gentle arms enfolded her in a hug. A whiff of sugar cookies and smoke. Cresca.

"I'm sorry too." Cresca hugged Thrash tighter. "I've been difficult. You've been difficult. I guess we're all just difficult weirdos."

Thrash laughed but it came out as a hiccup. Through her blurry vision, and a few strands of silver hair, she saw Saki slide off Surge's back and hold out a hand to Em. A moment later, Thrash found herself at the center of a messy hug. Four friends holding each other, hair tangled and cheeks stained with dirt and tears. Maybe *this* was a real portrait of a coven.

Thrash wasn't sure who broke away first, but eventually the arms came tumbling down and steps back were taken. When Thrash breathed, she felt like she was filling her lungs for the first time.

"If there's no point in going to NSU, what do we do now?" Thrash asked. "Do we just...go home?"

"No way," Cresca said. "We're not giving up and rolling over. This road trip started a movement, or helped a movement, whatever. Coco explained it all to me this morning. When your mom snooped around the ranch, Coco overheard her saying that you stole the Gift. Basically, Coco told every Magic Liberation person who would listen. That's why people are latching onto our trip as an anti-Gift protest—which I guess it kinda is."

"Do they think we can actually...change the Gift system?" Thrash asked.

"The MLM want you to find a reporter or something and expose what's inside the Gift of Glamour," Cresca explained. "According to Coco, the MLM already heard rumors about the Gifts muting knacks—apparently, the High Circle has done some shady shit over the years any time someone has gotten close to unveiling it. The MLM wants to prove that Gifts are bad news, ideally in a public setting with a lot of people watching so that the government can't deny it..."

In front of the eyes of the nation...

Thrash found her head bobbing, her foot eagerly tapping the asphalt leyline.

"We could still go to NSU," Thrash said. "The Justice wanted me to come to the university to choose a Gift in front of everyone, to make it clear I'm not anti-Gift and put this whole thing to rest—but I could expose the truth instead."

The rest of the Lunes were nodding—all but Em, who chimed in, "That sounds all fine and good, but how do we stop The Justice from seeing that we're coming? If she can see what you're going to do with the Gift of Glamour, she'll never let us within a hundred miles of a bunch of news orbs."

"Actually..." Saki raised her hand sheepishly. "I couldn't sleep last night, and I went for a walk through the gardens at the Brotherhood and I, uh, harvested this...without asking..."

Saki reached down her shirt and pulled out a bushel of fresh herbs, whose long green stems ended in leaves shaped like eight-pointed stars.

"You found warproot *again?!*" Cresca screamed. "I could kiss you, Saki. That is unbelievable. Unbelievable!"

"The Justice can't stop what she can't see!" Em clapped her hands together.

Thrash hoped that was true. At least it returned a fire to Cresca's eyes, one Thrash remembered seeing when Cresca first approached her at her Kindling and hinted that the world could be different, if only they got on the road and chose their own destinies. These girls looked ready to go to war—but did they understand the outcome?

"If we do this, and you all come with me," Thrash explained slowly, "The Justice, or the High Circle, will find some way to punish us. Are you all willing to risk your futures?"

Saki nodded without hesitation. Em considered it for a moment longer, but then her eyes hardened behind her glasses, and she gave Thrash a curt nod. That left Cresca, whose face had gone quiet and inscrutable for a moment while a thousand emotions warred underneath. Cresca, who would never get a Gift if she moved forward with this plan.

"You think I'm signing up for something called 'muting'

after all of this?" Cresca tossed her silver hair over her shoulder. "They're never gonna dim this sparkle."

Thrash smiled, and of all things, hugged Cresca again. Cresca felt so delicate in Thrash's arms, but she was made of harder stuff than she looked.

"I have just one question," Saki interjected. "How will we get there?"

Saki pointed across the road, and all of the girls' gazes landed on the wrecked car. It looked like a giant discarded soda can that had been rammed into a tree. Thrash thought, morbidly, that if she had to pass it off as a roadside attraction, she'd label it something like *World's Biggest Mistake.*

Thrash gathered her courage and finally said, "Em, I am *so* sorry. I swear I will find some way to repay you for the car, and I'll make sure your parents know I was driving—"

Em held up her hand. "We'll work it out."

"It *is* sad to see it like this..." Saki said quietly. She reached out, as if her long, delicate fingers could touch the cold metal from here, and then let her hand drop. "The times we had in this car—"

"Were literally so stressful that just the sight of this car makes me break out in hives." Em scratched her arms, either subconsciously or to make a point. "We can write about it fondly and remember the car via the Good Shit Jar. For now, our better bet is Surge."

The bear snorted, startling Thrash. The snort was not one of amusement.

"I must return to the Brotherhood," Surge said, his voice a low growl that no one dared cross. "You four must find your own way to New Salem."

Everyone's shoulders fell. No one knew what to say to that.

"Well, ladies, it looks like we're walking," said Cresca. She extended her arm to Thrash.

Thrash accepted, looping her arm through Cresca's. Saki joined next, linking herself beside Thrash. Em grabbed Cresca's other arm. Together, they took a step forward, wobbling a bit as they found their rhythm, unsure what they'd face next—but ready to face it together.

INTERLUDE

Dawn light filtered through the stable's generous windows. Familiars didn't sleep, not precisely, but Tempest needed a few hours of solitude every night to allow his innate essence to pool and clarify. It was a process Tempest likened to distilling a fine brandy—except nothing was being distilled at the moment, both due to The Justice's birds yapping all night and Tempest's own growing uneasiness.

Tempest didn't like New Salem and never had. Some clever writer once dubbed New Salem "the gold chalice of the nation," but in Tempest's opinion the port town hadn't glittered for over two hundred years. A fog clung to it that never quite burned off. The sea air ate at everything, casting its net indiscriminately over rusting fishing boats and musty brick mansions.

The university resisted the march of time by cutting itself off from the rest of the world with walls of solid ivy. Little about New Salem University had advanced since Tempest's last visit two decades prior, when Osmarra's young, hungry power shined like a beacon and drew him to these columned halls. In Tempest's humble opinion, it wouldn't be long before Thrash was attracting familiars of her own. Her ability to channel magic merely needed cultivation.

Two falcons landed on Tempest's stall door. He recognized Unbroken by his crooked beak and Strike by his lazy eye, always pointed somewhere it didn't belong.

"Strike thinks they will say The Justice's name for five hundred years," Unbroken chirped. "Whereas *I* think she will be on mortals' lips for a thousand years. Flood agrees with me."

Flood, stoutest of the birds, alighted by Unbroken's side. Despite his nonexistent neck, Flood was always nodding. The eternal yes-man.

"And? Why are you bothering me about it?" Tempest pushed his stable door open, forcing the birds to scatter. Unbroken settled onto the arm of a nearby candelabra, his talons curling around an iron branch.

"Will you stay with your witch, even if she fails?" Unbroken asked, head tilted.

Fails at what? Tempest didn't dare give the bird the satisfaction of asking for clarification, but the barb did what barbs were meant to do—it latched onto Tempest, and he couldn't shake it. Osmarra had suffered a few stumbles, but were they truly failures?

Unbroken saw his opening and continued, "It's not unheard of for the High Circle to urge a protectrix to retire early if a future as a Named Witch is not in the cards."

Tempest tossed his mane. "The High Circle ought to retire your beak. It has certainly served its duty, and we all deserve a break."

Unbroken narrowed his beady eyes and flew off to join the other chittering birds.

Tempest's skin prickled with electricity. If Osmarra's power crumbled, so did Tempest's tether to the physical world. But was the alternative a long life as a sycophant, obsessed with Osmarra's every accolade and how it might advance her name?

Tempest felt the tug of Osmarra's magic, of her reaching out to him via the bond they shared. He reached back and his vision expanded to include Osmarra's. She was cutting across campus, her pace brisk and relentless, but Tempest sensed something amiss.

"She wants to meet with me," Osmarra explained as she approached a line of prim cottages that housed visiting Named Witches and special guests.

At this hour?

"Apparently she saw I wouldn't be sleeping much anyway."

The Justice's self-fulfilling early morning meeting wasn't what baffled Tempest; it was Osmarra's aura of defeat. As she raised her fist to rap on the front door of The Justice's quarters, Tempest gently urged, *Don't forget your smile.*

Osmarra gave a grim little nod but avoided looking in the mirror on the cottage door. She knocked and the door immediately swept open, beckoning her inside.

In the small receiving room, The Justice sat at a modest table, gazing into her orb. She wore a silk robe, tied tight at the waist. Gone were her hat, sunglasses, and leather gauntlets.

Osmarra dipped her head. "An honor and a blessing."

"It's too early for that." The Justice waved Osmarra toward a seat at the table and asked, "Coffee?"

"Sure."

The Justice vanished into the kitchenette. Osmarra's hands fidgeted in her lap. She reached for the sugar dish and lifted the top, plucking out three sugar cubes and pocketing them for

Tempest. He sent Osmarra a pulse of appreciation and felt her relax into her chair.

The Justice returned with two generic purple NSU mugs. Both witches took their coffee black. They eyed each other as they sipped it.

"Congratulations are in order," The Justice said. "You are going to be a Named Witch."

I don't like this. There was a proper order to becoming a Named Witch, and it began with a golden letter arriving at their home in Belmar, with Thrash, Osmarra, and Tempest all drinking sparkling beverages and crying tears of happiness. There were supposed to be luncheons where Osmarra impressed members of both Circles, and those luncheons were supposed to turn into dinners, and those dinners eventually would land Osmarra at the Seven Trials. No one ever just said, "You get to be a Named Witch."

"What have I done to earn such an unexpected honor?" Osmarra asked carefully.

"It is not about what you have done, but what you *will* do." The Justice pursed her lips into a razor-thin line. "In a few short hours, you will meet your daughter at the gates. You will persuade her to accept the Gift of Sight. If you succeed, and I have seen that you can, I will convince the High Circle to grant you your Name."

Tempest felt Osmarra's pulse quicken. *The Triumph.* The Name had a glorious ring to it, but would it sound as winning when The Justice used it to call Osmarra like one of her errand birds?

"Protests are building around the country. People who can't even remember a time before the Gifts are calling for an end to them." The Justice shook her head. "Your daughter is a spark on a volatile pile of kindling that has been growing for years. The MLM has finally latched onto something that can't be ignored."

Osmarra swallowed. "Why send me? You've seen how she barely listens to me as is..."

"I would handle it if I could, but your daughter found a stash of warproot and it's interfering with my sight. I need you to go in my stead."

"Surely there has to be another way."

"Trust me, if I could throw up a few pyres outside the capital and blame it on the broom breakers, I would."

Tempest felt a flash of fury pass through Osmarra. He could feel her struggling to hold her tongue, and he urged her to follow that impulse and stay silent. Neither witch said anything for a time.

"I don't think you understand what's at stake," The Justice said at last. "The Gifts are the foundation of this great nation. Not just in terms of prosperity, but *stability*. With the Gifts, we have eradicated famine, reduced violent crime, prevented war and genocide."

Tempest remembered some of those times, and some of those witches. Before the Gifts, in the early 1800s, there was Alezandra of the Saltar Sea, a merciless witch which a knack for water manipulation. She hoarded resources until she was one of the richest people in the world. Then there was that cult leader, a male witch with a knack for mind magic who used it to make his death cult impossible to resist. Even earlier, there was the Great Fire of 1797, which burned down half of Elzborah City. It had been caused by an orphaned teenager with a knack that conjured flames. Not so different from Thrash's knack, really.

The Justice continued, "People think they want freedom, but what they need is law and order. It may start with the

Gifts, but once the foundation crumbles, the whole house will come down. They will come for the High Circle next."

"I understand," Osmarra said.

"Good."

The Justice stood suddenly and Osmarra scrambled to her feet, coffee left almost untouched. Osmarra knew a dismissal when she heard one. She bowed and began making her way to the door when The Justice cleared her throat.

"Your daughter *must* take the Gift of Sight," The Justice repeated. "Failure does not befit The Triumph."

Tempest burst out of the stable. Fresh air had never smelled so sweet, even if the grandeur of NSU felt a tad stifling. The impenetrable ivy walls grew so high that the only campus building visible from the street was NSU's ancient clocktower, whom the students called Grandmother. The ancient walls reminded students and townies alike: it was always better to be *in* than *out*.

Tempest found Osmarra sitting on a pristine granite bench, her head in her hands. What would Tempest do if Osmarra suddenly found herself *out?* When she looked up at him, wrinkles tugged at the corners of her eyes. Osmarra had let her glamours slip.

"I think I can do this," Osmarra said, all in a rush. "If I tell her that the Gift of Sight is what Duna would have wanted for her, I think I can convince her to take it. Thrash is willful, but she always listened to Duna."

Osmarra looked to Tempest for confirmation. He swallowed. Swallowing wasn't high on his list of physical pleasures, but he would miss it all the same if Osmarra's name faded and so did he.

However, what he would miss more than anything, he realized, was Thrash.

Osmarra couldn't see it, but she came alive around her daughter. Thrash could be infuriating, yes, but that little witch was also spirited, a light in a home that had grown dreary since Duna's death. That light should be encouraged, not extinguished.

"Are we sure that this is what we want?" Tempest finally asked.

Osmarra grew still and cold as the stone beneath her. "What do you mean? Where is this coming from?"

"You only have one daughter."

"And I'm trying to protect her."

"From whom? Not The Justice, clearly. That witch will say anything to get what she wants."

"I agree that her visions of total government collapse seem...unlikely. What worries me is how it will affect Theo. What if she is always seen as the girl who ripped the Thirteen States apart? She will never have a normal life after this."

"A life that looks like yours, you mean." Tempest leveled Osmarra with his most serious look. "What if she sees through your plan to invoke Duna? If she senses you're trying to manipulate her, it could backfire."

"'Manipulate' is a little dramatic..." Osmarra said, though she sounded less sure.

You humans invented drama, Tempest wanted to say, but instead he bit his tongue. The time for jokes had passed. Osmarra was nearing the cliff's edge, and this might be his last chance to steer her away from it.

"You often ask yourself what Duna would do," Tempest said. "I think she would ask herself, is a Name worth losing Thrash?"

Osmarra stood suddenly up from the bench, startling Tempest. She tugged her black uniform into place.

"You're my familiar," Osmarra said. "You are not her parent. Or mine."

The words felt like a slap. The gall of these mortals! To think that a human, even one he had pledged himself to, thought she held greater wisdom than Tempest, an eternal being who had possessed consciousness for over two centuries. It would have been laughable if it were not so pathetic.

"I tire of this," Tempest said coolly. "Do what you will but remember this: you could lose me too. Who will you have then?"

With a flick of his tail, Tempest trotted away.

19

Thrash picked her way through the thinning forest, a pebble lodged in her shoe. For the past hour or so, she had been following Cresca's knack with the rest of the girls, breathing in the scent of burning warproot as Saki waved a bundle in the air.

"Hey, can we take a breather?" Em asked. "No warproot-pun intended, but I could use a break."

The group slowed to a stop, and Thrash parked herself on a log and tugged off her sneaker. As she shook it out, Saki and Em plopped down beside her.

"Water?" Saki held her water bottle out to Thrash.

"Thank you," Thrash said, taking the bottle with a sheepish smile. "You know, I was originally planning to walk all the way to NSU alone. I basically looted the bottomless chest, but I never once thought to ask it for something as obvious as a water bottle."

"You wouldn't have survived long." Saki said it with such a grim certainty that Thrash almost choked on her gulp of water. Em laughed.

"Good thing you've got us," said Cresca. She stepped right into the sunlight, tilted her head back, and soaked up the warmth. Cresca always looked vacation-ready, but Thrash spotted an undercurrent of impatience in the way Cresca's fingertips fluttered, even as she laced her hands behind her back and sank into a stretch.

"Where to next, Captain?" Thrash asked.

Cresca dug into the pocket of her shorts and produced the rumpled, dirt-stained cigarette that she had been tossing every fifteen minutes or so.

"You sure we're heading in the right direction?" Em asked, eying the cigarette warily.

"Trust." Cresca winked at Em and then threw her hand to the sky, her rings flashing in the sunshine. The cigarette tumbled through the air. When it landed, Thrash leaned forward, pulled toward the cigarette like it was a magnet.

Cresca knelt down to read the cigarette and jumped back up with the spring of a trampoline.

"South!"

As Thrash wedged her foot back into her shoe, Em pulled the cane out of her hat. She snapped the pieces into place and sat on the hovering metal rod.

"Don't say anything," Em said.

No one said anything.

Cresca led the way, singing catchy songs with annoying call-and-response lyrics that Thrash had tried (and apparently failed) to exorcise from her days in her Wildergirl Troop. "Circle 'Round That Sad Trout" wasn't a bop, but at least it kept her mind occupied on something other than heat and discomfort.

The longer they hiked, the faster Cresca charged forward, her fingers drumming against her thighs with frenetic energy. Thrash felt herself falling further and further behind, and she wasn't alone. Not even Saki's long legs could keep up with Cresca's pace. For a second, Thrash actually lost sight of Cresca's bobbing silver hair in the trees.

Mercifully, she found Cresca stopped at the edge of the woods, gazing out at a parking lot and another indistinct craft station. Thrash dragged one leg after the other until she stood beside Cresca and paused to catch her breath.

"I don't think you're gonna like what my knack found," Cresca said, stepping to the side and gesturing Thrash toward the clearing like a reluctant magician drawing back a curtain.

Thrash squinted. All she saw was a craft station like any other, squat and welcoming and plastered in ads for whatever the traveling witch might need—maps, snacks, candles, etc. Nothing about the building seemed remarkable, and it boasted a very unremarkable parking lot as well.

But it was the car parked on that asphalt that was so remarkable.

"No," Thrash muttered under her breath. It could not be real, and yet it had to be. That cheap purple paint, those metal spikes gleaming like a vicious smile.

Madame Wiki.

"Yes," said Cresca. This wasn't a coincidence. "My knack led us here. That truck is our ticket to NSU."

"Maybe it's a trap," Thrash said. Always skeptical.

"Why would Rongo assume we need her truck?" Cresca tried her best to appear calm and level-headed despite her fingers buzzing with anticipation. With *magic.* "No, I'm pretty sure my knack led us here—to this."

Everyone was silent for a long moment. A question hung in the air.

"It's not stealing if we return it," Cresca said. "We're just borrowing the truck without permission. And Rongo shouldn't even be after us anymore, right? Em, didn't your parents cancel the bounty on your head?"

"They did..." Em chewed her lip. "But I don't know if Rongo knows it's cancelled."

"All the more reason to act now!" Cresca urged. "We'll return it when we're done, but we need to take this truck before this window of opportunity slams shut!"

"Uh, I think it's slamming shut." Thrash dropped to a crouch, tugging Cresca down after her.

Dressed in a camo coverall, Rongo surfaced from the craft station with a giant lavender soda in one hand and her staff in the other. It stood at almost five feet tall, made of tarnishing silver, with an orange ribbon wrapped around the top.

The big bounty hunter squinted at the sunlight and slid on a pair of the ugliest wraparound sunglasses Cresca had ever seen. Rongo set her staff against the wall and unzipped one of her uniform's many zippered pockets, pulling out her orb. Her fingers groped clumsily over the surface, like someone still getting used to scrying.

"We need the staff to drive the truck," Thrash whispered. Knowing that Thrash was on board made Cresca's heart pound harder. This was real. They were gonna do this.

"I have an idea," Saki said. "Make me invisible."

Wait, what? Everyone gaped at her.

"It makes sense. If Rongo catches wind that someone is sneaking up on her, I'll taste the danger. I can get out of there before she makes a move. And I'm fast."

Thrash nodded, thinking. "I mean, if you're okay with that, Saki. It does seem like our best shot."

"Coco, is that you?" They shouldn't have been able to hear Rongo from across the parking lot, but she was practically yelling into the orb. She held it at arm's length like Cresca's Nana.

Coco's response was too quiet to hear, but Rongo nodded and listened, eyes glued to her orb. Good. All that mattered was that she was distracted. Maybe they could actually pull this off.

Saki handed the warproot to Em, who clasped it in her fist as she scrunched her nose. With a *pop!* Saki became a near-invisible gleam of a girl.

Saki skirted the edge of the bushes and crept toward the craft station. Cresca yearned to bite her nails, tap her foot, light a cigarette—anything to make the tension more bearable.

"The gnats can't set foot on our property without a warrant," Rongo said. "No, that's dragonshit. You tell 'em that in Ji'ishland, that paper has to be signed by the Ji'ish Tribal Council too..."

Even though Cresca was staring right at the staff, she almost missed it move. At first, it only tilted, like someone was gently cradling it away from the wall. Then, inch by inch, the staff began floating away.

Saki didn't get far.

Rongo's head snapped up. Her neck swiveled immediately to the floating staff. The staff jerked forward, Saki bolting for it. Without hesitation, Rongo dropped her orb and her soda and lunged after the staff, all three hundred pounds of her moving swifter then Cresca could have imagined.

"Shit! Run!" Cresca yelled in a panic. She didn't have a plan, just a gut instinct that said, *Get to the truck!*

Cresca crashed through the bushes, Thrash not far behind her. When her feet hit the pavement, it felt like coming home, like taking her first sweet steps onto solid land after miles of uneven forest floor. Madame Wiki was only fifteen, maybe twenty, feet away, closer to Cresca than to the bounty hunter. Cresca could work with that. Somehow.

But when Cresca glanced at Rongo, she wasn't even running after Saki. She had stopped, bent over her boot. She pulled something out of it.

A stun wand.

In a flash of red, the staff dropped to the ground and Saki reappeared briefly, the glamour flickering back and forth as it battled with sparks of red electricity. A few seconds later, Saki collapsed to the ground in full color.

Before Cresca could react, Rongo turned and took aim at Cresca. *Oh crap!*

The magic hit Cresca in the chest like a lightning bolt. Her whole body felt like it was made of hot white fire, blinding in its intensity. Pain blew out her senses, searing her from the inside out.

When the burning subsided, Cresca toppled to the ground like a discarded cigarette pack.

Smell came back first. She inhaled the scent of dirt baking in the sun and then her eyes and ears adjusted. The world was turned on its side, the rocky ground cutting into her cheek. She saw another body lying in a heap, large and clad in black. Thrash. Did that mean...had Rongo gotten all of them?

"I saw your little friend there in the black steal a cheap wand on the news," Rongo said, though it was unclear who, exactly, she was speaking to. All of them? "Knew you couldn't get too far from those caverns, so I made a gamble and combed the surrounding leylines. Looks like it paid off."

Gravel crunched under Rongo's boots as she walked over to where Saki lay prone. Rongo knelt down beside her and picked up the staff. When she straightened, Rongo paused and sniffed the air.

"Now I know who stole my warproot!" Rongo said. "You

girls could get in real trouble for this. A few gnats just pulled me over yesterday, claimed someone tipped them off that I had it in my possession. That witch really has it out for me."

Rongo stared right at the bushes where Em must have been hiding.

"Come out, little fish," Rongo hollered. "I have your friends. All I need is you."

~

Em crouched behind the bushes, palms sweaty as she clutched the faintly smoking warproot in one hand. She didn't have a weapon or a clever plan. All she had was a bucket of guilt. If she had come clean to her parents sooner, then Cresca, Saki, and Thrash wouldn't be face down in a parking lot, splayed like wounded soldiers on a battlefield.

"Don't shoot!" Em yelled. Might as well get that out in the open. "The bounty is cancelled!"

Rongo gave a sharp laugh and barked, "These mind games won't fool me."

"Please, just lower your weapon and I'll come out and explain!"

"Oh, *you* will do *me* the kindness of coming out to explain?" Em could hear the dirt crunching beneath Rongo's boots as she crossed the parking lot. "No need. I will happily drag you out."

"Fine! I'm coming out!" Em snapped. She raised her arms high, wishing she could just run for the truck or stall in time for her friends to do something, but the harsh truth was staring her dead in the face: they were outgunned. Em would have to talk their way out of this and negotiate with the bounty hunter. She had to appear reasonable and diplomatic. Not exactly her strengths.

Em tugged her skirt free from the grasping bush and

stepped out into the open. Rongo looked like the last survivor standing after a dueling tournament. She leveled all five feet of silver staff at Em.

"My parents cancelled the bounty," Em repeated.

"So insistent, with this lie. Tell me, why should I believe they would suddenly call it off?"

Em's arms shot up higher. "Because I talked to them and I asked them to cancel it! I know that's not what you want to hear, but it's the truth. They're a little dramatic and they over-reacted, and I convinced them I was okay and I didn't need to be hauled home by a bounty hunter!"

A bead of sweat rolled down Rongo's forehead.

"Check your orb, if you want!" Em said. "Look up the bounty if you don't believe me."

"You're lying," Rongo said, but from what little Em knew about Rongo, she was almost as wordy as Em. She never gave a two-word answer. The bounty hunter was wavering.

"Go ahead, then. Turn me in. But you won't get your money."

Rongo's nostrils flared as she studied Em's face. She gripped her staff tighter.

Without warning, Rongo slammed the end of the staff to the ground, sending a pulse of magic through the earth. Em almost lost her footing as the ground hiccupped beneath her.

"Fuck!" Rongo growled. "You're not kidding with this, are you? Goddess Above, the things I've done for this job—and now there's no job?!" Rongo leveled the staff at Em again. "That money would've been *life changing.*"

"I can talk to my parents!" Em added quickly. Her arms were growing heavy. "You can earn the money another way. This is going to sound wild, but we need a ride to NSU. If you drive us there, I can convince my parents to compensate you—"

Rongo slammed the staff to the earth again and the world shuddered.

"I don't trust you witches," Rongo said. "No more mind games. *I* will take *you* to your parents, and we will see about that reward."

A few feet away, Cresca managed to pull herself up onto her elbows. Thrash and Saki didn't move, their muscles still fried by the after-effects of the stun wand.

"Coco," gasped Cresca. She threw her limp arm in the direction of the fallen orb. "Help us...for Coco..."

"Yes!" Em cried. "If you take us to NSU, that helps the Magical Liberation Movement! Coco's cause! They need to get Thrash to NSU."

Rongo's gaze cut to Thrash on the ground, confirming her identity. Her staff lowered, just a hair.

"She did mention something about that..." Rongo conceded.

"I can hear her on the orb," Cresca said. She was almost sitting up now. She coughed—or maybe it was a laugh. "She's pissed. Wants you to pick it up and talk to her."

Rongo wavered.

"You," she said finally, pointing the staff at Em. "Don't you dare move."

"Wouldn't dream of it!"

Rongo jogged over to the abandoned orb, crouching down to scoop it up. Em couldn't hear Coco's voice, but she could see Rongo nodding at the crystal ball in her palm. A minute later, she dismissed Coco's image and stalked toward Em, everything about her coiled body language screaming, *I don't like what I'm about to do, but I'm doing it.*

"I want to get paid," Rongo stated.

Em blinked, in part to consciously stop herself from rolling her eyes. "This is the *only* way you get paid. How many times do I have to keep saying that?"

"All you need is a ride to the university in Madame Wiki?"

"Exactly. You'll be helping us and the MLM. Not to mention sticking it to The Justice."

Rongo crossed the final lengths between them and snatched Em's hand out of the air, crushing her fingers as she shook her hand.

"We have a deal."

20

New Salem University was only an hour away, at least according to some quick calculations involving Madame Wiki's ancient speedometer. As they neared the coast, farmland and forests bumped up against suburban sprawl. Every town they passed reminded Thrash of Belmar because they were all made of the same Growth witch materials: pliable uppercrust stone and resilient pinefiber.

Thrash was feeling nervous, or maybe carsick, it was hard to tell. Her muscles ached from the stun wand (horrible experience, 0/5 stars), and she had somehow ended up in the middle seat, wedged between Saki and Em. A fog of warproot filled her senses, the bundle burning low and slow in Saki's fist. The herby scent almost covered up the stink of Madame Wiki's backseat, a mix of sweat and the metallic tang of dried blood. Animal blood, she hoped.

Rongo drove in relative silence. As Rongo's sister-in-law, Cresca automatically got shotgun. For the past hour, Cresca had been clutching her orb and feverishly watching captures about their impending arrival, occasionally coming up for air to inform Thrash that public opinion was slightly in their favor. Cresca's silver hair flapped in the breeze as Thrash watched two hula-girls wiggle their hips on the dashboard, one thin and black, the other round and brown. Coco and Rongo.

"It seems like a lot of people agree that the Gifts are sketchy," Cresca reported from the passenger seat.

Rongo grunted. "I coulda told you that. And I wouldn't have needed the orb to do it."

Cresca ignored Rongo and peered into her orb. Up ahead, the leyline ducked under a curved stone bridge that connected one half of the gray-beige suburbs to the other half. As Madame Wiki sailed toward the overpass, Thrash saw a bright orange banner hanging from the bridge. White letters proclaimed *Free the Witch, Ditch the Gifts!*

Eyes still glued to her orb, Cresca said, "A lot of people think you're dangerous, but slightly more people think you're brave. We can work with that."

"Glad to hear it," Thrash said, feeling anything but glad. Winning over public opinion was Osmarra's specialty, not hers. Thrash had never been popular. She was the sort of person who people forgot was even eligible for Yearbook Awards, and now she had to make an entire country not just like her but love her. She had to persuade everyone that she deserved her own magic, in the hopes that The Justice would break, or at least bend.

"Here's what you're gonna do," Cresca said with a mischievous smile. "When The Justice offers you the Gift of Sight, acting like it's an olive branch and everything, instead you just whip out the Gift of Glamour and open that baby. If the MLM is right, the fact that they mute magic is going to be too controversial to sweep under the rug."

Thrash nodded but she couldn't stop a sigh from escaping

her chest. So, she just had to do the exact opposite of what The Justice had demanded. That thought didn't exactly put her mind, or gut, at ease.

Cresca's head shot up and her eyes found Thrash's. "You okay?"

"Just worrying about the plan," Thrash said. She hesitated, then added, "And my mom."

"Ah, so nothing new." Cresca tempered her comment with a kind smile. "You know what works for me? Imagining what happens after I do a dreaded task. Like, sure you have to go to the dentist, but then you get ice cream."

Em piped in, "And then you get cavities and go back to the dentist. Circle complete!"

Cresca stuck her tongue out at Em.

"Even in the best-case scenario, I still have to go home and face my mom." When Thrash tried to envision her future, she didn't see NSU. She saw boxes of Duna's things looming over her in the stable. Osmarra had told her to do something this summer. Well, she had sure done *something*.

Thrash rubbed her temples, trying to banish an incoming headache. "I'm pretty sure I'm grounded for the rest of my life."

"It sucks," Cresca said, "but you learn how to sneak out at night and occupy yourself during the day. How do you think I perfected this eyeliner?"

"I just don't even know what I'll say to my mom. How do you stand up to your dad when you know he's judging you? Or that he doesn't approve?"

"Well, there's a lot of yelling," Cresca admitted. "At least at first. But I guess no matter how the fight goes, I always make sure I apologize."

Thrash fidgeted with one of the buttons on her hat, which

rested in her lap. "But what if you're not sorry? What if you didn't do anything wrong?"

"Are you telling me that if you hurt your mom's feelings, you wouldn't feel sorry? At all? To hurt the person who cares about you the most on this earth?"

Ooof, well, when Cresca put it like that...

"You have to listen to your inner voice," Saki said, twisting in her seat to face Thrash. "That's what you told me. Even when your parents disapprove."

"Yeah, if *my* parents can get over all of *this*"—Em said, waving at Rongo, herself, all of them—"we're all going to be fine. I can't believe I'm about to say this, but I'm actually kind of excited to see my parents again. I feel like we've put 'em through the ringer."

Rongo snorted. "I'll say. You girls've made me consider early retirement."

Everyone laughed at that, even Thrash. It felt good to laugh.

"Anyway, don't worry about Osmarra," Cresca said with a note of finality. "She's not the real person standing in your way."

As Cresca guided the conversation back to The Plan, Thrash found her gaze wandering out the window. Her thoughts washed over her with the landscape. When she pictured arriving at NSU's campus, she imagined a shining castle on a hill, because it had only ever lived in her imagination. But soon, it would be real.

Osmarra wasn't the obstacle she was about to face, but Thrash couldn't avoid her forever. Eventually, Thrash would have to look her mom in the eye. She thought of Duna's note, which urged her to believe in Osmarra's love. What did Thrash hope she would see?

It is within every person's power to accept the gifts they are given.

A tunnel of trees covered in twisting ivy lined the road leading into the town of New Salem. Thrash marveled at the green canopy, wondering if it was nature at work, or Growth magic. Either way, it was a spectacular welcome.

Madame Wiki emerged from the tunnel and the world turned from green to gray. The leyline sailed along a long strip of black ocean, heading down, down, down. Below the dip of the road, Thrash could just see New Salem's skyline, shrouded in clouds that hung low like tired eyelids.

Cresca navigated from the passenger seat, directing Rongo off the leyline and through the city streets. New Salem's proximity to the sea reminded Thrash of Belmar, but that was where the resemblance ended. For every mile crowded with struggling businesses and homes, there was a casual mansion taking up an entire block, festooned with white columns and high turrets.

The one thing all the buildings shared in common was that they had all boarded up their doors and windows. Was this because of Thrash's arrival? Were locals anticipating a full-scale riot or something? The truck cruised past a wall tagged with graffiti reading *All Witches Eventually Burn*.

"Turn right here, onto University Way," Cresca said. "This street should lead us right to the main gate."

"Cornelia's Gate," Em specified. "Famous Growth witch. Basically invented the Gifts and put NSU on the map."

The moment they turned the corner, Thrash's eyes landed on a poster of her own face plastered on a brick wall. Across her face, someone had scrawled, in big, bold letters, *Shut Up And Take It!* The inside of the truck got eerily quiet.

Well, they were on the right road, at least.

Ahead of them, the mishmash of warehouses and rundown houses ended abruptly, replaced by manicured bushes and tastefully spaced trees that would impress prospective students and university guests. Thrash could easily imagine students lazing on the grass, but there were no carefree students on the lawn today. Instead, a throng of protestors stood between them and the ivy walls of NSU, so thick that Thrash almost couldn't see the iconic wrought iron gate. Rongo had to slow the truck and inch through the crowds.

"I can't believe this," Cresca muttered. Thrash scanned their homemade signs, trying not to take the messages personally.

No Gift, No Diploma!

Typicals on Top!

Throw Her In The Thrash!

It sure didn't feel like public opinion was swinging in her favor. In fact, it was almost unbelievable that there were this many negative protestors...

Thrash leaned away from the window, angling herself so she could see the protestors retreating in Madame Wiki's side mirror. Except there were no protestors in the mirror.

"The protestors are a glamour," Thrash said. "You can tell if you look in the mirrors!"

As everyone craned to look, Thrash felt her blood boil. This was some next-level manipulation from Osmarra. The thought that her mom could write those posters as part of an illusion made Thrash's anger surge until Madame Wiki's side mirror suddenly splintered. The crack spread and then the whole mirror shattered, shards of glass tumbling and flying away.

"Goddess Above!" Rongo cried. "What the hell was that?!"

"I'm sorry!" Thrash blurted. She had to get her knack under control.

"Never should've agreed to transporting witches," Rongo grumbled.

"You'll get your reward," Em reassured her. "And then some."

Thrash closed her eyes and breathed, willing herself to calm down before she broke the rest of Madame Wiki's reflective surfaces. When she finally managed to see through the red, Thrash found Cresca twisting in her seat and angling a compact mirror at NSU.

"Up ahead, at the gate," Cresca said. "*Those* are real protestors."

As they pulled up to NSU's main entrance, Thrash felt even more intimidated. Ivy walls loomed over a chaotic scene as news wagons crowded around the campus and wandslingers in checkered black armor pushed back at the crowd using mirror-plated shields. Seeing the truck, the wandslingers surged forward, parting a sea of signs that cheered for Thrash and condemned her in equal measure.

"You sure you wanna be dropped off in this commotion?" Rongo asked.

"We're sure," Cresca answered for them. Rongo shrugged and edged Madame Wiki forward.

Thrash could just glimpse the university buildings through the spiked iron bars of Cornelia's Gate. The gate was grand, Gothic, and unwelcoming, a little like the vanity in Thrash's room that Osmarra wanted her to throw away. The entrance didn't scream *Welcome to NSU!* so much as *Outsiders: Stay Out.* As the protestors grew louder, Thrash imagined her head on one of the gate's impressive spikes.

The wandslingers expanded the circle of space around the truck, pushing back protestors, reporters, and onlookers.

Rongo drove Madame Wiki right in front of the gate and hovered there, waiting.

"Looks like we're at the end of the line," Rongo said.

"Hold on a second," Cresca said. "We just need The Justice to make her dramatic entrance—"

"Look up," Saki said, pointing to the sky.

One monstrous black falcon swooped down from above, its gleaming black feathers unable to conjure the same shine in overcast New Salem. The familiar landed in front of Cornelia's Gate, but it wasn't The Justice who dropped out of her familiar's saddle. It was Osmarra, dressed in her black uniform, a purple sash cutting across her torso.

Osmarra took a few steps toward the truck and pulled an amplification wand out of her coat. She held it against her throat so that all of the onlookers could hear her say, "Thrash. Be reasonable. Come out and talk to me."

Her mom had called her Thrash. She felt seen, but wary that it was just another tactic in her mother's arsenal. Beside her, Cresca caught Thrash's eye with a worried look that said, *Are you okay to do this?*

"I can do it," Thrash said, her voice almost a hush. "It's like you said, Cresca. My mom's the person who cares about me most on this earth, right? I should be able to convince her to want what's best for me."

The girls bobbed their heads, but no one spoke. Cresca chewed on her thumbnail, only looking half-convinced herself, until Saki nudged Thrash with her elbow.

"You *can* do it," Saki whispered. Her voice was soft, but her dark eyes glinted with steel. She pressed the smoldering bundle of warproot into Thrash's hand.

Em nodded. "Yeah, you know what? Anything is possible. Look at this truck! Look at *us!*"

"Look at *yourself*, Thrash." Cresca turned in her seat to face her. "You are honest-to-Goddess the bravest person I know. Just be yourself."

Thrash nodded, even though that was the problem in its essence: her mom didn't want her as she was. She wanted to carve Thrash into someone else, a thinner, more pleasant daughter in Osmarra's own image.

It had never been Osmarra's love that Thrash doubted, precisely.

It was her ability to accept Thrash as is.

Osmarra stood rigid, her spine straight as a ruler. She displayed a bland and welcoming smile, hands clasped before her like a living version of her portrait in Belmar's library. Thrash could've sworn there was something else there, too, an undercurrent of something unfamiliar. Regret? Sadness? Defeat?

"Hi, Mom," Thrash said. Though this situation was unprecedented, it also felt strangely ordinary. Like they could've been having a mother-daughter skirmish over dinner, if it weren't for the screaming protestors and reporters capturing every word.

"Thrash," Osmarra said, inclining her head. "On behalf of the High and Low Circle, I have the honor of offering you the Gift of Sight."

Should she pull out the Gift of Glamour right now and open it? No, she had to establish the basic facts, get the crowd and her mom on her side first. Thrash folded her arms, almost mirroring her mom's posture. She wanted to look calm and in control. She wanted to seem reasonable.

"I don't accept," Thrash said, raising her voice to be heard over the din. "You know I've already turned it down. Twice."

"A Gift of your choice, then—"

"I choose my knack." Thrash pointedly looked at the surrounding protestors. "And I think you'll find that I'm not alone. There are lots of young witches like me who don't want their magic muted."

"You are mistaken. It is *the Gifts* that bestow magic."

"That's a lie," Thrash said, losing patience. If there was no reasoning with her mom, then she might as well prove she was telling the truth. Thrash reached for her hat—

"Wait! Thrash, think this through for a second," Osmarra urged. "Your knack may seem like magic, but it is a symptom of it, and it can't be controlled. Your knack is dangerous."

"My *natural magic* is only as dangerous as I am." Thrash stared hard into her mother's unflinching face. *Do I look dangerous to you?* Osmarra's eyes darted away, settling somewhere beyond Thrash, on the onlookers who soaked in every word.

"Be reasonable, Thrash. This is a generous offer, and you have your whole future ahead of you."

"But if it's not a future I want, it's meaningless," Thrash said. "I don't want a Gift just because I'm supposed to have one."

"You don't know what you want because you're only sixteen," Osmarra said.

The fire inside Thrash flared, but she tamped it down with Duna's note. Osmarra loved her but had a hard time understanding her. What would it take to get her mom to see her —*really* see her?

"Maybe I don't know what I want, but I *do* know what I *don't* want." Thrash took a deep breath. "I don't want my natural magic muted. I don't want my options limited by a Gift or an HMU. And I don't care about whether or not that means I become a Named Witch, because that's all it is—a name."

Osmarra frowned. She cracked her knuckles, a brief and angry sound. Thrash wondered if that sound meant she had broken through to her mom, or if it was the opposite, and she was about to face the full force of the storm.

Thrash spoke before her mom had a chance: "Maybe 'want' is the wrong word. This isn't about what I want. This is about who I am."

Thrash's words had the opposite effect on Osmarra, whose anger suddenly swelled. She lashed out, demanding, "You think I don't know who you are?"

Thrash didn't know how to answer that. She suddenly felt like she was five years old, her life driven by the whims of capricious grown-ups—or maybe that was because she was suddenly standing in her bedroom.

The glamour was impressive. Thrash spun around, taking in her space, which wasn't quite right. In Osmarra's mind, Thrash's bed was made, her room was tidy, and posters retired years ago made a reappearance on the walls. The room was also mercifully quiet, free from the buzz of reporters and protestors.

Osmarra lowered the amplification wand and turned away from Thrash for a moment, composing herself. Thrash felt herself clenching her jaw and released it as her mom faced her.

"I know who you are," Osmarra said, the anger gone out of her voice like the tide returning to the sea. "I am your mother, Thrash. I know you better than you know yourself."

Thrash had a hard time believing that, but instead of firing that back, she paced around the room.

"Can they still hear us? In here?" Thrash asked.

"No," Osmarra said. "And I'm sure I'll get in trouble for it."

"With who?"

Osmarra nodded her head at a poster of The Justice on one of the bedroom walls.

"Well, that aged poorly," Thrash said. Osmarra gave a wan smile.

Thrash's gaze swept over her almost-bedroom again and she spotted Black Cat, her favorite stuffed animal, sitting prominently on her dresser. Thrash had always suspected that Osmarra conveniently "lost" B.C. during the move, because the beloved, tattered toy clashed with the house's aesthetic, but seeing the cat here...she wasn't so sure anymore.

"I just want what's best for you," Osmarra said.

"I know." And she did. Thrash felt it in her bones; her mom was telling the truth. "So why are you still trying to get me to accept a Gift?"

"Because children change. So rapidly." Osmarra reached out as if to touch B.C., but then pulled her hand back, remembering it was her own illusion. "You originally wanted the Gift of Sight, and it took me a few days, but I met you there. But by the time I was ready to concede, you had already moved on, to this nonsense about keeping your knack."

"If you had listened to me in the first place, about not wanting the Gift of Glamour—"

"I know you thought I was forcing the Gift of Glamour on you for selfish reasons, but the truth is—"

Osmarra stopped short. She rung her hands, considering what to say next.

"The Gift of Sight blessed Duna in many ways," Osmarra said, "but seeing her own death unfold...that was a curse. On both of us."

Thrash tried to remember Duna's final months, but those days were foggy. Had seeing the end made Mum suffer? The thought made her sick to her stomach. She could only imagine what that kind of revelation would have done to Osmarra.

Osmarra continued, "I never want you to endure that pain.

Granted, forbidding you from it may have been the wrong choice..."

"That...that makes sense," Thrash said. "I wish you would've just told me, because now I understand."

Osmarra eyes seemed so ancient, so tired, but she still managed to give Thrash a sly smile as she said, "I hope you have teenagers one day."

"What's that supposed to mean?"

"These choices are never easy. How could I know for sure that you were mature enough to handle the Gift of Sight, when you couldn't even face a few of Duna's boxes?" Osmarra sighed. "In all honesty, the Gift of Glamour seemed like the less complicated option."

"But that's not the only reason you wanted it for me, is it?" Thrash asked suddenly, fiercely. She swallowed. There was no turning back now. "With the Gift of Glamour, you hoped I would make myself prettier. And thinner."

Osmarra hesitated. "All I've ever wanted is to make things easier for you."

Is that how her mom was determined to see it? Thrash was so over this. Here she was, being the most honest, the most open, she had ever been with her mom—and it still wasn't enough. Thrash could feel tears prickling the corners of her eyes.

"But I was wrong," Osmarra said. Thrash looked up into her mom's eyes; there were tears there too. "I should never have made you feel that way. You are beautiful, just as you are. And so, so like her—"

Osmarra's face crumpled. Her hand flew to her chest, and at first Thrash thought her mom was having a heart attack— but it was just a sob caught in her chest. Thrash had never seen Osmarra cry beyond an artful tear. Not even at the funeral.

But now...now she was gasping for breath.

"I—I love you so much," Osmarra said, pulling Thrash into a hug. She sobbed into Thrash's hair. "If I ever made you feel otherwise...I am so sorry."

"I love you too," Thrash murmured. "And I'm sorry. I'm sorry I put you through this. I'm sorry I ran away..."

Osmarra sobbed into Thrash's hair, and Thrash let the tears pour down her cheeks until her posters blurred into colorful nothings.

Osmarra gave Thrash an extra tight squeeze and released her. From her coat pocket, she produced a handkerchief and offered it to Thrash. Thrash sniffled. Her eyes felt red and irritated.

"I don't want to be muted," Thrash said. "I don't want my natural magic erased. And I'm not the only one. This is bigger than just me now."

"I understand." Osmarra used her magic to whisk away her own tears. "Would the face of the revolution allow her mother to dry her tears with a little magic? Only if you want, of course."

"Sure." Thrash realized that, honestly, she didn't mind. A little glamour wouldn't hurt anything. As Osmarra swirled her fingers over Thrash's face, she thought about the MLM, the calls for revolution, and the Gift of Glamour tucked inside her hat. "How are we going to get out of this mess?"

Osmarra ran a smoothing hand over her hair. "Allow me to do the talking."

"But what about The Justice?"

"By the time you arrived here, I think there were very few paths left that led to the outcome The Justice wanted," Osmarra said. "Sending me to convince you was her best shot at making you accept a Gift. If that warproot isn't interfering too much, she has probably already seen that I failed. Now it's

just a matter of convincing her that accepting that fact is in her
best interests."

Osmarra put an arm around Thrash and guided her toward
the door that wasn't really there.

"There is a path forward," Osmarra told her. "It's just a
matter of finding it."

～

Thrash's bedroom dissipated around them, the glamour burning
off like morning fog. The black gate, the university, and the
crowds all came back into focus, followed by the rush of sound
that accompanied hundreds of people gasping and exclaiming.
It felt a bit disorienting, like waking up from a dream.

The Justice must have arrived while they were in the illusion because she was waiting by the gate with her arms
crossed over her chest. It was always difficult to gauge what
the Named Witch was truly feeling. Was that an undercurrent
of impatience in the tap of her boot?

"Let me do the talking," Osmarra whispered.

Thrash nodded and scanned the crowd for the Lunes. The
protestors and reporters inched forward, their numbers far
greater than the few wandslingers with shields. Thrash didn't
even see Madame Wiki; had the crowd closed in so far it had
overtaken the truck?

Then Thrash saw a flash of purple in the surrounding
bodies. A moment later, Cresca's unmistakable silver hair
bobbed above the crowd. Cresca scaled Madame Wiki and
extended a hand to Saki and then Em. Thrash could've sworn
she heard the distant sound of Rongo yelling at them to get
down, but her protests were lost beneath the cacophony of the
crowd. When Cresca spotted Thrash, she leaped like a cheer-

leader and almost fell when she landed on the hood of the car. Em screamed something unintelligible.

Saki looked solemn by comparison. Then she thrust her tattooed middle finger into the air. Cresca and Em caught on and joined her in what was perhaps the most heartfelt middle-finger salute anyone had ever received.

Thrash tried to wipe the grin from her lips as she turned back to face The Justice. The Named Witch reluctantly opened her arms and motioned to the crowd to settle down. The onlookers pressed forward, orbs out and eager to capture whatever happened next.

Osmarra cleared her throat and lifted her chin.

"We've reached an understanding," Osmarra announced. "Thrash will not take a Gift."

Thrash couldn't see The Justice's eyes behind those huge sunglasses, but she imagined them narrowing.

"Yes, you both have made that crystal clear." The Justice tried on a smile. It wasn't a good look. "I can see there will be no changing your mind. You are an exceptional young woman, Thrash Blumfeld-Wright."

Osmarra gave Thrash's shoulder a squeeze, but Thrash wasn't sure if it was a squeeze of reassurance or danger. It couldn't be this easy.

The Justice turned her body outward, projecting a little louder for the crowd to hear. "And exceptions must be made in exceptional circumstances. Your magic is unique, but it is also wild. Where, if not at a Historically Magical University, should a bright young woman such as yourself learn to harness such an exceptional knack?"

But Thrash wasn't an exception—that was the whole point. She heard a few cheers from the crowd and the sound transported her to her Kindling Day party, to that feeling of being paraded when it was truly Osmarra's show. Was she going to let this become The Justice's show?

"The High Circle would like to officially offer you acceptance to NSU, without a Gift," The Justice said, her voice dull and flat, as if reading lines from a script. "What do you say to that, Thrash?"

Thrash couldn't see the Lunes, but she could feel them watching. Brilliant Em, who had turned her knack into something innovative and new. Passionate Saki, who discovered that her knack could lead her down a path no Gift could. And Cresca. Impossible-to-adjective Cresca, who was only beginning to understand what her magic had in store for her.

"It's not just about my knack," Thrash said, but her voice was a shade too soft. With a swallow, she stepped toward The Justice, letting her mom's arm fall. She did her best to channel her mother's protectrix voice: "It's everyone's knacks. Because the Gifts mute knacks."

The crowd gasped, including Osmarra, who reached out to grab Thrash's hand. Thrash gave her an apologetic smile as she yanked her hand free and grabbed her hat. *Sorry, Mom. I can't take the easy way out.*

"And I can prove it." Thrash's hand closed around the leather book, and she pulled it from the hat, brandishing the Gift of Glamour for everyone to see. As the reporters with the news orbs clamored forward for a better look, she threw back the cover and exposed the false chamber.

"The Gifts mute all natural magic except for a single path, and they do it by using the very magic that the Gifts snuff out and the HMUs refuse to teach!"

This time, the crowd *roared*. Bodies surged forward and the wall of wandslingers shoved them back. Thrash retreated a step and bumped into her mom as the frenzied crowd grew louder and more furious. As people started chanting, "Ditch

Gifts!" she heard the sharp clap of a glass bottle breaking. What had she unleashed?

Meanwhile, The Justice stood absolutely still, ignoring the rioting crowd as she gazed off at something only she could see. Her hand flew to her head, and she winced. "Persecuting warproot."

A reporter broke past the wall of wandslingers and called, "Miss Blumfeld-Wright! Are you proposing that the High Circle abolish the Gift system? The very foundation of the Thirteen States?"

Is that what Thrash wanted? She couldn't hear herself think over the uproar.

Osmarra stepped forward, moving between Thrash and the encroaching orbs.

"Now, now, no one said anything about abolishing anything," Osmarra answered with a genial smile. The reporter leaned in toward her, pulled in by her magnetic charm. "What we really want, all of us, is a little more freedom. We want choices—and more than just three."

Beyond the wandslingers, people were hushing each other, straining to listen. A few were even nodding along. Osmarra put an arm around Thrash and squeezed her close.

"One size doesn't fit all. We can leave the Gifts for those who want them, but we don't have to force them on every witch. If my daughter has shown me anything this past week, it's that we have to listen when people tell us who they are and what they want. Many people"—Osmarra gestured to the circle around them—"are very clearly telling us that they want the same. Surely, The Justice agrees that we can loosen the ropes a bit?"

Osmarra flashed The Justice her most winning smile as the onlookers went quiet, holding their collective breath for an answer.

"Perhaps you are right," The Justice said, still cradling her head with one hand. "It is time we move forward. As a member of the High Circle, I will ensure that we work with the HMUs and reach an agreement that works for everyone."

The crowd lost it—reporters shouted into orbs, protestors cheered and screamed, and suddenly Osmarra was pulling Thrash into a hug. Was that it? Had they won? Thrash felt a rush of appreciation, a true sense that she wasn't alone; there were thousands, maybe even hundreds of thousands, of people on her side. Not everyone wanted a Gift, and that idea was so big that even The Justice couldn't stamp it out—at least, not here and now.

Over her mom's shoulder, Thrash glimpsed The Justice watching her behind those big black sunglasses. Osmarra had said the Gift of Sight could be a blessing and a curse. What futures had The Justice seen and what futures was she trying to prevent? It might be impossible to know, but Thrash couldn't help but wonder...had they bested the Named Witch, or played right into her hands?

The Justice tipped her hat, turned on her heel, and marched away.

EPILOGUE

Three Months Later

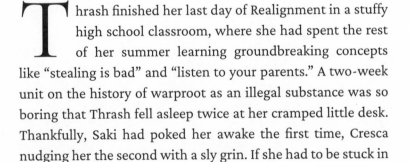

Thrash finished her last day of Realignment in a stuffy high school classroom, where she had spent the rest of her summer learning groundbreaking concepts like "stealing is bad" and "listen to your parents." A two-week unit on the history of warproot as an illegal substance was so boring that Thrash fell asleep twice at her cramped little desk. Thankfully, Saki had poked her awake the first time, Cresca nudging her the second with a sly grin. If she had to be stuck in that classroom for six hours a day, at least she was stuck there with her friends.

Thrash also knew she had gotten off easy with only three months of corrective education. The Justice may have wanted a harsher punishment, but she couldn't come after Thrash without making the High Circle look oppressive. Thrash was likely shielded by the fact that, for many, she had come to represent the increasingly popular anti-Gift movement—some were even calling it the Third Magical Revolution.

Despite the August heat, school started in a few days. Thrash was released from Realignment on Friday and spent all day Saturday going through the last of Duna's boxes. Earlier that summer, Thrash and Osmarra had struck a deal: Thrash would finally comb through Duna's belongings on the condition that she was allowed to keep anything she wanted. It was a compromise both of them could happily live with—Osmarra had less weighing her down, but Thrash still had Duna's treasured star-maps and journals tucked safely into the bottomless chest for whenever she was ready for them.

On Sunday, her last day of summer, Thrash woke up early, scarfed down a bowl of cereal, and ran through her mental checklist of "beach things." She had a towel and a water bottle in her hat already, along with a bag of Saki's favorite brand of BBQ chips and a conical orb stand Em recommended for amplifying music outdoors. For sun protection, she clasped the enchanted necklace with the silver *T* around her neck, the one Osmarra had given her on the day she got her knack.

That's when it hit her. A bathing suit! Thrash had almost forgotten the *essential* beach day item. Not that she was likely to get in the water, but she wanted the option. Thrash fetched the paper bag, still on her dresser, from her shopping trip with Cresca last week. A smile crept up her face as she tugged on the black one-piece suit, running her fingers over the bold cutouts along the side. Thrash twirled in the cracked mirror of the vanity. Osmarra offered to replace the glass, but Thrash wanted to leave the jagged split as a reminder of the most magical summer of her life—and where it had started.

Osmarra didn't push; she wasn't much for pushing these days. Despite fears that The Justice might pull strings to get Osmarra recalled, she was still Protectrix of Belmar, for now.

Her re-election was coming up next year and it wasn't looking good, but instead of obsessing over her public persona, Osmarra stayed out of the spotlight. She seemed almost peaceful, a word Thrash never would've associated with her mom mere months ago.

On her bedside table, Thrash's orb pulsed twice with soft white light. Thrash waved a hand over it and Em appeared in the glass. She sat behind the wheel of Saki's family's van, which Em had somehow convinced Saki's parents to trust her with for the day—so long as Em swore that the girls wouldn't take off on a spontaneous cross-country road trip.

"We're outside, witch!" Em said. "If you want a pastry, I suggest you get out here in the next two minutes!"

"I'm on my way." Thrash tossed her orb, and Em's dissipating face, into her hat. She yanked on a pair of jeans from her "lightly worn" clothing pile. It was too hot for jeans, but Thrash didn't have time to figure out how to manage the chub rub that came with wearing almost anything else.

Thrash fastened her hat and hopped down the carpeted stairs two at a time.

"I'm heading out!" Thrash called, unsure if her mom was getting ready upstairs or already out on her Saturday morning ride with Tempest. She might also be in the stables, which were roomier now that Thrash had finally gone through the boxes.

At the bottom of the stairs, Thrash heard voices coming from the living room. She stuck her head through the door and found Osmarra in her riding clothes, sitting stiffly on the edge of the couch and entertaining a guest. That happened, sometimes, but this was no ordinary guest. When Osmarra dropped the conversation, the stranger turned, following Osmarra's eyeline.

"Ah, Thrash, we were just talking about you," The Justice

said with a cold smile. The Named Witch looked so out of place in Thrash's living room that Thrash thought she might be dreaming...but no, that dark-clad woman on the cream couch was real.

The question was, why was she here? Thrash hadn't seen The Justice since that fateful day at NSU, presumably because she had bigger concerns to deal with. Sure, Thrash may have put the anti-Gift movement into motion, but it was a living thing now, wild and unpredictable. It would continue, with or without her.

"I wish I could stay and talk, but my friends are waiting for me," Thrash said. She didn't want to stay and talk, of course, but she was learning to pick her battles, and being rude to The Justice didn't benefit anyone right now.

"It's so good to have friends," The Justice said. "I was just saying to your mom how grateful I am to have her as a friend, here in Calypso."

Thrash's eyes flickered to her mom, who sat still as a statue. What could The Justice possibly still want from them? What had she seen in their futures?

"But friends also know when they've overstayed their welcome," The Justice said. She stood up and Osmarra hopped to her feet as well. "Thank you for the coffee. I can see myself out."

Osmarra bowed and The Justice saluted her with a tilt of her leather hat. Who wore a hat *and* sunglasses inside a house? It was hard to believe Thrash had ever idolized the woman.

Thrash bowed her head as The Justice swept by her. The corner of the Named Witch's mouth twitched.

"Until we meet again, try to stay out of trouble," The Justice said, and then she slipped out the front door, swallowed by bright daylight.

Thrash sank onto the arm of one of the couches. "What was that about?"

"My campaign," Osmarra said, eyes narrowing at Thrash sitting on the part of the sitting-furniture you weren't allowed to sit on. Thrash reluctantly stood up. "Nothing you need to worry about. Just go."

Though Thrash felt the pull of her friends, the beach, *freedom*, she hovered for a moment. Before she could talk herself out of it, Thrash threw her arms around her mom and gave her a tight squeeze.

"I'll be home for dinner," Thrash told her. "Seven still good?"

"Seven is great."

When Thrash pulled away, Osmarra hesitated a moment before releasing her.

"One last thing," said Osmarra. "I think Tempest is waiting on the lawn. Would you tell him I'll be outside in five?"

"Will I have to grovel for forgiveness on your behalf?"

"Quite the opposite, you may have to convince him to go. I've been trying to get him to go up into the canyons, but in his words, 'I've had enough adventure for the next 247 years.'"

Thrash rolled her eyes. "What did *he* do?"

Osmarra shrugged, but her eyes sparkled knowingly as she guided Thrash out the door.

Calypso's beaches were known for white sand, soft winds, and gentle surf—but Thrash only visited them once or twice a year. The vast, sparkling ocean waved at her as she trekked across the hot sand. They stopped a dozen feet from the water's edge and set up camp. Thrash kicked off her sandals and smoothed down her towel. The kiss of the ocean breeze was almost enough to make her forget The Justice's visit.

"Why don't I come here more often?" Thrash asked as she tilted her head back and let the sun and sea air caress her skin. "What's wrong with me?"

"Realignment wasn't great for summer plans," Cresca said. She flopped down on her towel and rolled her discarded sundress into a pillow. "Thank Goddess my dad let me get out of the house. Can you believe Coco and Rongo are staying *another* week?"

Thrash secretly cheered inside. After Rongo got her payout from Em's parents, she quit bounty hunting and fixed up Madam Wiki, while Coco started working officially for the MLM as an organizer and a speaker. They moved around a lot now, convinced The Justice was keeping tabs on them, waiting to pin some crime on them so she could justify throwing them in Realignment—the adult version of it, which involved a long stint in a real prison. During their stay in Belmar, Rongo boasted about fixing up her mom's cafe and taking the girls on a hunting trip someday. Thrash, for one, hoped she stuck around long enough to deliver on her promises.

"They're the worst," Cresca said, pouting. "Why is no one supporting me and my anguish?"

"Yes. You are right. Rongo and Coco are the worst," Saki stated with zero heart or commitment. Cresca groaned.

Meanwhile, Em pulled a small library out of her hat and placed the books on the corners of her towel to keep it from blowing away.

"Is that summer reading?" Cresca gasped.

"...Not exactly."

Saki picked up one of the books by the corner, like she was plucking a crab out of a pot and examining if it was still alive. "This isn't on the summer reading list, but I think seniors usually read it in the fall. Em, are you *pre-reading* books for the fall semester?"

"Senior year is the busiest year of high school!" Em said. "I'm trying to get a head start so I'm less stressed during the school year."

"Oh my Goddess, can we *please* not talk about school?" Cresca begged.

Em bit her lip. "How about college applications?"

"Snooze!" Cresca said. "Now that we're super famous, there isn't even any suspense. Sure, we don't have Gifts, but what HMU is going to turn down four badass, rebel witches who changed the course of history?"

Thrash laughed. "You *need* to let me read that college essay."

"Or we just forget about universities for a year..." Cresca said. "Gap year, anyone?"

Saki's hand shot up. Thrash chuckled, but Cresca wasn't laughing. Em frowned.

"I've been thinking about this..." Saki said, drawing swirls in the sand. "What can a university even teach me about taste magic? The Historically Magical Universities say they will admit a small number of non-Gift students next year, but who will teach us when no two knacks are the same?"

"Gap year!" Cresca chimed again. "Think about it. While the education system irons itself out, we travel Europa."

"The food," Saki said with a dreamy sign.

"The museums." Em was nodding now.

"The *adventures*," Cresca urged.

"We're gonna need a bigger Good Shit Jar," Thrash said to a chorus of laughs and cheers. As the girls continued fantasizing about what next year might bring, Thrash settled down against the bumpy sand. She copied Cresca and folded her sweater into a pillow. As the girls jabbered and the sun kissed her face, she closed her eyes and smiled.

After an hour of laying on the sand, Saki sat up suddenly, pushing her sunglasses to her head.

"It's ocean time," she said.

Cresca rolled over and stretched. "Holy House of Curses, it's getting hot. Thrash, I don't understand how you're wearing jeans and a shirt right now."

Thrash was the only one still clinging to her normal clothes, unless she counted Em in her tankini top and voluminous skirt. When Em stood up and shook off some sand, though, she slipped out of the skirt and revealed a pair of leggings made out of a shimmering green fabric.

Cresca hollered, "Sexy pants!"

"Thanks!" Em beamed. "My mom's trying to create a magical fabric that soaks in salt water and traps it for hours. In theory, it should let merpeople, like my dad, stay on dry land more than an hour or two."

As the girls oohed and aahed, Thrash felt an unexpected wave of anxiety. Looking up at her thin friends in their swimwear, with nothing to hide, they suddenly felt as far away and unreachable as when she stumbled on them at her library table.

"Thrash, you've gotta at least come stick your feet in," Cresca said, a real gentleness in her eyes. She reached out a hand to help Thrash up.

Would Thrash always be the girl who never got in the water?

Did she *want* to be the girl who never got in the water?

As Thrash peered into Cresca's eyes, she had to remind

herself: Cresca's friendship didn't hinge on how she looked. None of the girls cared about her backfat or her thick thighs. Hell, Thrash didn't even typically care about these things.

Thrash grabbed Cresca's hand. She had to have more faith in herself, and in the girls, if this messy but beautiful web of friendships—this coven—was going to last.

Plus, wearing a bathing suit really wasn't so bad. Thrash had stared down and overcome much worse.

She peeled off her shirt and her uncomfortable jeans. No one stared or commented, though Cresca couldn't help but crack a joke about Thrash having good taste in bathing suits. Before Thrash even had a chance to feel self-conscious, Em grabbed her hand and Saki had her arm.

Arms tangled like kite strings, they ran to the water.

A BRIEF HISTORY OF THE THIRTEEN STATES

1600s - WITCHES FLEE FAE persecution in Europa and settle in America.

1620-1712 - THE EARLY MAGICAL ERA, during which theories about harnessing and accessing magic are shared freely between the refugee witches and indigenous witches.

1712 - THE FOUNDING SISTERS DECLARE INDEPENDENCE, both national and magical, from Europa and move west across the continent, creating new colonies and forging new alliances.

1791 - THE FOUNDING SISTERS DRAFT and sign the constitution for the Thirteen States of America and establish a government.

1833 - THE CIVIL WAR breaks the Thirteen States of America into two contingencies: the First Nations and the Unified States.

1836 - IN THE AFTERMATH OF THE CIVIL WAR, borders are redrawn and three states are created with more autonomy and representation for indigenous Americans.

1865 - CORNELIA ST. JAMES invents the three Gifts–Glamour, Growth, and Sight.

1866 - THE GREAT IGIDAN DRAGON awakens in West Afrika and drives immigration to the Thirteen States of America.

1875 - NEW SALEM UNIVERSITY becomes the first university in the Thirteen States aimed at the education of Gifted witches.

1875 -1910 - THE FIRST MAGICAL REVOLUTION. The Gifts and higher education transform society in this period, also referred to as the Age of Aptitude.

1969 - THE FIRST PLATINUM WAND IS CRAFTED, ushering in a new era of innovation.

1970-1990 - THE SECOND MAGICAL REVOLUTION. Wands and orbs make basic magic accessible to non-magical persons, restructuring society.

1991-PRESENT DAY - THE MODERN MAGICAL ERA

AUTHOR'S NOTE: In creating a contemporary fantasy world that reflects the modern United States, the foundations of the Thirteen States echo, rather than fully erase, the United States' colonialist past. The worldbuilding of the Thirteen States intends to strike a balance between realism and idealism, but does not in any way condone colonialism or genocide.

DISCUSSION QUESTIONS

In the opening of *Fat Witch Summer,* Thrash lists her "love-hate" relationships. How do Thrash's strong opinions affect her and her relationships with others? Do you relate to her love-hate list?

When Thrash first meets Cresca, the "mean girl" defies Thrash's expectations by being genuine and kind. How does this early interaction shape the novel's message about beauty and the Gift of Glamour?

Thrash has strong opinions about the Lunes when she first meets them; are these impressions correct? How does Thrash's view of the girls change over the course of the story?

Thrash often clashes with her mother, Osmarra. What factors put a strain on their mother-daughter relationship? Can you relate to their struggles?

In the Thirteen States, mothers traditionally choose the Gifts, which represent maiden (Glamour), mother (Growth), and crone (Sight). How do feminine expectations and gender roles influence the world of the Thirteen States? How do they influence Osmarra and Thrash differently?

A recurring theme of the novel is "liking" versus "loving." Thrash mentions liking, but not loving, what she sees in the mirror. Later, she worries that Osmarra loves her, but doesn't like her. How are the paths to self-love, familial love, and friendship alike? How do they differ?

The book features interludes narrated by Osmarra's familiar, Tempest. What do you think this outside perspective brings to the story?

How do Cresca, Em, and Saki each struggle with body image? How do they overcome their insecurities over the course of the story?

Both Thrash and Cresca change their hair, with dye and magic respectively. Do you think both of them are rebelling against, or falling prey to, conventional beauty standards? How do you feel about magical versus non-magical body modification, or temporary versus permanent?

When Cresca takes off her rings, were you surprised by the changes she makes to her appearance? Is she a victim of toxic beauty standards, or a self-possessed young woman who knows what makes her feel confident?

Fat Witch Summer is described as a "body positive" novel, but Thrash is not always positive about her body. Do you think it's possible to practice "body positivity" at all times? What external factors (i.e. legislation, accessibility, religion) might limit someone's ability to fully embrace their body?

ACKNOWLEDGMENTS

Nothing gets accomplished without a coven to cheer you on and watch your back.

Thank you to Sarah Faulkner, who read at least two drafts of this manuscript, multiple synopses, and approximately one million text messages. Hazel Naylor, Katie Friesen, Genna Ford —I will stop sending you pages when I'm dead. Thank you for putting up with me and always giving great notes. Thank you Kristen Anderson, Camille Muth, Arielle Basich, Jenna Shively, Nick Franco, Maura O'Leary, and Ezra Miller for your enthusiasm and early feedback, and Patty Anderson for being my biggest cheerleader. Riley John Gibbs, Nidhi Patel, Molly Iker-Johnson, Alessa Winters, and Haley Kutulas, thank you for reading the first three chapters when I had no idea if the Thirteen States would make sense to anyone but me.

Thank you to Lauren Humphries-Brooks for your eagle-eyed editing and Amanda Elliot Panitch for your mentorship. Thank you to my colleagues who shaped this novel—Dave Beckerman, Julie Huey, Ken Narasaki, Yolie Cortez, Theresa Dorsey Mounce, Jayme Kusyk, and Bailey Magrann-Wells. Story analysts are not just lovely, well-read people—they also give great notes!

Amanda Julina Gonzalez brought the story to life with her beautiful cover illustration. Thank you for your gorgeous art, Amanda, and thank you Kiley Vorndran for making the introduction. Kalia Cheng, thank you for illustrating the vibrant map of the Thirteen States.

This book might come down a little harsh on moms, but I've been blessed with an amazing one. Thank you, Mom, for reading every manuscript, picking up every phone call, and supporting me at every turn. I love you! I'm also thankful for the time I had with my dad, an author who kindled my early love of books and stories. I miss you. Much love to the rest of my family for their support, especially my aunts and uncles, my cousins, my brother, and my wonderful in-laws. I know, this book is weird, but so am I.

Ben Kepner, your early excitement for my ideas keeps them alive. Thank you for eagerly reading my work chapter by chapter, a responsibility that was not included in our wedding vows. You have a sixth sense for seeing through the flimsy bits, knowing when to check my ego, and encouraging me to dream bigger. The Thirteen States wouldn't be as rich without your world-building expertise.

However, I still named Lake Chlala after our cat, against your recommendation. Sorry! I'm an *auteur* now.

Thank you to all the Kickstarter backers who believed in this project. A special shoutout to James Hudson, Chelsea Matthews, Joyce Kepner, Dru Kutulas, and Hazel Naylor for their support. If I've learned anything going through the publishing ringer, it's that every book is a miracle. To all the readers willing to take a chance on this book—who have bought it for friends, reviewed it, or shared their enthusiasm for a fat witch named Thrash—thank you.

ABOUT THE AUTHOR

Lizzy Ives grew up in the fog of the San Francisco Bay Area and now burns in the sun of Los Angeles with her husband, her cat, and their massive board game collection. She has a BFA in Film Production and has worked in various creative jobs for Marvel Studios, Lionsgate Entertainment, and Skybound Entertainment. She has a passion for books, movies, and comics, but above all, for stories well told.

 instagram.com/lizzytacular

 goodreads.com/lizzyives

 twitter.com/lizzytacular